Unlucky Money

Timothy J. Lockhart

Stark House Press • Eureka California

UNLUCKY MONEY

Published by Stark House Press
1315 H Street
Eureka, CA 95501, USA
griffinskye3@sbcglobal.net
www.starkhousepress.com

UNLUCKY MONEY copyright © 2022 by Timothy J. Lockhart. All rights reserved, including the right of reproduction in whole or in part in any form. Published by Stark House Press by arrangement with the author.

ISBN-13: 978-1-951473-57-0

Book design by Mark Shepard, shepgraphics.com
Proofreading by Bill Kelly

PUBLISHER'S NOTE:
This is a work of fiction. Names, characters, places and incidents are either the products of the author's imagination or used fictionally, and any resemblance to actual persons, living or dead, events or locales, is entirely coincidental.
Without limiting the rights under copyright reserved above, no part of this publication may be reproduced, stored, or introduced into a retrieval system or transmitted in any form or by any means (electronic, mechanical, photocopying, recording or otherwise) without the prior written permission of both the copyright owner and the above publisher of the book.

First Stark House Press Edition: February 2022

UNLUCKY MONEY

When Chinese American private-eye Wendy Lu takes on her first murder case, she doesn't realize how dangerous it's going to be. Probing into the murder of Susan Fontaine, the wife of her client, wealthy real-estate developer Whit Fontaine—the primary suspect in the case—Wendy fights to prove he was framed.

Wendy used to be a cop but quit after a rookie mistake caused the death of her partner. Now she leads a more traditional life, dealing with her guilt, feeling she has disappointed her parents. Yet despite hostility from Fontaine's arrogant business partner, opposition from the police, and violent threats on her life, she perseveres in the case.

And that's when Wendy discovers things that Fontaine, his partner Tom McKenna, and even Ryan Connolly, the police detective in charge of the murder investigation, would like to keep secret—that Fontaine-McKenna Associates is using criminal-syndicate money to finance the casino the firm wants to build. Now she is forced to use everything she's learned just to stay alive.

Timothy J. Lockhart Bibliography

Smith (2017)
Pirates (2019)
A Certain Man's Daughter (2021)

"...a modern master of pulp espionage ..."
　　　—Kristofer Upjohn, *Noir Journal*

"...this is quality pulp fiction. A thoroughly enjoyable read."
　　　—Paul Burke, *NB Magazine*

"A riveting, page-turning thrill ride ... Ten thumbs up."
　　　—Victor Gischler, author of *Gun Monkeys*

"...a great storyteller."
　　　—*Ship & Shore*

"The pages turned like uncovered clues. Made me want to plunge headlong into my stack of old PI paperbacks."
　　　—Rick Ollerman, author of *Truth Always Kills*

Acknowledgments

The author wishes to thank the following persons who kindly read and provided helpful comments on the manuscript of this novel:

Carmel Corcoran
Zhimin "Grace" Gong
Guy Holland
Lisa A. Iverson
Bill Kelly
Aaron M. Pomeranz
Warren L. Tisdale
Zhonglian WANG
Cina L. Wong
Bo "Bonnie" Xie
Allan Zaleski
Qi "Harry" Zhang

Special thanks, as always, to Greg Shepard and the rest of the fine folks at Stark House Press, with whom it is truly a pleasure to work.

Dedication
To Qi "Harry" Zhang and Bo "Bonnie" Xie
黄金万两容易得，一个知心最难寻。
(Huángjīn wàn liǎng róngyì dé, yí gè zhī xīn zuì nán xún.)
Gold is easy to get, a close friend is harder to find.

CHAPTER ONE

"Murder" is an ugly word. The act itself is an ugly thing to see and an even uglier thing to do. I've seen it before and now I've done it. I tell myself that I had no choice, that it was part of my job. Both of those things are true—or as true as any of the things we tell ourselves to be able to sleep at night.
But that doesn't make living with it any easier.

☐ ☐ ☐

When a light came on in the house, I turned off the novel I'd been listening to and picked up the video camera. I thumbed the power switch, made sure the "low light" setting was on, and focused the zoom lens.
The subject was in his kitchen, doing something with his hands that I couldn't see because they were below the window frame. He had on a dingy white tee-shirt and hadn't shaved that morning. Of course it was still early, a quarter after five, and there was only a hint of dawn in the eastern sky.
I'd been on watch since two a.m., sitting there in my dark, nondescript Toyota and keeping an eye on the unkempt suburban ranch house across and down the street. I don't care for talk radio or the late-night call-in shows that seem to attract people even stranger than some I have to deal with. So I'd brought a Megan Abbott audio book, knowing her stuff is so good it would keep me awake.
I'd also brought a bottle of water and a turkey sandwich. I hadn't eaten the sandwich and hadn't drunk much of the water. I didn't want to have to pee in the bushes of the nearby houses any more than I had to. Guys are lucky, I thought, not for the first time. They could just bring an old tennis-ball can. There was some special gear for women, but I didn't like to use it. Simpler just to squat in the shrubbery once I'd verified that the homeowners didn't have a dog that would react to my presence. Call it part of the supposed glamour of my job.
I'd been on this surveillance for the past three days, trying to get the evidence our insurance-company client wanted. Nothing much had happened over the weekend. The subject had driven in and out a few times, but we knew he was okay to drive, so there was nothing in that.
Today, Tuesday, might be more interesting. Yesterday afternoon he'd hosed off his boat, filled the gas tank from a big can, and hooked a

charger to the battery. Small, with a shallow draft, the boat was apparently meant for fishing, so I'd wondered if he might take it out this morning. I don't know much about fishing except that the people who do it like to start early, so I'd been on watch even earlier. I hoped I hadn't wasted my time.

The subject disappeared from the kitchen, leaving the light on. Then a light came on above the garage doors and light shone from the window on the side of the garage. One of the two garage doors went up, and I leaned forward as I began shooting, hoping to catch him pushing up the door. But it must have been a power door, because he walked out, wearing jeans and sneakers, as the door was still going up.

He was a big man, tall with broad shoulders but also with a jowly face and a gut that hung over his belt. We knew from our investigation that he smoked and liked to throw back a few beers—often more than a few. He was in his late fifties and beginning a slow slide toward retirement.

He had a couple of fishing rods in one hand and a large tackle box in the other. I shot him carrying them over to the boat, knowing that wouldn't help us much but hoping I'd get something better.

I did. After he put the fishing gear in the boat, he unhooked the battery charger and put it in the garage. He started his old pickup and backed it close to the boat trailer. Then he got out and walked to the rear end of the truck.

Fortunately for me the trailer was angled in the weedy yard so that I could see him on the far side of the trailer tongue. He bent to grasp the tongue. Then with an obvious effort—I could practically hear him grunting—he lifted the tongue and lugged it onto the hitch attached to the truck's bumper.

Jackpot! He'd told his employer that he'd hurt his back on the job and couldn't do any heavy lifting. Couldn't even bend over, he said, so his doctor, whose name surfaced in a lot of our insurance cases, had told him he should take several weeks off from his job at the warehouse. The report from the insurance company's physician was inconclusive—it's hard to disprove a claimed back injury—but the company thought he might be faking and asked us to find out. Now we had.

I kept the camera on him as he connected the trailer's brake-light wires and safety chains to the truck. I panned with him as he went back to the garage. When he didn't reappear, I figured he had gone inside the house, maybe to get his lunch or make a final head call before leaving.

After a few minutes the light in the kitchen went off. Then the lights in the garage. Soon he walked out of the garage carrying a small cooler in one hand and a phone in the other. I kept the camera on him in case he did something else I could put in our report. But he just put the cooler on the truck's seat and climbed in after it. He didn't move stiffly—maybe that was worth mentioning.

At that point I should have switched off the camera and left. He hadn't paid any attention to my parked car, and if he saw me drive down the street, he would probably think I was just some neighborhood resident going to an early job.

But knowing when to stop has never been one of my strong suits. That's why I'm not a police officer anymore. I decided to video him driving off to his fishing trip on a weekday when, but for his "injury," he would have been working.

There was more light in the sky now, and the sun had just pushed its upper edge over the horizon that showed in the gap between the subject's house and the one next door. Even this early I felt the warmth through the open driver's window, and I knew it was going to be another sweltering late-August day in coastal Virginia. Not a day I'd want to go fishing, but, good for me, our subject did.

I must have moved when I zoomed back to a wider angle in anticipation of shooting him driving away. Or maybe the rising sun flared on the lens. Something caught his eye, and he stared in my direction. Then he picked up a pair of binoculars—I guess he took them out on the boat—and used them to examine me.

The guy was dumb enough to fake an injury and think he wouldn't be caught but smart enough to figure out what I was doing. He dropped the binoculars on the seat, jumped out of the truck, and dashed into the garage. When he emerged seconds later he was carrying a baseball bat and running toward me.

I had my pistol with me, a SIG Sauer P365, small, lightweight, and easy to conceal. I always bring the pistol along on solo surveillance jobs, just in case, but that morning I didn't reach for it. I didn't think I'd need a gun to handle this guy, and showing it to him would work against me if we went to court.

I set the camera on the dash and raised the window. Then I slid out and locked the car. By that time he was halfway there, huffing down the street and carrying the bat at port arms. He was so close I could see the ugly look on his face. He certainly wasn't coming over to chat with me.

I crouched into a fighting stance, thankful once again that my father had insisted on my taking martial-arts training until I knew enough to protect myself. "You may need it," he'd said, giving me one of his looks that conveyed more than words could. And he'd been right—I had needed it a few times. This situation was shaping up to be another one.

The subject seemed surprised that I'd gotten out of the car and appeared ready to fight him. He slowed as he approached me, winded even though he hadn't run fifty yards.

He stopped about ten feet away, panting as he tried to catch his breath. He must not have noticed the camera on the dash, because he raised the bat in a threatening way.

"Who the fuck are you?" The anger was clear in his voice, but he was careful not to shout and wake the neighbors.

"Nobody." Unlike police officers, private eyes don't have to identify themselves.

"What are you doing here? You goddamned gook!"

That last was a mistake. Until he used that word, I hadn't wanted to fight him. But I've never put up with ethnic slurs. I don't make a big deal about being Chinese American, but I don't ignore prejudice.

"What did you call me?"

"You heard me."

"Yes, I did. And if you don't put that bat down, I'll kick your ass."

"Ha! A little girl like you?" He raised the bat higher and angled his body as though getting ready to take a swing at me. "I don't care how much karate shit you know. I'm the one who'll do the ass-kicking."

I'm not that little—five-six and usually just under 130 pounds—but I was a lot smaller than he was, and both of us knew it. Plus he had that bat.

Maintaining my fighting position, I took a step in his direction, but he didn't retreat. He moved the end of the bat in little circles, looking for an opening. I decided not to give him one.

Normally I would have gone for a knee, but I didn't want to risk putting him in the hospital. I leaped toward him and swirled into a roundhouse kick to his chest, barking out the attack words. "Ki hup!"

The kick staggered him, but he managed to swing the bat and hit my upper arm with a glancing blow. The arm went numb—I knew the pain would come soon—so I turned that side away from him.

He raised the bat again, but before he could swing it I kicked him again, straight-legged and harder this time. He fell backward onto the pavement, dropping the bat, which clattered on the asphalt. I grabbed the bat and threw it as far as I could onto the lawn of the house behind me.

Then he tried a kick, lying on his back and aiming for my ankle. I jumped back, making him miss. For a moment I thought he might get to his feet and see what he could do with his ham-like fists, but the fall seemed to have knocked the fight out of him.

"You hurt my back." He made a face that was supposed to show pain and touched his lower back. "I mean, even worse than it was. You're going to hear from my lawyer."

That was a familiar line. "Oh, sure, call your lawyer. But don't forget your baseball bat."

"Fuck you!"

"Another thing you can put on your list of 'nevers'."

He glared at me but didn't say anything else. I unlocked the car and got in. As I drove away I looked in the rearview mirror and saw him get to his feet, give me the finger, and walk over to pick up the bat. He bent over to do it, so I figured he couldn't be badly hurt.

Two blocks down the street I felt myself tremble from the rush of adrenaline. I hated confrontations like that. My mother had tried, without much success, to teach me to be nice, sweet, always helpful to others. Not subservient like the stereotype of Asian women but not a street-fighter either.

Well, it was just part of the job, I told myself. And I wasn't the one who'd been armed with a bat.

I noticed that the camera was still running, so I plucked it from the dash and switched it off. I checked the time on the car's clock. A little after six. Marcus was probably up by now—he'd been an early riser since his days in the Marine Corps. I punched the speed-dial for his mobile on my phone, and he answered on the second ring.

"Hey. How'd it go?"

"Good and bad."

He paused, and I could imagine the frown on his dark face. "Okay, tell me."

"I got good video. Him loading up the boat and then hitching the trailer to the bumper. It looked like a pretty heavy lift."

"Probably was. Sounds like just what we need. So what's the bad part?"

"He saw me and came after me with a baseball bat."

"Knowing you, I'm guessing he didn't get very far with that approach."

"No, I put him on the ground and took the bat away."

"You struck first." It was a statement, not a question.

"Yes. I didn't see any point in letting him take a swing at me before I did anything."

Marcus paused again. "And how bad is he hurt?"

"He got up as I drove away. He was well enough to flip me the bird."

Marcus chuckled. "Then he can't be too messed up. How about you?"

"He clipped my arm—nothing serious." My arm was throbbing now, but I didn't want to tell Marcus that. It wasn't broken, and I could stand the pain.

"Okay, I'll meet you at the office, and we'll see what you got."

"Fine. I'm going home first. Take a shower, change clothes."

"Sure. See you later."

He clicked off, and I put down my phone. That had gone better than I'd expected. Marcus Jefferson was a good boss, but he didn't tolerate stupid mistakes. Maybe I'd made one, maybe not. I'd know soon enough.

I took the interstate from Chesapeake to Norfolk and drove to my apartment near the intersection of Granby and Willow Wood. The place itself wasn't much, just a one-bedroom apartment with a combination living/dining room, but it had a great view of the Lafayette River. My parents thought it was odd that I now chose to live in Norfolk instead of Virginia Beach, where I'd grown up and where my office was, but I liked the old seaport's more urban feel.

I locked all my gear in the trunk and climbed the two flights of stairs to my place. I was tired from the surveillance and still jittery from the fight. In the cramped kitchen I opened a cabinet door and looked longingly at the bourbon, but then I closed the door and made a cup of green tea. I'd come too far to slide back now. I'd save that drink—or maybe two—for the end of the day.

I swallowed three aspirin for the arm. Then I took a shower, washing away the last of my anger along with the dust of the previous day and night and some of the tired feeling. I gingerly rubbed my arm under the warm water, and although a bruise was developing, the pain had begun to subside.

I'd shaved my legs recently, so I didn't have to perform that unpleasant chore, but I washed my hair. That was easier with the short cut: just above collar length, parted on the right, and combed to sweep down on the left.

I'd kept my hair long in the Navy as many servicewomen do, trying to hold onto some femininity in that mostly male environment. I'd worn my hair pinned up in my Navy uniforms just as I had in my police officer's uniform, but I'd had it chopped off ... afterward. I hadn't given cutting my hair much thought at the time, but now I realized it was one way of doing penance.

Not the only way of course. The drinking and the nightmares saw to that. And were still seeing to it.

Bobby had liked my hair long. He'd said so several times, watching me as I undressed and took out the pins. I'd let what I thought of as my "long, black tresses"—all that reading as a child!—flow down my bare back. Then Bobby would hold me in that special way he had, firmly yet gently, kissing me long and deep as he wrapped his fingers in my hair and pulled me to him.

My face felt hot, and I realized it wasn't just the shower. I was crying, crying again for what I'd had and lost. Killed. Buried. Tried to forget.

But could never forget.

CHAPTER TWO

I got to the office about nine-thirty. As usual I'd found little food in my refrigerator, so I'd taken time to have breakfast at the pancake house in Ward's Corner, the one with framed photos of old Norfolk on the walls. I hadn't finished reading last Sunday's paper, so I did that as I ate my ham and eggs.

I knew what my mother would have thought about the food. She still fixed a traditional breakfast every morning, usually white-rice soup—congee—or a different soup made with sticky-rice dumplings. I remembered how annoyed she'd been when my little sister and I, seduced by Saturday-morning cartoon commercials, begged for the sticky-sweet cereals we'd seen kids eating on TV. My mother finally gave in but only to the extent of buying cereal for us, continuing to make breakfast for my father and brother and herself.

When I got to our office building, the parking lot that we shared with a dental practice, a real-estate company, and a beauty salon was only about half full, so I was able to snag a spot near our front door. There's no name on it, just the street number. Our business cards don't even list that, only a post office box along with the telephone number and a generic e-mail address.

Simone, our office manager who doubled, or tripled, as receptionist and administrative assistant and was also Marcus's wife, was at her desk when I walked in. A former model still gorgeous in her fifties, she had her headphones on and was transcribing dictation, her long, slim fingers flying over the keyboard as she typed in a report by Marcus or Larry, our agency's other investigator.

I gave her a little wave and mouthed a silent "hi." Simone took one hand off the keyboard long enough to waggle her fingers at me and then continued typing, the keys clicking like furious knitting.

I went back to Marcus's office. He was on the phone but gestured me in and pointed to a chair.

The person on the other end was doing most of the talking. Marcus just said "uh-huh" and "okay" occasionally while taking notes on his yellow legal pad. Marcus had told me once that using those pads gave him more credibility with the lawyers we dealt with—both those who were our clients and those on the other side. I'd followed his lead in that practice as I had in some others. But as Marcus has pointed out to me a couple of times, I'm too stubborn not to do most things my own way.

As I waited for the telephone conversation to end, I wondered what my next assignment would be. I hoped it wasn't another worker's comp investigation with those long hours of surveillance. Maybe I'd get a shoplifting case and pretend to be an employee while I watched to see which of the real employees were stealing. It might be a divorce matter—collecting evidence of infidelity—even though Marcus knew I disliked divorce work and gave most of those cases to Larry, who didn't seem to mind spying on people having sex in motel rooms.

You learn a lot about human nature in this job. Most of it isn't pretty. My father had wanted me to be a lawyer or an accountant, a well-educated person with a prestigious job. My mother had wanted—still wanted—me to marry and have babies she could spoil. I knew that to at least some extent I was a disappointment to them. But I had also disappointed myself. More than once.

Marcus finally said, "Okay, see you at noon," and hung up. He looked at his notes for a moment, then looked at me, a pleased expression on his face. "Whew! Got something big for you, girl. Something juicy."

"Yeah? What is it?"

"I'll tell you in a minute. First let's see what you got from that surveillance."

I dug the camera out of its black canvas bag and used the cable that Marcus handed to me to plug the camera into the big video monitor on the wall. As I switched on the camera, Marcus clicked the remote a couple of times, and my video appeared on the screen.

Marcus watched silently as the subject loaded the boat and hitched the trailer to his truck. When the subject bent over and lifted the trailer hitch, Marcus froze the action.

"Perfect! That's all we should need. Man going fishing on a weekday morning, too hurt to work but not too hurt to pick up a boat trailer. The insurance company will be happy with this."

"That's good. But keep watching."

"There's more?"

"Yeah, the part with the baseball bat."

Marcus glanced at me before putting the subject into motion again. After a few seconds he said, "Okay, now he sees you ... gets the bat ... and runs toward you, mad as hell." He stopped the action and turned toward me. "What made you keep shooting? You should have just driven away."

"I know. But I got mad too. I was just doing my job—I wasn't the one faking an injury."

"Hmm. Can't afford to be too emotional in this line of work."

The words stung, but I made no reply.

"Well, let's see the rest of it." He clicked the remote, and we watched the brief fight. When it was over and I was finally driving away, he clicked the remote again, and the monitor went dark.

"That's not too bad. The guy was clearly threatening you, and he was bigger and armed. It was reasonable for you to defend yourself."

"You don't think his lawyer will try to claim that I started it? And maybe that I hurt the guy?"

"Sure. And then we'll offer to show the entire video, which proves that the guy's not just faking an injury, he's well enough to run across the street and try to beat you with a club. The facts are against him more than they're for him. You were smart to keep the camera running—now it won't be 'he said, she said'."

That made me feel better. "Thanks."

"Notice I didn't say you were smart to take the guy on. You should have left the scene. You had what we needed, and there was no need to risk getting hurt—or hurting our case."

I sighed. "I know. But I guess hindsight's always twenty-twenty."

"Yes, it is. Trite but true. Next time remember what I told you."

He waited until I said, "I will."

"Good. Now let's talk about what came in this morning."

"Okay. What's that?"

"A murder investigation."

I let the words hang in the air a moment. Murder? I'd never worked on a murder investigation, not even as a cop.

"Who was killed?"

"Susan Fontaine, wife of the real-estate developer Whitaker Fontaine. Ever heard of them?"

"No, I don't think so."

"They're well known around town. They're rich—by most people's standards anyway—and give a lot of money to charities. Children's Hospital, Chrysler Museum, things like that. Always going to black-tie events. A power couple—well, at least they were."

"What happened?"

"The police found them in their bedroom late Saturday night. She was dead by gunshot, and he was passed out drunk. His pistol was on the floor near his hand. There was a short item in the paper yesterday morning. You didn't see it?"

I shook my head. "Haven't gotten to it yet—on the stakeout. Why were the police there?"

"Fontaine had been at a business dinner with his partner, man named Tom McKenna. Apparently Fontaine had been drinking heavily, and McKenna tried to take his keys. Fontaine got nasty, told McKenna to go fuck himself—this was in front of their investors—and insisted on driving. When McKenna got home he called Fontaine, but there was no answer. He got worried and called the police, asked them to check the house."

"Doesn't seem like they'd respond to that sort of call."

"No, not usually, but both Fontaine and McKenna donate money to the toy drive the police run every Christmas. And they're friends of the mayor. So the police sent a patrol car to the Fontaines'—a big house in the Lochhaven section of Norfolk. Rich folks' neighborhood."

I nodded. I knew where that was—large two- and three-story houses shaded by tall trees. Several had docks jutting into the Lafayette River. When you drove through you could see the water glinting like silver beyond the green expanse of the well-tended lawns.

"Fontaine's car was there, which normally would've ended things, but the front door of the house was open." Marcus glanced at his notes. "This was after midnight, so a little late to be walking the dog or anything like that. The patrol team went up and rang the bell but got no answer. They thought maybe someone had picked the lock and gone inside."

"So they checked the house and found the Fontaines."

"Right."

"Sure looks like he did it."

"Yeah, it does. But his lawyer says he's pleading not guilty. That's who I was on the phone with just now. The information he gave me he got from Fontaine and the police yesterday."

"Who's the lawyer?"

Marcus grinned. "You're going to love this. Scott Cushman."

"Oh, great—'The Cash Man'."

"Exactly. I know how much you like him."

Which was not at all. He and his partner Jacqueline Taylor—both married but widely rumored to be engaged in a long-term affair with each other—had a busy personal-injury, DUI, and criminal-defense practice. They knew Marcus from when he was on the Virginia Beach police force and often retained us to do investigative work. In the eight months I'd worked for Reliable Investigations, I'd had several dealings with each of them.

I got along fine with Jackie. We kept our relationship businesslike and just did our respective jobs.

But Scott was a little too friendly, always complimenting me on my appearance and touching me on the arm or back. He hadn't quite crossed the line—at least not yet—but he'd come uncomfortably close to it, and he often looked at me as though imagining me naked.

Maybe he had "yellow fever"—a fetish for Asian women. It's more common than you'd think and usually pretty obvious. It's also a major turn-off. Who wants to be wanted not for herself but because she fits some male fantasy?

"I'm not wild about him, but I can work with him. I'll be strictly professional—and hope he'll be too."

"He will." Marcus paused for effect. "Especially if Jackie's around."

Both of us chuckled at that.

"We're meeting them for lunch, talk about the case, what to do next."

"Fine. When and where?"

"Noon. The Tidewater Yacht and Country Club."

"The country club? Then I need to go home to change."

Marcus looked at my beige chinos, casual top, and low-heel shoes. Other than having long sleeves to hide the bruise, that sort of outfit was my standard working uniform in this kind of weather.

"You're fine. The club's not fancy—I've been there before."

"Easy to say when you're wearing a suit."

"Well, there's no time. I want you to read the newspaper story and then research Fontaine. Dig up as much as you can before we meet Scott and Jackie."

I started to protest but then saw the look on his face. "Okay, I'll jump on it."

"Good." Marcus checked his watch. "We'll leave in about an hour and a half. On the way there you can fill me in on what you learn."

Allowing myself the relief of a mental sigh, I went to my office, small and windowless but functional, and got to work.

Who was this Whitaker Fontaine? And if he hadn't killed his wife—which seemed like a pretty big "if" at this point—who had and why?

That's what we had to find out.

CHAPTER THREE

We headed for the country club in Marcus's Buick. Marcus liked big domestic cars—"American iron," he called them—partly because he was a big man and wanted to be comfortable but also because of all those years riding in their patrol-car equivalents. As he drove I scanned my notes and hit the highlights of what I'd learned from my research.

"Whitaker Randolph Fontaine III—his friends call him 'Whit'—age fifty-two. Norfolk native from a prominent family that had money until his grandfather made some bad business deals and lost most of it. Got his bachelor's degree from the University of Virginia, spent six years in the Navy, then went back to UVA for a master's in business."

"Navy, huh? Find out if he qualified on the pistol range."

"He wouldn't need experience with a gun to shoot someone in the same room."

"No, but Scott and Jackie will want to know, and if he got a pistol ribbon, the other side will use that against him."

"Okay." I made a note. "Next he worked for a couple of local investment firms before he and Tom McKenna—that's Thomas James McKenna, originally from New Jersey—started Fontaine-McKenna Associates about ten years ago. Fontaine is more the finance guy, and McKenna is more the construction guy. They built a number of hotels, office buildings, and strip malls, mostly in Virginia Beach. Both men made a lot of money—and still do."

"And the wife?"

"Susan Elizabeth Blackledge, forty-six. Originally from Richmond. Her family made its money more recently, running a chain of discount furniture stores, but still has it. Susan sold her share of the company to her siblings after she married, and Whitaker used some of the money to start Fontaine-McKenna Associates. She met Fontaine while he was getting his M.B.A.—she was an art history undergraduate at UVA. Married him right after she graduated. No children and nothing in the public record to say why."

"Any history of domestic violence?"

"No. At least not in the record."

"You checked with the Norfolk police?"

"Yep. Used your name, and they confirmed that Fontaine's clean except for the occasional parking ticket."

"Huh. I'm surprised they still remember me. That liaison job was only for six months."

"Well, they do. Sergeant Zack Spencer said to say hello and to ask you about the New Year's Eve party at his house on Willoughby Bay. The one where you, and I'm quoting now, 'won a bet by doing the polar plunge at midnight—in the buff'."

Marcus grinned but rubbed his face to try to keep me from seeing it. "Hmm, my memory's a little hazy on that one."

"The sergeant predicted you'd say that. He also said to tell you he thinks he still has the pictures somewhere."

That got a laugh. "The son of a bitch probably does. Okay, back to business. Any more on the wife?"

"Nothing that stands out. She worked for the Chrysler Museum for a few years but left when Fontaine started making big money. Then she mostly served on the boards of arts organizations to which they donated. Got her picture in the paper and *Virginia Living* a lot, mostly from attending those fancy events you mentioned."

"Anything else?"

"Well, she was very attractive. Beautiful, I'd say. Fontaine is also good-looking. The sort of couple who seemed to have everything. Here's a magazine photo of them."

I held up my phone, and Marcus glanced at the picture as he turned off Hampton Boulevard into the entrance to the club. "Yeah, that sort of couple. But not anymore."

I looked down the driveway that ran through the emerald golf course and past the clay tennis courts, finally curving up to the enormous stone clubhouse. Beyond the corner of the building I saw a forest of sailboat masts, some with jaunty flags snapping in the breeze. The brick pillars that flanked the driveway bore polished bronze plaques that read, "Members and Guests Only."

"No," I said, "not anymore."

The inside of the clubhouse was cool and quiet and seemed dim after the noon brightness outside. When she saw us the receptionist hesitated a moment before nodding politely as we passed her desk.

Marcus led the way upstairs to a gleaming oak door marked "The Grill." He pushed it open, and I followed him inside. Scott and Jackie were sitting at a table by the picture window that overlooked the harbor and all those boats, each costing more than I made in a year. Maybe in two years.

Scott rose as we approached. "Hi, folks. Thanks for doing this on such short notice." He shook Marcus's hand, and leaned over to kiss my cheek. I let him do it but then stepped back and went to a chair that put me next to Jackie and across the table from him.

Jackie lightly touched my arm. "Hey, Wendy, how are you?"

"Fine, thanks. Good to see you." I noticed the obviously expensive coral-and-white summer dress she was wearing and was immediately self-conscious about my casual attire.

The men and I sat. The server appeared with menus and asked what we wanted to drink. Scott ordered a scotch and urged Marcus to do the same, but he demurred. Jackie ordered a chardonnay, and Marcus asked for sweet tea, the national drink of the South. I wanted a bourbon with a splash of water—I was tired and my arm ached—but I settled for my usual hot tea.

We made small talk while we sipped our drinks, looked over the menus, and ordered lunch. Once the server had collected the menus and departed, Scott said, "Well, this is going to be a tough one. No witnesses, but the circumstantial evidence is damning."

The club wasn't busy on a Tuesday, and no one was seated near us, but Scott kept his voice down anyway. So did Marcus. "Were Fontaine's prints on the gun?"

"Yes, but that's not surprising. It was his gun after all. But there were no other prints on it, and no one had wiped off all the prints, so that evidence points to Fontaine."

"Doesn't mean no one else could've done it."

"No, but it's not good for us."

"No, it's not." Marcus thought for a moment. "So what happened after the police found them? The usual drill?"

"Uh-huh. The police took Fontaine to their Ops Center on Virginia Beach Boulevard and questioned him while the CSI team checked the house."

As I jotted more notes on the pad I'd brought in the small briefcase I used as my "job purse," I could picture the crime-scene investigators photographing everything before an ambulance took Mrs. Fontaine's body to the morgue. Then they would have started looking for prints and any other physical evidence.

"What did they find?"

"I don't have any details yet. We may have to wait for their formal report plus the autopsy report—could be three or four weeks, maybe longer. But my guy in the lab told me about the prints on the gun."

I wondered how much cash The Cash Man was slipping his guy to get advance information like that. Apparently enough money to help Scott win more of his criminal cases than his competitors could. Unethical but shrewd—really shrewd, which was a good description of Cushman himself.

"If you've got someone on the inside, we might get the preliminary autopsy report sooner," Marcus said.

"Yes, but there doesn't seem to be any doubt about the cause of death. The news reports say—and my source confirmed it—that she was shot twice in the chest."

"That'll usually do the job."

"I guess there's no chance it was suicide?" I knew I was reaching, but two-shot suicides, although rare, are not unknown.

"No, apparently either wound would've been fatal," Scott said. "Plus, her prints weren't on the gun. And I'll bet the lab won't find any gunpowder residue on her hands. I'm glad you thought of the possibility though—that's the sort of brainstorming we're going to have to do to save Fontaine."

So at least Scott hadn't thought the question was completely stupid. That made me feel a little better about having asked it.

Perhaps to save me from any embarrassment, Marcus quickly asked, "Did Fontaine talk?"

"No, or at least not much. The police started their 'gotcha' routine—bright lights around a hard, wooden chair—but Fontaine told them pretty quickly he wouldn't say anything without speaking to a lawyer, so they had to stop after about half an hour."

"Good. He might have said anything if they'd done one of their eight-hour marathons."

"Even confessed," Jackie said, "to something he's now saying he didn't do."

"It's been known to happen," Marcus said, and I knew he was thinking about the Norfolk Four—Navy sailors who'd confessed to raping and killing another sailor's wife in 1997 and then recanted. Their confessions were so implausible, even contradictory, that all four were eventually released from prison but not until each of them had served several years. A fifth man, the only one linked to the crime scene by DNA evidence, said from his prison cell that the four had been stupid for talking.

Although that case had occurred some time ago, news reports on the men's lengthy quests for pardons had kept the memory of it alive, and I was familiar with it although not as much as Marcus was. He'd known the detectives involved, including the one later convicted of extorting money for lenient treatment of criminal suspects. Marcus hated corrupt cops, and he shook his head every time he mentioned that man.

Scott was surely familiar with that case. "Well," he said after a pause, "thankfully, we don't have that situation. When they let Fontaine use the phone—that was on Sunday morning after they'd taken him to the Norfolk jail and he'd been booked and fingerprinted—he called his business lawyer, who referred the case to me."

Jackie raised her eyebrows at Scott's remark that the referral was to him, not to their firm, but she didn't say anything.

"Have you been able to talk to Fontaine?" Marcus asked.

"Yes, briefly, right before his arraignment yesterday morning. The judge said he's going to be charged with second-degree murder and use of a firearm in the commission of a felony. Depending on what facts the police investigation reveals, the prosecutor might bump the murder charge up to first degree."

"What sort of sentence is he looking at?"

"Well, he has no criminal record, so thirteen to twenty-one years for second degree, twenty-three to thirty-eight for first degree. The firearm offense is three to five."

Marcus let out a soft whistle. "That's a lot of time."

"Yes, it is—if he has to do it. He'd probably get a lot less if he claimed the shooting was the result of a drunken argument. I told Whit that if he'd recall the scene that way, I could probably convince the court it's true. But he won't let me try—not yet anyway. He may change his mind if we can't find anything to raise reasonable doubt."

Neither Marcus nor I said anything to that, so Scott continued. "Anyway, the judge set the preliminary hearing for next week and scheduled a bond hearing for this Friday."

"Do you think the court will grant bond?" I asked.

"That's a tough call, given the charges, but maybe. Fontaine's a prominent citizen with longstanding ties to the area. Plus he's done good things for the community. I might be able to get him out on a two-fifty bond."

That meant $250,000. Fontaine could either post that much in cash or use a bail agent and pay a fee of ten or maybe fifteen percent. A lot of money either way, but my research indicated that Fontaine could raise it.

The server arrived with our food—salads for Jackie and me and something more substantial for the men. We were silent as he distributed the plates. After he left Marcus looked at Scott. "So, what do you want us to do?"

"The circumstantial evidence seems so damning that I don't think we can just try to poke holes in the state's case. We're going to have to come up with a plausible theory about how and why someone else killed Susan Fontaine."

"That's going to be hard to do," Marcus said, "unless someone else really did it."

"Yes, it will," Scott said, spearing a piece of his grilled trout almandine, and I could tell he thought Fontaine was as guilty as the evidence suggested. So did I.

"But that's the only way to create reasonable doubt," Jackie said.

As I nodded in agreement, I noticed that although Scott had almost finished his drink, Jackie had barely touched hers. Well, maybe Scott didn't like to drink alone and she was just accommodating him. I could understand that—from both perspectives.

"So we've got to find someone with motive, means, and opportunity." Marcus looked at Scott, then at Jackie. "Any suggestions about where to begin?"

"A few." Jackie took a slim stack of index cards from her Burberry bag and handed them to Marcus. "I made some calls this morning. I know people who move in the same circles as the Fontaines, and although most of them wouldn't tell me anything, a couple of them did."

Marcus slowly thumbed through the cards while the rest of us ate. "Looks like the Fontaines weren't getting along too good. Both of them said to be having affairs. And, despite outward appearances, Fontaine-McKenna Associates may be in a slump. Maybe Fontaine and McKenna haven't been getting along so good either."

He handed the cards to me and took another bite of his cheeseburger. I read the notes Jackie had made in her small, precise script. "Well," I said, "this is something to go on."

"It's a start," Jackie said, "and I may be able to find out more."

"I'm surprised anyone told you this much," I said. "Doesn't seem like the act of a friend, if these people are supposed to be friends of the Fontaines."

Jackie smiled. "Where there's a lot of money and success, there's also a lot of jealousy. And plenty of people are jealous of them—or were before this happened."

"That's not enough motive to shoot Susan Fontaine."

"You wouldn't think so. But if her husband didn't do it, the killer's motive could have been jealousy—a love triangle gone wrong."

"We'll see," Scott said. "Marcus, I want you to check out this house this afternoon—the police told me they'll be finished with the crime scene today. They released Fontaine's keys to me." He handed a key ring to

Marcus.

"Okay, but I doubt we'll find anything they didn't."

"Maybe not, but it will tell you something about Fontaine. And his late wife."

Marcus nodded and dropped the keys in his coat pocket.

"You can interview him tomorrow. I told him you'd be working on the investigation."

"Actually, I'm going to give Wendy the lead on this one. It looks like there's a lot of digging to do, and she can devote more time to it than I can."

I blinked, and my mouth hung open for a moment before I thought to close it. I'd assumed I'd assist Marcus with the investigation, not run it. I glanced at Scott and saw that he was as surprised as I was. He looked at Jackie, raising his eyebrows.

Then he looked at me. "You think you're ready, Wendy? You've helped us with a lot of little cases, but investigating a murder ... that's a big responsibility."

My ears burned, and I started to make a sharp retort, but Marcus waved his hand to stop me. "Of course she's ready, Scott. I wouldn't put her in charge if she weren't."

Jackie gave me a sympathetic look but didn't say anything. Apparently our sisterhood extended only so far.

Scott paused. "Okay, Marcus, you know your business. But we need to move quickly on this. If a murder investigation isn't successful within a week—"

"It'll probably never be successful," Marcus said. "Yeah, I know. Don't worry—we'll do our best."

"I'm sure you will." Scott reached into his inside coat pocket and pulled out a white envelope. "Here's a letter stating that we've hired your agency to work on this case."

We'd need that letter to meet with Fontaine in jail and perhaps for other things. Marcus silently handed the letter to me, and I slipped it into my briefcase along with the index cards and my notepad.

As I did so, Scott signaled the server to bring the check. "Good luck, Wendy. We'll be in touch."

"Thanks." While Scott signed the check, I took the last sips of my tea, thinking hard. Was I really ready for this? I would have been comfortable in a number-two role, but taking the lead? I wasn't sure.

Then it hit me—maybe I'd gotten too comfortable, working what Scott called "little cases" and backing Marcus up on bigger things. Maybe I needed a challenge. And maybe Marcus knew that and was betting that if he gave me this assignment, I'd step up to meet the challenge.

I looked at Marcus, who gave me an enigmatic smile and then pushed his chair back from the table. "Thanks for lunch, Scott, Jackie. It's good to see both of you. We'll get going on the investigation."

"Great," Scott said as we all stood.

Scott shook hands with Marcus and gave me another peck on the cheek. Jackie touched my arm again and nodded slightly, which I supposed was her subtle way of telling me that she thought I could handle the responsibility. It occurred to me then that she was always careful not to get too far out in front of Scott—just another of those small compromises.

We walked downstairs and out into the parking lot, which was cooler than most because of the trees planted at intervals. Marcus turned to look at the boats clustered in the harbor.

"Remind me, Scott—which one's yours?"

Scott smiled. "That power cruiser with the blue trim. He pointed, his gold cufflinks flashing in the sun. "*Naut Guilty.*"

I groaned inwardly. That was a bad one, but I guessed I should have expected it.

"Nice boat," Marcus said. "Well, this case should earn you enough to gas her up a time or two."

"I think so. This one should be good for all of us."

And for Fontaine? I wondered how the case would turn out for him. Virginia had abolished the death penalty, but there was a high probability that he'd end up in prison for most of the rest of his life—maybe all of it.

I hadn't met Fontaine yet, but some people would rather be strapped to a table and take that needle than rot in prison for decades. Which kind of person was he?

In any event I needed to lower the odds against him—flip them if I could. And if I couldn't do it within a few days, I probably wouldn't be able to do it at all.

Marcus had said I was up to it. Well, we'd see.

CHAPTER FOUR

Marcus drove to the Fontaine house, following the directions I read to him from my phone. The house was even bigger than I'd imagined, a sprawling place, looking fairly new, on a large lot that adjoined the water.

"Modest little cottage," I said.

Marcus chuckled. "I bet they bought a tear-down and had this custom-built. I'm sure the neighbors were thrilled with the design."

He was probably right. The house was tasteful—if you like modern architecture—but most of the nearby houses were more traditional, with wooden siding and large windows flanked by shutters. Many were painted in Williamsburg colors—creamy whites and soft greens and yellows. The rest of the houses were mixed—a Tudor here and there, a couple in Mediterranean style, and a few with red brick and *Gone With The Wind* white columns. What they all had in common was being expensive and well-maintained.

Marcus pulled into the broad concrete driveway and parked beside the police car that was near the closed garage. A uniformed officer was moving around on the front steps, cutting and bunching up the yellow tapes emblazoned with "CRIME SCENE—DO NOT CROSS" in big, black letters.

We walked up the steps as the cop finished rolling the tapes into a big ball. He put the ball under his left arm and let his right hand hang free. "Yes, can I help you?"

"Marcus Jefferson and Wendy Lu, Reliable Investigations. We're working for Mr. Fontaine's defense counsel."

"Do you have some ID?"

"Sure," Marcus said easily.

I could tell that Marcus was annoyed but trying hard not to show it. He pulled out his wallet and showed the officer the state-issued identification card that displayed his name, picture, and private-investigator registration number. I did the same thing.

The officer looked the cards over carefully and nodded. "Okay, wait here."

He stepped back and closed the door.

"He's a nice, friendly fellow," Marcus said.

"Just doing his job."

"I guess. Maybe I'm getting crotchety in my old age."

I smiled. "You won't be old for at least a few more weeks, and you've always been this way."

Marcus put on a surprised expression. "Think so?"

Before I could answer, the door opened again and a tall, late-thirtyish man in plain clothes—obviously a detective—stared at us. "Hello. I'm Sergeant Connolly, NPD. You're working for defense counsel?"

Marcus nodded. "Yes, Cushman and Taylor."

"'Cash Man?' Great. I knew this was going to a fun case. Say, didn't you used to be with the Virginia Beach police?"

"Yep, for twenty-five years. My partner was too."

"Just for three years," I said.

"I've heard of you, Jefferson. They say you were a good cop. Honest and fair."

"I tried to be."

"And you're Ms. Lu?"

"Wendy Lu." I was sure Connolly had never heard of me unless it was in connection with how I left the force. Apparently he hadn't—he gave no sign that he recognized my name. But something, maybe his tone or the way he was looking at me, made me add, "I'll be the lead defense investigator."

I could tell that surprised him, but he was too professional to say so. Instead he gestured for us to come inside. "Well, come on in. We're done. I was just doing a final walk-through to make sure we didn't miss anything."

We went into the house, which the air-conditioning was keeping quite cool, almost cold. From the living and dining rooms flanking the large foyer I got an impression of hardwood floors, oriental rugs, expensive furniture, and original art. The air smelled faintly of floor wax and furniture polish, but what I thought it really smelled of was money—the kind of money that was supposed to insulate people from the violence that had happened in this house. The kind of money possessed by people who thought murder happened only on back streets, in squalid apartments, and at sleazy motels, not in their tastefully decorated bedrooms.

But in this case they were wrong.

I noticed Connolly watching me as I glanced around. Then he turned to Marcus. "Look, you were both on the force, so I'll do you a favor. Show you around, save you some time."

I was about to say that we'd be fine on our own, but Marcus spoke first. "Okay, thanks. Of course we may take another look ourselves."

"Sure, if you think you need to."

With the uniformed officer bringing up the rear, Connolly led the way down a long hall toward what I assumed would be the master bedroom. "There are more bedrooms, two bathrooms, and a home gym upstairs, but this was their bedroom and bathroom. Hers, anyway. It opens onto the back yard and the pool."

Marcus looked at Connolly. "What do you mean 'hers'?"

"It doesn't look like he slept there much—none of his things are in or on the dresser or in the closet. Looks like he used a bedroom upstairs."

"That doesn't mean they didn't sleep together. Maybe he just liked to have his own space to get dressed."

Jotting notes, I paused at their use of the past tense, implying Fontaine would never live in this house again. There was a good chance he wouldn't, at least not past his trial, but still it sounded odd—speaking of a living person as if he were dead.

"Look at this," I said, pointing to the gold-framed wedding picture on the wall just outside the bedroom.

They say all brides are beautiful. I don't know whether that's true, but Susan Blackledge certainly had been a beautiful bride, a slim blonde with bright blue eyes and a dazzling white smile set off by an equally dazzling white dress that her mother might have worn at her own wedding.

Fontaine looked very handsome beside her, tall and well-built, almost a James Bond double in a tuxedo that looked custom-made and probably was. But although he was smiling, there was an odd look in his dark eyes. Not exactly that of a deer caught in headlights, but something that said he wasn't quite sure what he was getting into.

I thought of my parents' wedding picture—both of them looking very stiff and formal but also impossibly young in their traditional clothing. The photo, its colors considerably faded, had been taken in China several years before they immigrated to the United States. Suddenly it struck me that I was now older than they were in that pale picture.

Contrary to what you sometimes see in the movies or on TV, there was no outline of where Susan Fontaine's body had been. Chalk or tape contaminates the crime scene, so real investigators don't use it. Sometimes they use fluorescent paint to mark the position of people killed in traffic accidents, but that's about it. The investigators would have taken plenty of photos to show where the body had been.

The bed was unmade, the covers thrown back and the pillows at different angles, but otherwise the room was remarkably neat for a murder scene. For example, there were no clothes strewn about and nothing broken. A large TV sat on the long, low dresser, and near it several pieces of expensive jewelry glittered on a mirrored tray, which, unfortunately for Fontaine, seemed to rule out robbery as a motive for the murder.

The only thing out of the ordinary was a stain on the carpeted floor, the dried blood such a dark crimson it was almost black.

"They found her lying here?" Marcus looked at Connolly.

"Yes. She was on her side where the bloodstain is, and he was on his back over there not far from her. The gun was between them."

"How were they dressed?" Marcus stepped close to the stain and measured distances with his eyes.

Connolly pulled his own notebook from a pocket of the tan sport coat he wore over a dress shirt with no tie. The well-tailored coat, brand new or nearly so, looked good with his dark-brown trousers, also well cut. As he flipped open the notebook, I glimpsed a slim gold wristwatch, an elegant opposite of the large, gaudy "aviator watches" common in the Navy.

He consulted his notes. "Let's see ... she was wearing a silk nightgown. Pale blue, if you're interested. Barefoot, no jewelry but her engagement and wedding rings. He was wearing gray pants, a light-blue shirt, a navy-blue blazer, and loafers. Wedding ring and wristwatch."

"Blood only on her?" I kept my tone unemotional despite imagining how the red of her blood must have looked against the blue of her nightgown. I even felt a little sick but was determined not to show it.

"Yeah, just her. Not that much actually—apparently she died quickly and didn't bleed a lot."

"Not even from two in the chest?" Marcus sounded skeptical.

Connolly looked at Marcus. "Either one would've been enough. Both bullets caused major damage. I'd bet they couldn't have saved her if they'd gotten her to the hospital right away instead of at least an hour after she was shot."

Marcus nodded. I made another note, and then a thought hit me. "Wait a second—you say he had a coat on?"

"Yes, he did. He'd worn it at dinner."

"Okay, but doesn't it seem odd that he wore it in here? I mean, most guys would've taken their coat off as soon as they came through the front door. Probably dropped it on a chair—like that one." I pointed to an armchair in the corner.

Connolly frowned. "Remember—we don't think he slept in here. At least not routinely. All of his clothes are upstairs."

"I know, but I don't think he would've worn a blazer around the house. Especially not at the end of a long day in the summertime."

"She has a point," Marcus said.

"Could be that he was just unusual in that regard. I've heard he's a snappy dresser. Or maybe he was so drunk he didn't followed his normal routine. Plus there's one other thing."

"What's that?" I wondered what I might've missed.

"He came into this room planning to kill her, or they quarreled once he got here and then he decided to kill her. Either way he was in a highly emotional state. It's impossible to know what he would or would not have done—he certainly wasn't acting normally."

I thought about that. "No, I guess not. But you're assuming he killed her."

"All of the evidence says he did. Oh, I know you'll try to find something that will incriminate someone else or at least raise doubts about Fontaine's involvement. But I think you're going to have a hard time—a very hard time."

"We'll see," Marcus said.

I went over to the walk-in closet and opened the door. Not to stereotype my own gender, but you can tell a lot about a woman from her closet. This one was full of expensive, fashionable clothes that told me Susan Fontaine had cared about her appearance and spent money to enhance it. Either she was neat or had a maid who was, because the hanging clothes were grouped by type and color and the sweaters and casual clothes, all neatly folded, were too.

On a top shelf I saw a blanket—not needed this time of year—a couple of extra pillows, and an empty plastic bag, large and rectangular with zippered sides. It was some sort of storage bag, and I wondered what was normally kept in it. I hadn't seen anything in the closet or the bedroom that would seem to fit the bag.

"Anything else, Wendy?"

Marcus's question ended my probably idle speculation. I turned and went back into the bedroom. "I'll want to see the crime scene photos of course. But now I want to go through the rest of the house."

Connolly gave me a look. "There's nothing else to see here."

I forced myself to pause before replying. "I'm sure you're right, but I'd like to walk around anyway. Consider it part of my training."

"Okay, if you have time to waste." He turned to the uniformed officer. "Rick, we finished the checklist, right?"

"Yes, sir, everything on it."

"Fine. Jefferson, can you lock up when you leave?"

"Sure, we have a set of keys."

"All right. We'll be going." He looked at me again. "Good luck, Ms. Lu."

"Thank you. I may need it."

He held my gaze another moment but didn't say anything. Then he nodded at Marcus and left, followed closely by the other officer.

I waited until I heard the front door close behind them. "Cops. All the same."

Marcus chuckled. "Yes, we are. And so are you."

"I know."

"Connolly's a good detective, or so I've been told. I'm friends with another plainclothes who plays in Connolly's weekly poker game, and he generally speaks well of him. Except that Connolly sometimes bets more than he should and can be a sore loser."

"He may be good, but it sounds as though he's already made up his mind about Fontaine."

"You can't blame him for that—under the circumstances."

"No, I guess not. Well, let's see the rest of it."

We walked through the empty house, our footsteps and occasional comments making the only sounds. Connolly was right—there was nothing else to see, at least on the first floor. We'd already seen the living room and dining room, and the kitchen, pantry, and powder room were what you'd expect in this sort of house.

The den was at the back of the house and, like the master bedroom, opened onto the back yard and pool. It was a rather dark room with what I thought of as masculine décor—wood paneling, deep leather chairs, and a big built-in bar. Given the lighter and more delicate decorating in the living room and dining room, I thought the den was mostly Whit's hangout, not Susan's.

Upstairs I took a couple of minutes to poke around Fontaine's bedroom. He had expensive clothing too although less of it than I'd expected. A bookcase contained several books on how to succeed in business, a couple of international thrillers by best-selling novelists, and several framed pictures, mostly of Fontaine and others standing in front of construction sites.

I pointed to a picture that had turned up in my research. "That's Tom McKenna, his partner." McKenna was a bit shorter than Fontaine, a slim, pale redhead dressed in khakis and holding a construction helmet.

Marcus picked up the photo and studied it. "He looks like a foreman, but then you said he was more the construction guy."

"That's right."

"You'll want to question him. Right after Fontaine, I mean."

"Sure—if he'll talk to me."

"Why wouldn't he? No reason for him to lawyer up."

"No, I guess not."

A desk that matched the bookcase sat next to it. The desktop held a small brass lamp, a black Bose Wave radio/disc player, and some modern jazz CDs. The man seemed to have good taste in music.

The center of the desk was conspicuously empty, and I ran my fingertips across the space. "Think he used a laptop here?"

"Maybe. If he did, the police have got it and are searching it now. Ask Connolly about that when you look at the murder photos."

I nodded and checked the desk drawers. The bottom drawer held an oily rag and a gun-cleaning kit.

I made a note. "Looks like he kept his gun here."

"Yes, but that doesn't mean it was there on the night of the murder. It could have been somewhere else in the house, or he could have carried it in his car or even in his coat pocket."

"Or someone else could have had it."

"Yes, if someone else was the shooter."

"Someone who knew where he kept the gun—or maybe someone who took it away from him."

"Doesn't narrow the field down much, does it?"

"No."

His bathroom was as neat as hers although there were fewer bottles and tubes. The mirrored cabinet above the sink didn't contain any prescription medicine, just aspirin and some over-the-counter allergy pills, but there was a bottle of some stuff to hide gray hair. One of those "so gradual no one will notice" preparations. No one but everyone who knows you, I thought. Well, we all have our little vanities, and from what I'd seen so far, Fontaine had fewer than most.

We finished our walk-through and retraced our steps downstairs. At the front door Marcus turned to look back into the house. "Big place for just the two of them. I wonder why they never had any kids."

I wondered that too but realized only Fontaine had the answer. "You never know about a thing like that. You just never know."

Marcus and Simone had two children, both grown and both quite successful—a lawyer and a computer scientist. He loved being a dad, so it was probably hard for him to imagine why a married couple wouldn't have at least one child. But all he said was, "Yeah, I guess that's right."

Marcus locked the door behind us and handed me the keys. "It's all yours now, Wendy. Time to earn your paycheck."

CHAPTER FIVE

Back at the office I spent the rest of the day reviewing my notes and planning the investigation. By five-thirty I was tired, having been up since about one in the morning and working most of that time. I yawned as I put my papers in order and shut down my computer.

Carrying my briefcase, I went to Marcus's office and stood in the doorway. He was doing one of his least-favorite things—reviewing and revising draft bills to our clients. He noticed me standing there and put down his pen.

"Big day, huh?"

"Yes. And I'm going to see Fontaine in the morning."

"That'll be interesting."

"I imagine. I suppose he'll stick to his not-guilty story."

"Sure, at least for the time being. He may switch closer to the trial if Scott tells him he's likely to be found guilty. Fontaine might try to cut a deal at that point."

"Depending on what I find, he may have to. Why don't you go home? I think Simone already left."

"Yeah, she's home cooking dinner. I'll go soon. Just wanted to finish these bills." He looked down at the one in front of him. "Ms. Henderson isn't going to like hers."

"Divorce case?"

"Yeah, and it took Larry a while to catch the husband in the act. He's a slippery devil. Larry finally found him and his girlfriend at a motel in Chesapeake. Fortunately for us, they didn't close the curtains all the way." Marcus chuckled as he moved the bill from one pile to another.

Having been the "girlfriend" myself, I didn't find the situation amusing. At least there hadn't been a private eye on our tail—not that I knew of. I'd thought it was just a matter of time before Bobby and his wife split up. And maybe they would have if ….

I struggled to push the thought out of mind. After all those months I expected the pushing to be easier. But it wasn't. I wondered if it ever would be.

"Well, I'm going to take off."

"Sure. Big plans for the evening?"

"If you call having dinner with the parents big."

He must have noticed my tone. "Hey, your parents are nice people. They love you very much."

"I know."

"Then what is it?"

"Let's just say they're not wild about my life right now—the way I'm living."

Marcus nodded. "I can understand that. As a parent you just want your kids to be happy. And you tend to think that what makes you happy—or, worse case, would've made you happy—will make them happy."

"I didn't know you were such a philosopher."

"Well, there's a lot you don't know yet. But you'll learn fast—especially in this job."

"Maybe more than I want to know."

"Probably. I have. Now scram."

"Yes, sir, boss." I gave Marcus a mock salute and headed for the door.

My parents lived in Virginia Beach in an ordinary ranch house in a quiet, middle-class suburb. The only thing that made the house stand out was the beautiful lawn—well landscaped and meticulously maintained. My father liked to work in the yard—he said it relaxed him—and he'd told me once that he and my mother were determined not to give their neighbors a reason to sniff at the home of "those people." So he mowed the grass twice a week, kept the flower beds weeded, and pruned the shrubs with the electric trimmer I'd given him as a birthday present.

I pulled into the driveway and parked. The double garage door was open, so I could see the neatly kept space and my parents' cars—Dad's basic Chevy for his daily commute and Mom's nicer but less-driven Chrysler.

I walked through the garage to the door that led into the house. Although I'd lived in that house for most of my life and knew the door probably wasn't locked, I rang the doorbell anyway. I just didn't feel comfortable walking into what I know thought of as my parents' house— my home no longer.

My mother opened the door. When she saw me, she smiled and said, "Hello, Wen," in Chinese, or more precisely in Mandarin, using my actual name. My mother could speak English but not very well, even after more than twenty years in the United States, and she preferred to use Mandarin. That's all she spoke with my father and my brother. With my sister, who barely spoke it at all, she reluctantly used English.

And with me, well, things were more complicated. Technically, Mandarin was my first language because I spoke it before I learned any English. My family immigrated to the United States when I was four, and I had little exposure to English until I started kindergarten.

I was so humiliated that I couldn't talk like the other kids. But I picked up English fast and after that used Mandarin only at home and then only when I had to, which was with my mother. My father's English was good—he'd studied in the United States in his twenties—and he didn't mind conversing with me in it.

But my mother never liked speaking to me in English. She thought that because I was born in China, I should always be more Chinese than American.

For my part, I consider myself American, but sometimes I do think in Mandarin. And on rare occasions I even dream in that language.

Things like that make me wonder, whenever I happen to look in a mirror, who is that woman looking back at me? Who *should* she be? I don't really know. I've never known.

I said hello to my mother and restrained my impulse to lean down and give her a hug. My parents were seldom physically affectionate with us kids, and I knew a hug would make her uncomfortable. So I simply returned her smile, slouching a little in an effort to minimize the difference in our heights.

"Have you eaten yet?" She used the traditional Chinese "politeness" question—the equivalent of the Western "how are you?" Then she added, "You look tired."

Thanks, Mom, I thought. "I am a bit tired. I had to work last night—well, early this morning."

I thought my mother might make another of her critical remarks about my job, but she didn't. "You'll feel better after a good dinner," she said, leading the way into the kitchen. "I'm making things you like—dumplings and noodles with bean sauce."

They were two of my favorites—jiao zi , dumplings stuffed with pork and cabbage, and zhá jiàng miàn, wheat noodles topped with zhá jiàng sauce made from ground beef and soybean paste. Mom was able to get the right ingredients because Hampton Roads' relatively large Asian population, including thousands of Filipino Americans drawn by the Navy, meant the area had several Asian grocery stores.

"Great! Thank you." I noticed that she named an even number of dishes—an odd number, as served at a funeral dinner, would be unlucky. But so would four, sì, sounding too close to s , or death. In China, especially Northern China, people probably wouldn't serve these particular dishes together—just one or the other with a small side dish—but after so many years in America, my mother was more relaxed about such things.

"But you didn't need to go to so much trouble on my account."

"It's no trouble—I like to cook."

She did and was very good at it. My mother came from a town near Beijing, so her native cuisine was Jing style—"cuisine from the capital"—influenced by the emphasis on seafood and vinegar in Shandong, the coastal province just east of the capital. However my father was from Sichuan Province, so she had learned to make several of the spicy dishes for which that area is known. Although she didn't brag about her cooking, she liked seeing her family and other people enjoy the food she prepared, and she liked receiving compliments on it.

I remembered my mother had told me that people always prefer the type of food they had growing up. "Your stomach never forgets," she'd said, which I thought was a good way of putting it and in keeping with the Chinese partiality for "purity," meaning simplicity and consistency, in cuisine as in other areas of life.

I liked both styles of dishes that my mother made, but I preferred the pungency of Sichuan food. The less I said to her about also liking American food, the better—with its many international influences it wasn't "pure" no matter how tasty it might be.

I felt awkward standing there as my mother bustled about, stirring, tasting, seasoning. "Is there anything I can do to help?"

"No, I'm just about done. Your father's in the den, watching the news. Go sit with him, and I'll call you when dinner is ready."

"Okay." I walked out of the kitchen, which I noted was looking a bit dated. I did the mental math on how long they'd had the house and was surprised. I hadn't realized it was so long. Time moved so much faster now than when I was a child and didn't know about bad things such as insurance fraud and theft and adultery.

Or worse things. Such as murder.

My father was in his chair, reclined just enough to be comfortable but not so far back as to imply laziness. There was nothing lazy about him, especially his mind, which was honed as sharp as the knives in my mother's kitchen.

"Hi, Dad," I said in Mandarin. "What's new?"

He gestured toward the television set. "Oh, mostly the same people arguing about the same things," he said in his lightly accented English. "And not getting anywhere. Sometimes I find it frustrating."

"I'm sure you do." I slipped back into English myself.

My father muted the sound and turned to me. "You look thin. Are you eating right?"

"I'm fine. I've been going to the gym a lot lately. And working some long hours—surveillance mostly."

"I see. Are you enjoying this job?"

"Well, it's okay, and I need to be doing something after ...."

"Yes, I know." My father smiled gently, and I was relieved that he didn't seem to want to talk about the past any more than I did. "I think it's good that you're keeping yourself busy."

"I suppose so."

He rose from his chair. "Would you like a cup of tea before dinner? It will give you a good appetite."

"Sure, if you're having some."

I knew that if I weren't there, he'd probably have a small glass of scotch before dinner. I'd never acquired a taste for scotch, but over the years Dad had become something of a connoisseur. He and some of his friends occasionally met at the bar of a local Chinese restaurant, and he'd badgered the owner into stocking several brands of scotch that he liked. He'd tried to get his friends interested in scotch too, but most of them preferred beer.

None of the men ever brought their wives, and despite being rather Western in many ways, my dad was no exception to that rule. My mother didn't drink, and she disapproved, although silently, of the fact that my father and I did.

Both of them knew that after Bobby died I'd tried to crawl into a bourbon bottle and stay there. It hadn't worked out too well. I might still be there if Marcus hadn't come by my apartment that bleak fall afternoon and offered me a job. Marcus had met my parents when I was still on the force, and I wondered if perhaps my father had said something to him about my ... condition. But I knew better than to ask Dad and "lose face" in his eyes.

My father returned with two delicate teacups on a wooden tray. "Your mother says that by the time we finish this, dinner will be ready."

He held the tray out to me, and I took one of the cups. He took the other, put the tray on a table, and sat back in his chair. I waited until he raised the cup to his lips before drinking any myself.

We were silent for several moments, both of us savoring the delicate flavor of the tea. After a polite pause he said, "Are you working on anything interesting right now?"

"Yes, something that came up today." I didn't want to bring bad luck into the house by mentioning murder, but I felt I had to say something. "The Fontaine case. It's been on TV—the story about that rich woman." I was careful not to refer to that *dead* woman. "And her husband of course."

"Oh. Yes, I saw that." He shook his head. "An unfortunate thing."

"Really unfortunate for her. And for him too—he's our client."

"So you are trying to prove he is innocent?"

"Exactly. Or at least find another plausible suspect."

My father sipped his tea thoughtfully. "My life is so different from yours. Teaching economics, writing articles, going to all those faculty meetings. What you do seems much more interesting."

"Most of it's just routine. Asking people questions—often the same questions—and trying to fit the answers into some sort of pattern that makes sense. It isn't like what they put in those TV shows."

"Wen, please let me have my illusions. I like to think of you—the professional you—as being a detective in one of those movies you enjoy so much." He paused. "What's that French term you use?"

"French term? Film noir?"

"Yes, dark movies, dark stories. But I hope it isn't dangerous like that."

I thought of the guy who'd come after me with a baseball bat. That seemed like a year ago, but it was just early this morning. "No, it isn't really dangerous. It's actually boring sometimes."

"All jobs are—or can be. Sometimes. But I think you are good at this, so perhaps it is what you were meant to do."

I wondered if my father meant that. I hoped he did, but being a PI was a lot different from what I knew he'd imagined for me.

"Still, please don't tell your mother about this new investigation. She worries enough about you as it is."

"Okay."

My father nodded and unmuted the television set. We finished our tea as we watched the rest of the news program. Then my mother called us in to dinner.

Because it was just the three of us, we ate in the kitchen. I helped my mother put the platters of food on the table and then sat in my traditional place.

"Thanks, Mom. I can use a home-cooked meal."

"I'm sure you can. We hardly ever see you anymore."

I tried to ignore the implied criticism. "Well, it's good to be here." I knew that the dinner—and my favorite dishes—were her way of showing she appreciated my visit.

"I hope you mean that." She gave me one of her skeptical looks.

"Of course I do. And I appreciate your going to so much trouble."

"It's for your father too. I think the only reason he married me was because I know my way around the kitchen."

My father smiled at her. "That wasn't the only reason. Just a big one."

My mother smiled too. Then, perhaps to cover her feelings, she said, "Wen, do you want a knife and fork? Or will chopsticks do?"

"Chopsticks are fine, Mom." I picked up the platter of jiao zi and, in the traditional way of respect, served some to my father. "Here, Dad. You begin."

As we ate my mother peppered me with questions about my job, my apartment, and my life in general. I gave her general answers about my job—not using the "M" word or even mentioning the Fontaine case at all—and more specific ones about my apartment. I said little about my personal life. I could tell that made her impatient, but I knew she was frustrated that I wasn't dating anyone, and I didn't want to have a discussion about why not.

Trying to change the subject, I asked, "How are Chong and Nannan?"

"Fine," my mother said. "Your brother is doing well with his job, and Nannan is busy with the children."

"And Meihua and Greg? How is she feeling?"

"Her pregnancy is going fine—just a few more weeks now. Greg is … Greg."

I knew my mother didn't care much for her American son-in-law, but she never said anything really negative about him. At least not to me.

"I can't wait to meet my new niece! Another chance to be the best aunt ever."

"You are a good aunt, Wen." My father looked at me. "And maybe one day you'll have children of your own. I've always thought you'll be a good wife and mother—if you have the chance."

I chewed and swallowed, the food not tasting quite as good as it had seconds earlier. "We'll see. But I'm not in any hurry."

My mother made a dismissive gesture. "You can't wait too long. You don't want to be alone all your life."

"I'm not alone, Mom. I have my family and friends and my work."

She frowned. "You know what I mean."

I laid my chopsticks—delicate, hand-carved teak—on their matching rest. "Yes, I know, Mom. And I know you just want me to be happy. But I need some time …." Not wanting to bring up anything, I didn't finish the thought: to get over *him*. I wiped my eyes with the napkin and picked up the chopsticks.

Watching me, Dad came to my rescue. "Isn't it good to have Wen here to share dinner with us? You remember when she was in the Navy and out at sea on her ship? We used to look at the map and wonder where she was."

"I remember." My mother paused. "I thought, so, now my older daughter is in the Navy. How will she like it—will she fit in? And I was always afraid that something would happen and you'd never come back."

I smiled at her. "Don't worry, Mom. You know I'll always come home no matter where I go or what I do."

That made her smile, and the rest of the meal went fine.

Driving back to my place I thought about my mother's comment on my Navy service. I knew that she and my father were proud of me for serving even though they'd never said so—they had other ways of showing it.

When I got home I turned on a single lamp, fixed myself a drink, and sat outside on my tiny balcony. The air had cooled enough not to be uncomfortable. I sipped my drink and watched the river slip past. The water was dark except for the occasional wink of a reflected light. There was no sound except that of my breathing and the tinkle of the ice in the glass when I lifted it.

I sat there a long time. When fatigue and whiskey finally let me stop thinking, I went to bed. And for once I didn't dream.

CHAPTER SIX

My appointment to see Whitaker Fontaine was at 10:00 a.m., so I got to the Norfolk City Jail, located in the resuscitated heart of downtown, at 9:30. I parked in a nearby city garage and walked to the sprawling gray building that, with 1,700 beds, was the largest and most overcrowded jail in the Commonwealth of Virginia. Not much to be proud of, I thought. Well, at least USS *Wisconsin*, a World War II battleship, was moored nearby, and Nauticus, a popular maritime museum, was next to that, so the children of inmates could visit those attractions after they'd been to see their fathers in jail.

The inside of the building gave the impression of modern technology layered onto the steel bars and concrete cellblocks from some James Cagney gangster movie. The sheriff's department, not the police, ran the jail, and they'd installed what they called the "VUGATE" video system for making visitors' thirty-minute chats with inmates more efficient.

Inmates were generally allowed only one or two visits per week, but that rule didn't apply to attorneys or to those working with attorneys. So I'd been able to make an appointment to see Fontaine even though Scott Cushman had visited him twice earlier in the week.

Knowing I wouldn't be allowed to keep my briefcase and phone with me, I'd left them in the car. At the security checkpoint I showed my driver's license as ID, dropped my keys, pen, and sunglasses into the plastic bucket, and went through the metal detector. The bored deputy let me carry my notepad through, and I retrieved my other items.

Attorneys who were willing to sign a waiver form could visit their clients in the cellblocks, but because of the obscene catcalls and lewd gestures from the prisoners, almost all female attorneys and most of the males prefer to use the small visitation rooms. I'd chosen to do that, not because I was afraid of some guy grabbing his crotch and leering at me but because I wanted my conversation with Fontaine to be private.

I rode the elevator to the sixth of the jail's eight floors. A deputy met me and took me to the room where Fontaine was waiting. He was sitting in a metal chair with his hands folded on the table in front of him. I recognized him from his picture even though the prison uniform and the strain on his face made him look almost like a different person.

I took the chair across the table and handed him my card. "I'm Wendy Lu, a private investigator. Scott Cushman has asked my agency to assist with your defense."

Fontaine looked briefly at my card, then dropped it on the table. "He mentioned that. He said something about a retired Virginia Beach detective. That can't be you."

"No, that's my boss, Marcus Jefferson. But I'm also a former cop."

He studied me. "You can't have been on the force very long. You look pretty young."

"Long enough to learn the business. That's why Marcus appointed me lead investigator in this case."

My tone made him pause for a moment. "Okay, I get it. You know what you're doing. Well, you'll need to for my case. All the evidence is against me."

"It is now, but that's our job—to find evidence in your favor."

"You're assuming there is some."

I looked him in the eye. "Well, there must be some. Scott tells me you're pleading not guilty."

"Yes, because I'm not guilty!" He leaned across the table. "I didn't do it. I mean, I don't remember certain things about that night, but I know I couldn't have killed Susan." He looked into my eyes, trying to convince me. "They found me next to her body and the gun, sure, but that doesn't mean I shot her."

"No, it doesn't." I opened my notebook and clicked my ballpoint. "Tell me what you do remember."

He slumped back in his chair. "I've already told the police everything. Scott too. There's nothing left to tell."

"Maybe not. But maybe something else will come to you if you tell it again. I've seen that happen."

He looked annoyed and seemed about to say something sharp in reply, but after a few seconds he shrugged. "Okay. I guess I've got nothing else to do."

I waited.

"Tom and I had these Japanese real-estate investors in town, and—"

"That's Tom McKenna, your partner?"

"Yes, for almost ten years now. He was the one who set up things with the Japanese. Usually I handle the investor side of things, but Tom knows a guy here who knows these people. We met them at our office at two o'clock, spent the afternoon showing them some of our developments, and then went back to the office and talked for a couple of hours. After that we took them to dinner."

"I understand that you were doing some drinking that night."

Fontaine shifted in his chair. "Well, yeah, I guess I was. It had been a long day, and Tom was being a pain in the ass. Acting like he was the brains of the outfit and I was just along for the ride."

"Was that unusual?"

"I'd heard he said stuff like that occasionally, but he'd never done it in front of me. Maybe he was just trying to impress them—I don't know. All I do know is that it pissed me off."

I made a note. "Where did you take them to dinner?"

"Lynnhaven Dock House. We figured they like seafood, so we took them to a seafood place. Plus it has a great view of the ocean. Then we got there, and they all ordered steaks."

"They can get all the seafood they want in Japan. But not steaks like ours."

"I guess so. Steaks and scotch—that's what they wanted. And to go to a strip club afterward. Like the ones they'd been to in D.C.—lots of naked blondes. I had to tell them there aren't any like that in Virginia Beach. Too many Bible thumpers."

He caught himself and looked at me to see whether I was offended by that last remark. I wasn't. To the extent I have any religion, I'm a Buddhist. And I was no more surprised by the desire of the Japanese businessmen to see blonde strippers than I was by their wanting to eat beef. Things like yellow fever can work both ways.

"Did anything unusual happen during dinner?"

"No, not that I remember. We just kept the liquor flowing and laughed at their jokes. The dinner went on for quite a while—well past ten, I think."

"Is that where your memory starts to get hazy?"

He looked embarrassed. "Yes. I guess I was drunk at that point. I could still walk, sort of, but I was slurring badly. Tom tried to take my keys. I remember that. And I think he said he'd call me a cab."

"How did you get home?"

"I drove. I don't remember doing it, but I must have, because when the police arrested me the keys were in my pocket and the car was in the driveway."

"And you can't remember driving?"

"No. Like I said, there are a lot of things I don't remember about that night." He looked at me. "That isn't going to help, is it?"

"No, it's not." I scanned the information I'd jotted down the previous day. "Why was the front door open?"

"I don't know. I guess I left it open."

"But you don't remember."

He shook his head. "No. But it's hard to believe I left it open—I never do that. Not even when I get the newspaper off the walkway in the morning."

I made another note. "Okay. This next part may be hard. Was your wife already dead when you got home?"

"I don't remember." He shook his head again, harder this time. "I wish I could, but I just don't! God, I wish I hadn't had so much to drink that night."

"Okay, take it easy. You don't recall anything about the shooting—no loud noise or anything like that?"

"No, nothing."

"Well, tell me anything you do remember."

He squeezed his eyes shut and sat that way for a moment. When he opened them, he looked down and off to the side. "There's nothing to tell—nothing more. All I know is that I didn't do it. I had no reason to, and I wouldn't have done it even if I'd had a reason."

"She was shot with your gun."

"I know."

"Who else knew where you kept that gun?"

"No one. Just her."

"Are you saying it was suicide? From two shots?" According to Scott, the evidence ruled out that remote possibility, but I wanted to see whether Fontaine would grasp at any straw.

"I don't know! Goddamnit, I've told you—I don't remember! I'm just sure I didn't kill her."

I paused, giving him some time to cool down. "That's not going to be much of a defense. All right, let's try it this way. Who might have had a motive to kill your wife?"

"I can't think of anyone."

"No one at all? I understand that she may have been ... seeing someone else."

He laughed bitterly. "I'm sure she was. Maybe more than one person. She's been—had been—unfaithful to me for several years now, on and off."

That was a motive for murder, but he didn't seem very upset about her infidelity, and apparently it had been going on for a long time. If he'd killed her—*if*, I reminded myself firmly—the motive must have been something else.

"Could one of them have done it? The current guy or an earlier one?"

"Why would a lover want to kill her?"

"Sometimes affairs end badly." Mine had—very badly—so I knew what

I was talking about. "Anyway, it's a place to start. Do you know whom she was seeing recently?"

"No, she was always careful. No calls to the house or anything like that, at least not when I was around. After all, this is a small town in some respects—even if you lump Norfolk and Virginia Beach together."

That was true. Bobby and I had always tried to be careful about being seen in public, at least in civilian clothes. We never knew where or when we might run into somebody.

"But people would tell me that they'd seen her having dinner with another man, or she'd come home at two in the morning with some story about having been 'out with the girls'. Women her age don't stay out that late—not with other women unless they're lesbians, and Susan wasn't. She just liked men."

"You have no names at all?"

"I know she was seeing Colin Huntsman for a while. She dated him in college before she met me. He married afterward, but the two of them got together four or five years ago. I thought they'd broken things off but maybe not."

"Anyone else?"

"Dan Wallace. She served on a board with him. Roger Covington. They played tennis together—at least that was the first game they played."

I made notes. "That's all?"

"All I'm aware of, and I don't think any of them would've killed Susan. They had no reason to. I mean, she wasn't blackmailing them, threatening to tell their wives or expose the affairs in some other way."

"How do you know?"

He thought about that. "Well, I guess I don't *know*. But there's absolutely no evidence of anything like that. Plus I don't think Susan would've done such a thing."

"You'd be surprised what people are capable of." I hesitated a moment but knew I had to ask. "Why did she do it? The affairs, I mean. Were the two of you unhappy?"

"Not at first. And not for a long time. Then—well, we couldn't have a child, and Susan had a hard time dealing with that. Especially because …."

"Because what?"

"She was infertile. Endometriosis. So she blamed herself."

"It wasn't her fault."

"Of course not. I told her so a thousand times. But she wanted children."

"Did you consider adoption?" That question didn't have much to do with the murder investigation, but I couldn't help thinking of the adopted children I'd known at the Hampton Roads Chinese School. Their parents, almost all white, seemed so happy with their little Chinese kids.

"I would have, but Susan didn't want to. She said she wasn't sure she could love some other woman's child as much as her own. She became depressed after the doctors told her she couldn't conceive. Then she sort of slipped into drinking too much and running around with men." He paused, remembering. "I just buried myself in my work, and that didn't pan out much better than what Susan did."

"And you've had your own affairs." I kept my tone carefully neutral.

"I'm not proud of that, but I won't deny it. Susan found out, of course—well, after the first two. We had a terrible fight. That's when I moved to the guest bedroom."

"Have you been seeing anyone lately?"

"Yes, but I'd like to keep her out of it."

"I'm sorry, but you can't. Not out of the investigation. We don't know yet whether she'll need to testify." I held my pen poised over the pad. "Well?"

He sighed. "Maxine Walters. She's a commercial real-estate agent with the Gartner Group."

I'd heard of it. The Gartner Group was one of the biggest property-management companies on the Southside—the five Hampton Roads cities south of the James River and the southern tip of Chesapeake Bay. People who aren't from Virginia usually think "Hampton Roads" means roads on land, but the name actually refers to the maritime "roadstead" formed by the intersection of the James and other rivers as they empty into the bay. Many folks who've lived here a long time call the area "Tidewater," a name that I think makes more sense.

"You met her through work."

"That's right, about a year ago. At first it was just business—I mean we got along well from the start but didn't see each other apart from work. Then one day we didn't get back from a construction site until that evening, and I invited her to dinner." He paused and looked at me. "Things just sort of progressed from there. You know how it goes."

Yes, I knew. I remembered the first time Bobby and I had dinner—the way he'd smiled at me across the table. The way he'd made me laugh even after a long patrol shift. How I'd felt inside. Yes, I knew quite well.

"Is she married?"

"She was. Been divorced for a few years. No children. I don't think she ever wanted any. And she didn't seem to mind that …."

"You're married." I finished the thought for him.

"Right again."

"Were you going to divorce Mrs. Fontaine and marry this woman?"

"I hadn't planned to. Maxine and I never talked about marriage. She doesn't seem eager to try it again, and I felt that, well, that I owed it to Susan to stay with her. To try, at least, to make her happy."

And now it's too late for that, I thought, jotting more notes. "Do you think Ms. Walters could have killed your wife?"

"Of course not! Why would she do such a thing?"

"Perhaps to free you to marry her. But you say that's not something she wants."

"No. At least I don't think so."

"Well, I'll talk to her and see what she says."

He frowned. "Who else will you have to drag into this?"

"I don't know yet. I'll have to see where the evidence leads. I'll have to talk to your partner and maybe some other people at your office. Maybe these men your wife was seeing. But remember it's to keep you from spending most of the rest of your life in prison."

He looked around at the cold, bare walls. No windows, no sun, nothing green and living. Nothing that could make him forget, even if only for a little while, that he was in a cage.

Then he turned back to me and simply nodded. I could tell that being in jail was already getting to him. I understood how he felt—it would have gotten to me too.

I glanced at the wall clock. My time was almost up.

"One more thing." I needed to ask the question even though I was sure what the answer would be.

"What's that?"

"I understand that your wife came into the marriage with family money."

"Yes, she did. We invested most of it, primarily in stocks and bonds, keeping it for … our children."

"And you left it there even after she knew she couldn't have children?"

"Yes. I was making a lot from the business by then, and we didn't need Susan's money. I suggested that she give half of it to a charity and then oversee what the charity did with it. That would've given her something useful to do."

"She didn't want to do that?"

"Well, at first she seemed to like the idea, but she never went forward with it. Maybe her depression held her back. I don't know. But the money's still invested—about six million now."

"And who gets it?"

He shifted in his seat, not looking at me. "The will says I do."

"All of it?"

"Yes ... all."

Well. I knew what the prosecutors would call that—six million reasons to kill her. We'd need something strong pointing another way or Fontaine was going to stay inside for a long, long time.

I made a final note and stood to go. As I did, someone slammed a door down the hall, and the sound made him jump.

"Easy," I said. "Take it one day at a time. We'll do the best we can."

He nodded again and stared at the tile floor.

As I walked out, a guard came in to take Fontaine to his cell. For a moment I was tempted to wait and give him a goodbye wave. But then I thought of how his wife must have looked, lying dead on the floor with two bloody holes in her chest. I kept walking and didn't look back.

CHAPTER SEVEN

I went back to the office, typed up my notes, and, still sitting at my desk, ate the salad I'd brought for lunch. As I was finishing, Marcus appeared in the doorway.

"What did Fontaine have to say?"

"Not much. He says he doesn't know anyone who would've wanted to kill her."

"He'd better think of somebody. Otherwise he's done."

"I know. I think he knows it too. Maybe some ideas will come to him when he can think more clearly."

"Maybe. Let's hope so. What's next?"

"Talk to his partner, Tom McKenna. Then his girlfriend."

"His girlfriend?"

"Yep. The current one at least." I checked my notes. "Maxine Walters. Works for the Gartner Group as a commercial real-estate agent."

"That figures—keep it all in the family."

"Well, affairs are often that way." The words were out of my mouth before I realized what I was saying.

Marcus looked at me for a moment. I was afraid of what he might say next, but it was only, "Okay. Good luck with McKenna."

I put my lunch things back in their insulated nylon bag and stuck the bag in a bottom drawer of my desk. It occurred to me that if I were Philip Marlowe, I'd have a bottle of bourbon in there. Or scotch—wasn't he a scotch drinker? But given my history, an office bottle didn't seem like a good idea.

I picked up my briefcase, notebook, and pen, got my goes-with-anything black jacket off the hangar on the back of the door, and headed for my car. Twenty-five minutes later I was parked in a visitor's spot in front of the multi-story office building that housed Fontaine-McKenna Associates. The building was modern, all stone and glass, and surrounded by what amounted to a small park, mowed and trimmed almost as neatly as my parents' yard.

There was a wooden bench under the trees, and I thought how pleasant it would be to sit there in the cool shade for a while. Maybe to read. Maybe to think. Or maybe just to sit and do nothing at all.

But I was on the clock, so I went through the revolving door and walked across the marble floor of the lobby to the tenant directory mounted on the wall. Fontaine-McKenna was on the fourth of the six floors—high enough to have a good view but not so high as to pay the highest rent.

I punched the elevator button and waited for the car. Two women came through the front door and crossed the lobby to wait with me. They looked like co-workers returning from a late lunch. Both were young bottle blondes with good tans and expensive clothes.

They looked at me but didn't say anything. I didn't say anything either. The doors opened, we got in, and rode up in silence. I could tell that the women would have been chatting with each other if not for my presence. They got off at three, and as they exited, one glanced at me and said, "Have a good day."

"You too," I said, because that's what we always say even though it has no more meaning than our perfunctory "how-are-yous." But politeness is what sands away some of the rough edges of life. The others prick us and sometimes we bleed.

The reception area of Fontaine-McKenna was spacious and tastefully decorated. Large framed photos of what I assumed were some of the company's major projects hung on the walls. The receptionist gave me a practiced, professional smile as I walked over to her desk.

"May I help you?"

"I'm here to see Tom McKenna."

"Do you have an appointment?"

"No."

Her smile dimmed but didn't quite vanish. "I see. What name shall I give?"

I liked that use of "shall." Maybe she was a fellow member of the tribe of readers. We can't always recognize each other by appearance.

"Wendy Lu. I'm a private investigator working on the Fontaine murder case."

Then the smile did vanish. "Please have a seat. I'll see if Mr. McKenna is available."

She waited until I sat in one of the uncomfortable modernistic chairs. Then she lifted her telephone handset and spoke softly into it. I couldn't make out any of the words.

She listened for a moment and put down the handset. "Mr. McKenna said he'll be right out."

"Good. Thank you."

In less than a minute a slim man of medium height strode briskly from a side corridor that led into the reception area. He had a pale face dusted with freckles, and his rust-red hair was clipped unfashionably short. I recognized him from the picture I'd found, the one I'd seen again at the Fontaines' house.

He looked at me and then glanced at the receptionist, who nodded slightly. The man stepped over to me. "I'm Tom McKenna. You must be Wendy Lu."

"Yes." I gave him a business card. "Mr. Fontaine's lawyers have hired our agency to investigate the murder of Mrs. Fontaine."

He read the card and then tucked it into the pocket of his dress shirt, worn without a tie. "A terrible thing. I can't believe that Whit did it—I just can't."

"Well, we're going to try to raise reasonable doubt about that."

McKenna paused for a moment, then glanced again at the receptionist. She was pretending not to listen, seemingly fascinated by whatever showed on her computer screen. "Let's go back to my office."

"Certainly."

He retraced his steps, and I followed. We passed a secretarial bay where an older woman wearing thick glasses sat in front of a computer, typing away. She glanced at me but didn't say anything, and McKenna didn't introduce us.

His office was what I expected—a large room furnished in an expensively tasteful but not overdone way. Lots of pictures everywhere, some of Fontaine-McKenna projects and some of McKenna sailing or playing golf, mostly with other men. A couple showed McKenna running in races, a number card across his chest and a look of grim determination on his ruddy face.

There was only one picture that showed Fontaine and McKenna together. It was a posed photo of them standing in the middle of a line of uniformed police officers and presenting something—it looked like a check—to the senior officer, a captain. I didn't recognize him, but I did know a couple of the other cops, and I spotted Connolly at the far end of the line. He'd been younger then, probably promoted to sergeant just in time to stand there stiffly with the others.

I didn't see any pictures that looked like family photos. I glanced at McKenna's left hand—no wedding ring. Of course that didn't mean he wasn't married. I knew from long experience that some married men don't wear wedding rings. And some don't pay much attention to the ones they do wear.

And, I reminded myself, some women fall in love with married men.

McKenna closed the door, and I took the seat that he waved me toward. I took out my notepad and pen while he seated himself behind the big desk.

I opened my notebook and smiled, trying to put him at ease. "Thanks for seeing me, especially without an appointment. In a case like this we have to work pretty fast. Leads get cold quickly."

McKenna nodded. "I understand. I'm happy to be of any help I can although ...."

I held the pen poised above the paper. "What?"

"Well, it seems pretty cut and dried. I mean, the news reports say they found him in her bedroom, and the gun was right there. Who else could have done it?"

"Somebody—anybody—who wanted to frame him. It's been done before."

"Yes, but how likely is that?"

Not very, I thought. But I had to consider that possibility, no matter how remote. I parried his question with one of own. "How well did you know Mrs. Fontaine?"

"Susan?" He frowned. "Oh, reasonably well, I guess. I was a guest in their home many times and entertained them myself over the years. She was always trying to get me involved in her charitable causes, but I steered away from that. I donated money from time to time, but I never agreed to serve on any boards. I just don't have the time."

"I see." I made some notes. "But about their marriage—how did they seem as a married couple?"

"What do you mean?"

You're smart enough to figure it out, I said to myself. Maybe he just didn't want to speak ill of the dead—or his partner. "I mean did they seem devoted to one another? Was the marriage stable, secure?"

"Oh, who can tell? Except the people in the marriage?"

Good point, I thought. Yes, he was that smart. "Well, did either of them have affairs?"

He frowned again. "I think I'd rather not say."

"She's dead and beyond slandering, and he may be looking at a long prison sentence. I think you need to say."

He thought about that for several seconds, rubbing his chin. "Okay, I guess you're right. Yes, I think that both of them were involved with other people from time to time."

"Do you have any names?"

"No. Sometimes I could tell from things he said and did that Whit was seeing someone. This is a pretty small firm, so it's hard to hide much."

He didn't look at me when he said it. That's often a "tell" that someone is lying, and I had the feeling he was lying to me. If Fontaine had been seeing Maxine Walters, a prominent real-estate agent, for as long as a year, McKenna almost certainly knew about their affair.

I wanted to keep him talking, so I didn't call him on the lie. "How about Mrs. Fontaine?"

"All I know is that he spoke to me once or twice about his suspicions regarding Susan. I just listened—I didn't know what else to do. It made me pretty uncomfortable, frankly."

"I imagine so." I made more notes. "Well, can you think of anyone who would want to kill Mrs. Fontaine? Or put Mr. Fontaine in a bind? Perhaps do both?"

He paused but didn't rub his chin this time. "No, I'm sorry but I can't."

"I knew it was probably a long shot, but I had to ask." I scanned the list of questions I'd jotted down at the office. "How were the Fontaines doing financially? Any money problems?"

"Not as far as I know. Whit never mentioned anything like that."

"And Fontaine-McKenna Associates? How is the company doing?"

He laughed and glanced away as though looking at some of the project pictures. "Well, we could always be better. It's not easy doing developments in this economy. But we're paying the bills, keeping the lights on. I'd say business is fair."

That might mean something, I thought. I looked at him closely, waiting to see whether he'd continue. But he didn't say anything further, just checked the big watch on his wrist.

"Is there anything else, Ms. Lu? I have a conference call scheduled in a few minutes."

I looked over my notes. I wanted to ask him about the dinner that he and Fontaine had hosted on Saturday night but not when he was pressed for time, and in any case I wanted to talk to someone at the restaurant first. "I think that's all for now. I may—probably will—have some follow-up questions. Is there anyone else here I can talk to? Mr. Fontaine's assistant, for example?"

"Is that really necessary? We're all pretty busy around here."

"I think it's necessary. And I'm sure you want to help Mr. Fontaine all you can."

"Well, of course, but none of the staffers know any more about this than what they've heard on the news."

"They might—you never can tell."

He paused, looking annoyed. "Well, all right, if you insist. Whit and I share an assistant—Betty Partridge. She's sitting outside." He pressed a button on the phone. "Betty, there's a woman here who wants to talk to you about Mr. Fontaine's ... situation. Her name is Wendy Lu. I'll send her out to see you."

He stood up, indicating that our interview was over. I gathered my things, and he walked with me toward the door. He opened it and spoke to the woman at the computer. "Betty, this is Ms. Lu. She has some questions about Mr. Fontaine."

The woman adjusted her glasses and gave me an anxious look but nodded.

McKenna turned back to me. "That's it then. Goodbye, Ms. Lu."

"Goodbye."

He didn't offer to shake hands, and I didn't either. I heard the door close behind me as I stepped over to the woman's desk.

"Hi." I held out my card. "I'm a private investigator hired by Mr. Fontaine's lawyers to help with his defense."

She took the card in her hand, read it carefully, and nodded again, all her movements small but quick. The bird-like motions certainly fit her name.

"Is there somewhere else we can talk? Perhaps a conference room?"

"Yes, if it's free."

The room was vacant, and I took a moment to enjoy the view as we stepped inside. Above the suburban sprawl of Virginia Beach the sky stretched away, clear and blue with a few wisps of white cloud for contrast, and on the horizon I could see the water of Chesapeake Bay glinting in the sun. You're never very far from water in Hampton Roads, and that's one of the things I like best about the area.

I turned and looked at Betty Partridge. She was definitely nervous. "Nice view," I said. "I'll bet you enjoy it."

"Yes, I do—when I have time to look at it."

"I imagine they keep you pretty busy."

"Most of the time, especially Mr. McKenna. Well, Mr. Fontaine too, when he was ...."

"When he was here?"

"Yes."

"Let's sit down." I took the chair at the end of the table so that I wouldn't be sitting across from her.

She sat next to me and folded her hands in her lap.

"Maybe Mr. Fontaine will be back soon," I said. "That's what I'm working on—trying to get him out of this mess."

She glanced at me and then looked down at her hands. "I hope you can do that. He's a nice man. I can't believe he—well, I can't believe he would do such an awful thing."

"So you like working with him?"

"Oh, yes. He's easy to get along with, never harsh or demanding. He has high standards, but there's nothing wrong with that."

I made a note. "No there isn't. How long have you been with the company?"

"I came right after they opened. I'd been with a law firm but wanted something with more regular hours. My children were still little then, and I'd just gone through a divorce, so I needed to be able to drop them off and pick them up at the same time every day."

Like McKenna, she wasn't wearing a wedding ring, so apparently she hadn't remarried. Except perhaps to her two bosses and this job. "I understand. So you've seen the business grow over the years."

"Yes." She looked at me, inclining her head a bit. "We're been quite successful. Mr. McKenna and Mr. Fontaine were—are—good partners. They work well together, and the firm did well. That is, until ... ."

"Until what?"

She shifted in her seat. "I think Mr. McKenna could explain things better than I could."

"He asked you to talk to me. And this is important—Mr. Fontaine's entire future is at stake."

"Yes, I know, but ...."

"What?"

"Well, there's been some friction lately. I'm not sure about what. But I've heard them arguing a few times—more than a few, actually. Never in front of me, always behind closed doors. But I've heard them."

"And what were they saying? What were they arguing about?"

"I don't know. I mean, I couldn't make out the words."

I made a note, thinking about how to phrase my next question. "And you never stepped closer to the door? Never, perhaps, put your ear against it?"

She blushed even though there was no need. Under those circumstances eavesdropping was only natural—just human nature.

"Uh, well, yes. One time I did, but someone caught me, so I never did it again."

I'd have been surprised if she hadn't done it but not surprised if she'd lied about it. She was more truthful than most people I'd met on the job.

"And that one time—could you tell what they were arguing about?"

"No." She shook her head. "I wasn't able to listen long enough." She paused. "You ... you won't tell them, will you? Neither of them?"

They likely know, I thought, especially in an office this small. Whoever had caught Betty in the act had probably told her bosses to curry favor with them. Unfortunately, that's the way the world works.

But there was no need to burden her with my speculations. "Of course not. I can see that you want to help Mr. Fontaine. By the way, do you always call both of them 'mister'?"

She blushed again but not quite so much this time. "To people from outside the firm I do. Mr. Fontaine asked me to call him 'Whit', so I do that. Mr. McKenna is more formal. I tried calling him 'Tom' once, and he didn't say anything about it, but he gave me such a look that I never did it again."

I could imagine that look. I skimmed over my notes, thinking about what to ask her next. "I'm just beginning this investigation and don't have a lot of facts yet, so anything you can tell me about Mr. Fontaine may be helpful—especially his relationship with his wife, any personal or business troubles he was having, that sort of thing."

She didn't reply.

"Anything at all that you think may be relevant."

Then she spoke but without looking at me. "I, uh ... I don't know of anything that might help you other than what I've already said. I've been under a lot of strain myself lately—nothing to do with my job here—and I may seem somewhat distracted, but if I knew anything that might help Mr. Fontaine, I'd tell you."

"What about anything that might not help him?" I'd need to know that sort of thing too.

She shook her head and her spoken "no" was so soft that I could barely hear it.

I waited, but she didn't say anything else. "Okay," I said, putting away my notebook and pen. "I guess that's all for now. I may have some follow-up questions."

"I can't think of anything else I could tell you—anything that would be helpful, I mean."

"You never know what may be important in a case like this."

"I suppose so."

She sounded doubtful, but I didn't debate the point with her. "Well, you have my card, so if you do think of anything that might be useful, anything at all, please get in touch."

"I will. Thanks, Ms. Lu."

"No, thank you. And 'Wendy' is fine." I stood to go.

"Wendy. That's a nice name." She got out of her own chair and followed me toward the door. "Like that redheaded girl on the hamburger signs."

I'd heard that one before. "Sort of—my real first name is Wen. But using

'Wendy' just seems easier."

"Well, I like it."

Something made me feel sympathy for her, this nice but obviously nervous woman who'd been caught eavesdropping at work. I gave her a smile and said, "Thanks. So do I."

CHAPTER EIGHT

The Virginia Beach traffic was the typical Virginia Beach traffic, so it was almost five by the time I got back to the office. Simone was tidying up and getting ready to leave.

Even after a long day Simone looked great. I could see why she'd been selected to pose for *Playboy*'s "Women of the ACC" when she'd been a senior at North Carolina State. Marcus had mentioned that once, and I'd been curious enough to find the photo on the Internet although I never told Marcus or Simone. It was a tasteful nude, but I don't think I'd have been brave enough to pose like that, even at twenty-one, and my parents—or at least my mother—would have stopped speaking to me if I'd done it.

Simone paused when she saw me. "How'd it go today?"

"Fine, I guess. Hard to tell. I feel like I'm not making much headway."

"Well, you just started on this case, so it's too soon to hope for much."

I dropped my briefcase on a guest chair. "I suppose. Is Marcus still here? I thought I'd give him an update."

"No, he's out meeting with a potential client. He said to tell you that he'd see you in the morning."

"Okay. Well, have a good evening."

"You too. And don't spend it here." She smiled so that her admonition wouldn't sound quite so much like what it was. Simone had been successful in business—hospital administration—before Marcus persuaded her to join him at our little agency and help run the office. He wasn't good at paperwork and she was, so I knew it was due largely to her that I got paid every two weeks

As I walked back to my office I saw Larry sitting in his, and I stopped in the doorway to say hello.

"Oh, hi, Wendy." He put down the file he'd been reading. "How's the big case going?"

"Okay. No breakthrough yet."

"Give yourself time. You'll get there."

"Sure. What are you working on?"

"The usual." He grinned and sang in his fine tenor, "'Your cheatin' heart will tell on you.'"

"Surveillance tonight?"

"Yep, starting about eight. Chain motel near the oceanfront. The wife found a credit-card slip from there, so she thinks it's their 'low rent rendezvous'."

Larry was an amateur actor and singer who like to drop lines from plays and songs into his conversation and then watch to see whether people recognized them. He'd used that last line before, and I knew it was from "Third Rate Romance." The Amazing Rhythm Aces—good name for a band, but whatever happened to them?

I liked Larry even though we didn't have much in common other than our jobs, and he seemed an even odder fit as an investigator than I was. I'd asked him once why he didn't go into acting and singing full time—I was sure he would have preferred that to what he was doing—and he'd said, "Because I'm not good enough. To be a professional, you have to be a lot better than I am. Plus, you have to want it more. I'm lacking in both talent and desire, so here I am, Larry Kilgore, PI." He'd paused, looked uncharacteristically serious for a moment, then grinned. "And I have a beige trench coat to prove it."

Most people think that being a private eye must be exciting. It's not. You spend most of your time asking strangers nosey questions, poring over printed and electronic records of various sorts, and conducting surveillance, *i.e.*, sitting somewhere and waiting for something to happen. It gets exciting only when something goes bad, like when someone comes after you with a weapon, most often a gun but sometimes with something else as had happened to me yesterday morning.

"Well, I hope you get what we need from the surveillance. Say, how's Kevin?"

"He's fine, thanks. He's not teaching this summer, so he has more time to work on his dissertation. If the Old Dominion University gods are kind, he should be Doctor Kevin by the end of spring semester next year."

"I want to read his dissertation when he's finished. I like a lot of those pulp novels from the fifties that he's writing about."

"I'll tell him. I'm sure he'll be flattered."

"Does he plan to stay at ODU after he gets his doctorate?"

"If they'll hire him. We like Hampton Roads and don't want to move."

"Or maybe he can get on at one of the other local colleges."

"We'll see. He's been talking to the English Department at William & Mary, but that would be a bit of a commute from Virginia Beach."

"I suppose so. But I'm sure things will work out fine. Please say hello for me."

"I will. We should have you over for dinner soon. Kevin's been trying some new recipes."

I smiled. Larry couldn't cook any better than I could, but Kevin was a whiz in the kitchen. He'd even considered going to culinary school and becoming a chef, but his love of literature had won out. "Just ask. I'll be there."

Then I went to my office. Typing up my notes from the afternoon didn't take long. I finished by a quarter to six and decided to hit the gym. I hadn't been in a couple of days, and my body was telling me it needed exercise.

I said goodnight to Larry, wishing him luck on the stakeout, and walked past Simone's vacant desk on my way to the door. I keep a gym bag in my trunk, so I headed straight to the closest Y. I move around a lot in my job, and the Y membership lets me use any of the facilities in Hampton Roads.

I usually do about two miles when I run outside in the morning, but I didn't know the neighborhood around that Y, so I stayed inside and used a treadmill. I get bored on a treadmill, so I just did a mile and then started on the weights. When I was about halfway through my routine, I noticed Vanessa Hoang coming out of the locker room in workout clothes. She saw me, waved, and walked over to the weight rack.

I put down the two dumbbells I'd been lifting and toweled my face. "Hi, Vanessa. Taking the evening off from the big law factory?"

She laughed. "Yeah, for once. How are you?"

"Can't complain. Well, I could, but who'd listen?"

She laughed again, one of the things I'd liked about her since we went to high school together. But Vanessa, a better student and more ambitious than I, had gone straight to college and then to law school, returning to Hampton Roads to take a job with the biggest firm in the area. She was a mid-level associate in the corporate department and, I was sure, headed for partner. But she'd stayed in touch with me over the years and never acted superior about the differences in our educations, jobs, or incomes.

"I know, right? I haven't seen you around lately, Wen. You must be busy."

Vanessa, who had a Vietnamese middle name she seldom used, was the only person outside my family who always called me by my real name. I knew that one reason we got along well was our common ethnicity. Both of us had a variety of friends, but with a fellow Asian American everything was just ... well, easier.

"Very. And working crazy hours, some of it doing nighttime surveillance." I wanted a mental break from the Fontaine case, so I didn't mention my new assignment.

"Sounds like both of us could use a break. Say, want to get a drink afterward? Maybe something to eat?"

"Sure." I didn't have any plans for later that evening, and it would be good to catch up with Vanessa.

"Okay, I'll be ready to go in about forty-five minutes."

"Sounds fine. See you out front."

Vanessa smiled and went over to a stair-stepper. She was petite but athletic. She'd been a good soccer and tennis player in high school and probably still was, not that she had much time for either sport.

I finished my routine and headed for the locker room. I stripped and stood under the shower for a moment, then went into the steam room. A woman wrapped in a towel was sitting on the bench. She seemed surprised when I spread out my towel and sat on it. I'm not an exhibitionist, but I'm comfortable in my skin, and I don't see why women should have to cover up more than men do. Or more than I've been told they do. Maybe I could have posed like Simone after all.

By the time I came out of the steam room Vanessa had finished her workout and was stuffing her shoes, shorts, and tee-shirt into her gym bag. She still had the trim, muscular body I remembered from high school.

Towel in hand, I stopped on my way back to the showers. "I don't see how you do it."

"Do what?"

"Stay so slim. I know you don't have much time for the gym these days."

"Well, look at you. You must do a thousand sit-ups a day to keep your stomach that flat."

"I have to work at it. And watch what I eat."

"Don't we all? But I'll admit I got lucky in the gene lottery. My mother never seems to put on weight."

"One more reason for me to be jealous of you."

"Oh, you needn't be." At my puzzled expression she added, "I'll fill you in over drinks."

I nodded and went to take a shower. Moving my face from side to side under the warm water I thought about how Vanessa had looked standing there in her panties and sports bra. I'd never had romantic feelings toward another woman, but I supposed that if I did, that woman would be Vanessa.

One rainy Saturday afternoon in junior high we had been alone at her house and had practiced kissing, telling ourselves it was just so that we wouldn't be as awkward the first time we did it with boys. It hadn't thrilled me, but it hadn't been bad either. Her lips were soft on mine, and as we "practiced," each of our tongues found the other.

But we'd been right—it did make things less awkward the first time I'd kissed a boy. Johnny Zhao, that shy kid with glasses who'd had an obvious crush on me. I wondered what had happened to him. Probably married now with children. Maybe he thought of me once in a while. Or, more likely, didn't.

I was almost dressed by the time Vanessa got out of the shower. I finished as she unwrapped her towel and took her underwear out of the locker. Careful not to stare, I said, "See you out front," and headed for the lobby.

I checked e-mails while I waited for her. There was nothing urgent.

Vanessa came out in her expensive, well-tailored suit and coordinated high heels, and, as I had been at the country club, I was conscious of my more casual clothes. Well, each of us dressed for her job, and I couldn't do mine in her outfit. What if I'd been wearing something like that when Mr. Baseball Bat came after me? But I liked her fashionable look and told her so.

"Thanks. Where should we go for a drink?"

"How about The Shack? We can sit outside and enjoy the view."

"Kind of a dive, isn't it?"

"Not kind of—it *is* a dive. That's why I like it."

Vanessa smiled. "Okay. I'll have my private eye to keep me out of trouble."

"Yeah, but who'll keep me out of trouble?"

We drove separately to the eastern end of Chic's Beach. Chic's—often spelled Chick's—is near the Little Creek Navy base and spans both Lynnhaven Inlet and the border between Virginia Beach and Norfolk. The suburban area is home to a number of bars and restaurants, some nicer than others, but most not nearly as upscale as the newer places along the Atlantic Ocean in Virginia Beach proper. Chic's is a "local's beach" with a funky, down-to-earth feel I don't sense when surrounded by all the tourists at the oceanfront.

The Shack, right off Shore Drive and right on the beach, looked like its name. We were able to squeeze into the small parking lot, where my Toyota blended in but Vanessa's BMW not so much.

We told the hostess we wanted to sit outside, and she led the way to the deck, which, on a Wednesday evening, wasn't very crowded. The view was spectacular—a crimson sunset over the rippling blue-gray water, the panorama bisected by the long bridge-tunnel that runs to Virginia's Eastern Shore. Gulls wheeled and cried against the wispy white clouds that floated in the inverted indigo bowl of the sky. A few people were walking along the shoreline, and occasionally a sport-fishing boat slowly entered or left the inlet, running lights glowing in the falling darkness.

We sat at the scarred wooden table the hostess indicated, and a good-looking guy with a deep tan came to take our order. When he wasn't waiting tables, he probably lived on a surfboard. I ordered a Jim Beam with a splash of water, and Vanessa surprised me by asking for the same thing instead of her usual white wine. We also ordered the stuffed-mushroom appetizer to share.

As the server walked away I admired the snug fit of his narrow khaki shorts. I noticed Vanessa doing the same thing and winked at her. "Nice view, isn't it?"

"Yes, it is. In more ways than one." She laughed but sobered quickly. "I wish I got to do this more often."

"I know it's hard for you to get away from the office."

"Sometimes I feel like I live there. I don't mind working hard, but I'd like a life too. And maybe …."

"What?"

"Well, a husband and kids eventually. We're closing in on thirty, Wen, and neither of us married. No children."

"You're not seeing anyone?"

"No, not in a while now. Guys don't like that I have a law degree and make more than they do. Plus I have so little free time, and I often have to cancel plans at the last minute to work on some rush project. I see why most women lawyers in private practice are either married to other lawyers or …."

"What?"

"Well, married to their jobs." She looked at me. "I didn't think it would be this way. Did you?"

I'd told her about Bobby, of course, but she was too good a friend to bring up that painful topic. "You were always more of a planner, Vanessa. I just take things day by day. But you don't have to do it, you know. There are other jobs."

"That's true. But I'll confess—I like the money. I've gotten used to having some, and I'd find it hard to give that up."

I didn't know what to say, but the server saved me by arriving with our drinks and appetizer. "Cheers," I said. We clinked glasses and each had a sip. Then Vanessa put her drink down and began slowly turning it in a circle, watching the glass revolve in the ring of condensation it was leaving.

She looked at the glass for a moment, then looked up at me. "Do you remember when we were little and used to get lucky money?"

"Sure." At the Chinese lunar New Year—ch n jié, the first new moon of midwinter—my parents had given each of us kids a red envelope containing two dollars. We called the envelope hong bao—literally, "red packet"—and were always excited to get it, both for the money and for the luck it brought.

The Vietnamese also celebrate the lunar new year, which they call t t, one of the few Vietnamese words I know. They give their children lucky money too, and Vanessa and I had eagerly compared our envelopes, noting the differences and similarities between the Chinese and Vietnamese versions.

"That's a nice custom," Vanessa said. "My parents still do it for me, but I guess this is the next-to-last year. Once you're thirty, no more red envelopes."

"My parents stopped when I turned twenty-five. By that time I hardly noticed."

"Lucky money." Vanessa turned her glass a bit more, then drank from it. "I used to think money was always lucky. Now I'm not so sure."

By that time the sun was gone, but from beneath the horizon it painted the western clouds blood red. The water was black, and I couldn't see the ripples any more. Lights glowed here and there, and the headlights of cars winked along Shore Drive and over the inlet and bay bridges. The temperature hadn't dropped much, but suddenly I felt a chill. It must have been from the ice in the drink I was holding.

I had some of the whiskey and felt the familiar burn in my throat. Too familiar, I thought. Well, it was only one drink. The stuffed mushrooms looked good, but I noticed that neither of us had touched them.

Vanessa was silent, and I didn't interrupt her musing. I had musing of my own to get to, but I'd been doing too much of that recently, and I just wanted to sit for a while. Sit and try not to think—which sounds easier than it is.

After a minute or so I gave it up. I finished my drink and put down the glass. "Want another?"

The question brought Vanessa back from her reverie. "No, I guess not. I still have some work to do when I get home."

"Take the mushrooms then. Something to snack on while you work."

"You sure? You don't want half?"

"No, my mother stuffed me full at dinner last night."

Vanessa laughed—I knew she could relate to that experience. Then she tried to pay the check herself, but I insisted on splitting it and the tip.

As we walked out, for some reason I thought about those big homes in Lochhaven—the ones like the Fontaine's—with their swimming pools and boat docks and views of sparkling water. I also thought about the bronze signs on the brick pillars that guarded the country club.

And those red envelopes. Lucky money—all of it.

Or maybe not.

CHAPTER NINE

I hadn't had time to buy groceries, so I ate breakfast at the pancake house again.

The gray-haired woman at the cash register smiled as she counted out my change. "You're getting to be a regular."

I hadn't slept well—maybe it was my leftover-pizza dinner—and didn't feel very chipper, but I tried to smile back. "I guess so."

"Well, thanks for coming in. My grandson knows how to say thank you in Chinese and Japanese, but I don't."

I could tell she was making an attempt to connect with me. "It's 'xiè xiè' in Chinese. I don't speak Japanese."

"Shay shay?"

"Yes, that's pretty close."

"Well, shay shay then. We appreciate your business."

"You're quite welcome."

I felt a little better as I walked to my car. The breakfast had helped, and so had the woman's friendliness.

Of course, you *are* a repeat customer, I thought, and then chastised myself for being so cynical. Getting that way is an occupational hazard in this business—you get used to so many people lying, trying to cover up things. It doesn't take long before you begin to wonder if anyone is telling you the truth.

First on the day's agenda was Maxine Walters, Fontaine's current girlfriend. Sitting in my car, I searched for the Gartner Group and then dialed its phone number.

"Gartner Group—how may I help you?" The receptionist's cheery tone suggested that she'd slept better than I had. And probably with someone. Maybe someone like that guy in khaki shorts, for instance.

"Hi, this is Wendy Lu—the last name is spelled L, U." I did that with strangers over the phone so that people wouldn't think I was Mary Sue's first cousin. "I'd like to speak to Maxine Walters, please."

"May I say what this is regarding?"

"I'm doing a routine background check on a friend of hers." Except for the "routine" part, that was almost true.

"Hmm, I'll see if Ms. Walters is available."

The receptionist sounded skeptical, but I didn't care. It's something else you get used to in my business.

After a longish wait the line clicked and a voice said, "Hello, this is Maxine Walters."

"Hi, Ms. Walters. I'd like to make an appointment to talk to you for a few minutes today. It's important."

"I believe Janice said you're doing a background check on a friend of mine. Who's that?"

"Whitaker Fontaine."

The wait wasn't quite as long this time but almost. "Whitaker Fontaine?" She made it sound like a question although she couldn't have been surprised. At least she shouldn't have been. After the news came out about his wife's murder, she must have known that someone would link her to Fontaine.

"Yes. You do know him?"

"Well, professionally, of course. I'm not sure I would call him a friend. You see, I—"

"Probably don't want to discuss this over the phone. Sorry to interrupt, but I think we should speak in person, don't you?"

"Uh, yes, I suppose that's a good idea. But not here."

"Where? We'll need a place where we can talk privately."

"I understand. How about Extra Perks on Virginia Beach Boulevard? The morning crowd should be thinning out now."

I'd heard of that coffee shop. I hadn't been there but thought it shouldn't be hard to find. "All right. I'll meet you in half an hour. What are you wearing?"

"What? Why do you ask?"

"Just business—I need to be able to recognize you."

"Oh, I see. Well, a white linen dress. Sleeveless. A large gold necklace—a bit gaudy, I'm afraid."

"Got it. See you there."

I clicked my phone to end the call. Maxine Walters sounded smart and direct. Maybe she could tell me something that would help.

A quick search showed me that Extra Perks was near the intersection of the boulevard and North Witchduck Road. Tourists are always amused by that name, but I'm sure it wasn't amusing to the colonial woman actually "ducked," or tried by water, for allegedly being a witch. If I'd been around then, they probably would have done the same thing to me—someone who didn't always follow the rules and had strange eyes. "Bewitched" if not necessarily bewitching.

I headed out of the parking lot and got onto I-64 eastbound. Once I was on the interstate I moved over to the far left lane and noticed a black car behind me do the same thing. Figuring the driver might want to go faster than I did, I moved one lane to the right. The black car—it looked like a Lexus—did the same.

Hmm. Didn't seem like coincidence. The car stayed behind me—not too close but not letting another car get between us—as I took the exit for I-264 East toward Virginia Beach. In my rearview mirror the driver appeared to be a white or maybe Asian male wearing sunglasses. All I could really tell was that he had dark hair and narrow shoulders. I didn't recognize him and didn't think he was planning to ask me for a date.

I would have taken the exit for North Witchduck Road, but I didn't want to lead the guy to my meeting with Maxine Walters. So I went past that exit, got off at Independence Boulevard, and worked my way through the narrow merge area. I got lucky and a car trying to get onto 264 westbound got between me and my friend. I gunned the Toyota and shot down to Virginia Beach Boulevard.

The black car was now two cars behind me. The light facing me was red, but there was an opening in the traffic, and I took it without stopping, heading east on the boulevard as fast as the other cars would let me. I knew that the traffic enforcement camera monitoring the place where I'd turned had videoed my failure to stop and that I'd soon get a ticket in the mail, but I shrugged that off. I just wanted to lose that black car.

I went a couple of blocks, turned right, went a few more blocks, and turned right again. I was on a twisting road that would take me back to Virginia Beach Boulevard near its intersection with Witchduck. I checked the rearview but didn't see the car.

I let out the breath I hadn't realized I was holding and let the car slow down a bit. I checked the mirror again to be sure and still didn't see the car, so apparently I'd lost it.

Then it hit me. The driver must've followed me from the pancake house. How had he known I'd be there? I didn't go every day and hadn't planned on going today. The odds were too long that he'd staked out the place in hopes of finding me.

No, he must've staked out my apartment and followed me from there to the pancake house. That meant he knew where I lived.

A cold finger ran down the length of my spine. How could he know that? I didn't have a home phone, and because of my job, I told very few people where I lived. An online search wouldn't have revealed the address.

So maybe it was someone I knew. Maybe some guy I'd dated and brought over to my place. That wasn't a long list. And no one on it had a car like that—or at least not when we'd dated. But it's not hard to trade cars, so that factor didn't mean much.

I had no idea who might be following me. Was it related to the Fontaine matter? That seemed unlikely. Some cop still pissed at me because of Bobby's death? That seemed a lot more likely. I knew that some of them were angry about it and probably would stay that way. I hadn't forgiven myself, so why should all of them forgive me?

I sighed. I didn't need someone on my tail at any time and certainly not in the middle of a murder investigation. I knew I should tell Marcus but didn't want to. He'd probably believe me about the car and not just think I was paranoid, but in case it was a cop, I didn't want to remind him about Bobby. Not that Marcus had forgotten, of course. But at least he didn't hold it against me.

I came to Virginia Beach Boulevard and waited until the light let me turn left. Then I went a couple of blocks to the coffee shop. It was in a nondescript strip mall with an auto parts store on one side and an insurance place on the other. The sign on the window showed an old-fashioned coffee pot with a handle and spout. The pot had a smiling face and happy-looking cups dancing around it. Under other circumstances I might've smiled at the image. But not now.

To make my Toyota more difficult to spot from the street, I parked on the far side of a car perpendicular to the insurance place, which anchored the right end of the building. As I walked to Extra Perks, I checked the street but didn't see my friend with the black car. It was okay with me if I never saw him again.

But somehow I knew I would.

Extra Perks' conditioned air was almost uncomfortably cold but had a pleasant coffee-and-pastry smell. Maxine Walters had been right—although there were a few customers, the place wasn't crowded.

A woman who fit the description I'd been given sat by herself as far away from the counter and other customers as possible. She had a newspaper and a cup of coffee in front of her but didn't seem focused on either. She glanced nervously around the shop, and when she noticed that I was looking at her, she stared back. I gave no sign of recognition.

I went to the counter and looked at the menu posted on the wall. The offerings were all espresso this and latte that. Designer coffee for people who'd never had to drink a cup of Navy joe. I ordered a cup of regular coffee from the fresh-faced teenage girl at the counter and then at the fixings area off to the side added sweetener but no cream.

I carried the coffee over to Maxine's table. "Hi there. Didn't know I'd run into you here. Mind if I join you?" I spoke just loudly enough to be heard by the nearest customers.

She glanced around to see if anyone was looking at us. No one was. "Sure. Please sit down." She pitched her voice to match mine.

I put my cup on the table and sat, smiling to make her more comfortable. I waited a few moments to give her time to relax as much as she would. While I waited I sipped my coffee. It tasted good but was too hot, the way most places serve it, so I put the coffee to one side to let it cool.

"Thanks for agreeing to meet." I lowered my voice so I wouldn't be overheard.

"Okay, but I'm not sure what I can tell you."

Again she had the good sense to keep her voice down, but I found her comment odd. Was she saying that she didn't know how much she could tell me? Or that she didn't know what story to give me? Well, I'd find out.

"You can tell me about Whitaker Fontaine."

"Tell you what about him? I said I know him professionally."

"I'm sure you do. And I'm also sure you know him in another way. Start there."

She gave me a cold look and lifted her cup, probably to buy time. After a sip of coffee she said, "Did he tell you?"

"Yes. He didn't want to, but I told him that he had to. We've got to talk to everyone who might be able to help with his defense."

"Well, I don't know anything that could help."

I ignored that. "How long have you been seeing him?"

"I've known Whit for a couple of years now."

I just stared at her.

She sighed. "Okay, I've been seeing him—socially, I mean—for about a year."

Socially. That seemed an odd way to describe an affair, but I didn't point that out. I guess we're all entitled to our little evasions. And rationalizations, I told myself. Don't forget rationalizations.

"Where?"

"What do you mean?"

"I mean where do you go after the social things—drinks, dinner, maybe a movie. Where do you go for ... dessert?"

She jerked her chin up. "You sound like you know what you're talking about."

"Maybe I do. But we're talking about you now—you and Whit Fontaine."

"Yes, I'm quite aware of that. Well, mostly we went back to my place. I hate the motel-room thing. Or even a good hotel unless you're out of town. Then it's different."

"Have you taken trips together?"

"Let's say we've gone on trips that had the same destination."

I knew what she meant, so I didn't ask her to elaborate. Given our supposedly chance meeting, I didn't want to pull out my notepad in that public place, but I jotted some things on a napkin.

"Anywhere else?"

"Such as …?"

"His house."

She glared at me. "You really mean their bed, don't you?"

I met her gaze, held it steadily. "Yes, I do."

"What difference does it make?"

"Maybe none or maybe a lot. Please answer the question."

She looked down at her cup. "Well, okay. Although I don't see how this can possibly help Whit. But, yes, we did it in their bed—her bed really—a few times when Susan was out of town. Want to know how that made me feel?"

"If you want to tell me."

"Dirty. Slutty. But thrilled at the same time. Like he was finally mine, and I could really be his wife."

Oh, I could relate to that. Yes, I surely could. I forced the picture of Bobby's bedroom out of my mind and focused on doing my job.

"Is that what you want—to marry him?"

She nodded. "Yes. I love Whit. I have almost from first meeting him."

"Did the two of you discuss marriage?"

She shifted as though uncomfortable. "No, not really. I tried to bring it up a time or two, but he changed the subject. Still, I'm sure he knows that's what I want, ultimately."

I remembered what Fontaine had told me. Obviously, they weren't on the same page about this. Well, they weren't the first.

"You say that's what you want. Do you still want it?"

"Yes, if … I mean …."

"If he didn't do it."

"That's right. And I can't believe he did. He didn't love her, hadn't for a long time. But he couldn't have killed her. He couldn't kill anyone."

I remembered crime scenes I'd been to—many of them the aftermath of violence, usually senseless violence. You can't know what someone is capable of, I thought, until that person crosses the line. I thought of a book I'd read once, a novel about what war's violence brings out in people: *The Thin Red Line.*

Of course people have free will—they don't have to cross that line. This woman was hoping Whit Fontaine hadn't, but it was only that, a hope.

"What about you?" I asked.

"What? You mean, could I ...."

"Yes, kill someone."

"I didn't kill Susan Fontaine."

"I'd hardly expect you to admit it if you had."

"There's nothing to admit!"

One or two people looked our way. She noticed and lowered both her head and her voice before adding, "I didn't do it."

"Where were you on Saturday night?"

"Home."

"All evening?"

There was the barest hesitation before she answered. "Yes, from about five o'clock on."

"Were you alone?"

"Yes."

I made a note. "Were you waiting for Whit?"

She paused. "Like I said before, you sound as though you know how it is."

"Trust me, I do. So you waited at home, hoping he'd come over."

"Yes. He said he had a business dinner and would try to come by afterward."

"Did he often stop by like that?"

"As often as he could. But I suppose he couldn't get away that night."

"Apparently. Is there any way you can prove you were home all night?"

"No, I guess not."

Not much of an alibi, I thought. She didn't seem like the type to kill her lover's wife, but you never knew. Maybe if she wanted him badly enough. But if she'd done it, why had he been found next to the body? Unless she was trying to frame him for revenge. Talk about cutting off your nose to spite your face.

"But I'm telling you I didn't do it!" She was as insistent as before but remembered to keep her voice down.

She must have thought I looked skeptical. Maybe I did. I had some of my coffee—cooler by then—while I thought about my next questions.

"Did you know where Whit kept that gun?"

She didn't try to pretend she didn't know which gun. "Uh, I ... well, Whit said they had a gun for protection against prowlers."

"That isn't what I asked. You slept in Susan Fontaine's bed. Was there was a gun in the nightstand? Or was it somewhere else?"

I was annoyed with her, and maybe I spoke more loudly than I'd intended. In any event she glanced around the coffee shop to see whether anyone was listening to us. I did the same but didn't see anyone who seemed to be giving us special attention.

Keeping my voice down, I pressed her. "Where was that gun?"

She stood, plucked her purse from where it hung on her chair, and looked down at me. "I think I've answered enough questions."

"I'm just trying to help Mr. Fontaine."

"Well, attacking me won't help him."

"I wasn't attacking you. And I didn't accuse you of anything. I just need to know what you know about him and the death of his wife."

"I've told you all I can." She glanced around again, then leaned toward me and added in a harsh whisper, "I have no idea who killed her—or why."

I stood too. I was a couple of inches taller than she was, and I took my turn to look down at her.

"Thank you for your time."

She started to say something—I don't think it was "you're welcome"—but held back the words and headed for the door. I sat again and read over my notes as I finished my coffee.

I was sure she'd known where that gun was.

CHAPTER TEN

Sitting in my car, I phoned Marcus and filled him in on what Maxine Walters had told me—and what she hadn't.

"You think she did it?" Marcus sounded skeptical, which is usually a good attitude for a cop or investigator to take.

"I don't know. She had a motive and, assuming she knew about the gun, the means. But you'd think she'd have a better alibi."

"Yes, and there's the matter of him lying there. Unless she's trying to frame him."

"If she's that angry with him, you'd think she would've shot him, not his wife."

Marcus chuckled. "It's been known to happen. Larry's seen women that mad a few times. Well, what's next?"

"I guess I'll go to the Lynnhaven Dock House and see what they can tell me about that dinner on Saturday night."

"Probably nothing that will help, but I guess we have to cover all the bases."

"Yes, we—hey, wait a second." My mouth still stung a little from the too-hot coffee, and maybe that's what prompted the idea. You know, we're assuming that Mrs. Fontaine was killed shortly before the police found her and Whit Fontaine lying there."

"Sure, because that's how it looked."

"But what if it was meant to look that way?" I felt a rising excitement as I thought through the possibilities.

"What are you getting at?"

"What if she'd been killed earlier? And the killer was able to keep the body warm somehow?"

Marcus was silent for a few seconds. Both of us knew that body temperature was an indicator of the time of death—not the only indicator but an important one.

"Okay, I guess that's a possibility," he said, "depending on what's in the lab report. But then why was Whit there?"

"Maybe he was so drunk that when he saw her body, he just passed out. Or ...."

"What?"

"Maybe he was there to fit a frame."

"Well, if he was, somebody put him there."

"Sure, but who?"

'Don't ask me, girl. You're the lead investigator on this case. Who've you got so far?"

"Hmm, Maxine Walters. Maybe. Or a husband of one of Fontaine's several girlfriends. That's it."

"What about the partner—McKenna?"

I thought about that. "I don't think so. No apparent motive."

"Nobody else?"

"Not so far."

"Well, you're just getting started. Keep digging. I'll ask Scott if he has any information about the time of death."

"Okay." I wondered if I should tell Marcus about the guy who'd followed me, but I decided not to, not right then. I didn't want to sound like a scared little girl. I could deal with him, whoever he was. At least I hoped so.

I said goodbye and headed for the Lynnhaven Dock House. The restaurant was on the water at the southern end of Chesapeake Bay, a little way east of Chic's Beach. It was large place, built to look from the outside like a weathered gray boathouse. Fishing nets, life rings, and other marine gear hung from the outside walls. A few wooden benches sat in front to accommodate people who had to wait when there was a line to get in, and a wooden pier jutted into the water for those who came by boat. The third generation was running the place, and it was well known for good if somewhat pricey food and the spectacular view from the big deck out back.

I crunched across the oyster-shell parking lot, which was about half full from the lunch crowd, and parked next to an expensive-looking pickup that bore a bumper sticker displaying crossed casting rods and the legend "Fish Fear Me." Hampton Roads has a lot of well-to-do people who seem faintly embarrassed by their financial success and compensate by acting more down-home than they really are. Fortunately, I'd never had to do that—I'd never had enough money to be embarrassed by it.

I went inside and the hostess greeted me. Although the day was warm, edging toward hot, I asked to sit outside, and she led me to a table on the deck shaded by a large green umbrella. The shade and the sea breeze made being outside comfortable enough, and I enjoyed inhaling the salt air and watching the waves chase each other to shore.

I had the deck to myself except for one couple sitting close together by the far rail. After watching them for a moment or two I figured that they were illicit lovers having a noon rendezvous. Now I was embarrassed—by my personal experience with that scene.

I'd read the newspaper at breakfast, so over my lunch of a seafood salad with unsweetened ice tea I read a copy of *The New York Times Book Review*. It was an old issue because I never seem to have time to stay current with my reading. Over the years two or three ex-boyfriends had chided me for reading so much, and that was probably one of the reasons they were now exes.

I lingered over my lunch, partly because I enjoyed sitting where I was and partly to let the restaurant clear out. By 1:30 there were only a few diners left, so when the server asked me for the third time if I wanted anything else, I said no and paid the check.

No one was sitting at the bar inside. I chose a stool at the far end and sat. The bartender, an older man who looked as though he'd heard everything and seen most of it, asked me what I wanted. I wanted a bourbon but ordered a club soda with lime.

The bartender didn't give me the disappointed look that most of his brothers and sisters do when someone orders something other than alcohol. He merely nodded and fixed my drink in a few deft motions. He laid a white paper napkin in front of me and placed the drink on it with the slight flourish of someone doing something he knows he does well.

"Thanks." I slid a card in front of him. "I'm on a case. I'd like to talk to servers who were working on Saturday night."

He took his time looking at the card before he slid it back to me. "Well, that was the dinner shift, so I'm not sure any of them are here now." He thought a moment. "Maybe Judy. She normally works days, but I think they moved her because they had so many reservations that night."

He caught the eye of a busser cleaning nearby tables. "Arturo, see if Judy's here, will you?"

The slim brown man stopped what he was doing and gave me a curious glance but didn't say anything. He dropped a stained white cloth on the tabletop, put his gray plastic tub on a chair, and walked away. In a minute or so he returned, followed by a petite brunette dressed as one of the restaurant's wait staff.

He gestured toward the bar and went back to the table he'd been cleaning. The woman continued on to the bar. She looked at the bartender inquiringly, and he motioned toward me. "This young lady wants to talk to you."

I showed her the same card I'd showed the bartender. "Hi, I'm Wendy Lu. I'd like to ask you a few questions."

She crossed her arms. "Why?"

"I'm investigating the death of Susan Fontaine, the wife of a man who was here for dinner on Saturday. Someone murdered her that night."

"Oh. I see." She didn't uncross her arms, but the mention of murder made her slump a little.

"Do you have a minute?"

"Well, I guess I could take a short break now."

"Good." I paused and looked at the bartender. He read my mind the way good bartenders can with people, went to the other end of the bar, and busied himself with doing bar things.

"Please sit down, Judy."

"Okay." She took the stool next to mine, nervously drumming the fingers of one hand on the bar.

"Don't worry, this isn't about you." I took out my pad and pen. "But I understand that you were on duty Saturday evening. Correct?"

"Yes. That's not my usual shift, but we were going to be really busy, so Sam—he's the manager—told me to come in. I didn't mind because you can make good money on a Saturday night, and—"

"That's fine, Judy. I just want to ask you about Mr. Fontaine and his party."

She blinked to refocus. "Mr. Fontaine?"

"Yes. He and his business partner were here with some Japanese men. Do you remember?"

"Oh, sure. I didn't have their table, but I had ones next to it, and I remember them. There were three, I think. Yes, three."

"You mean three of them plus Mr. Fontaine and his partner, Mr. McKenna."

She gazed into the middle distance, and I could tell she was trying to picture the group of them. "That's right. Five altogether."

I made a note. "Okay, tell me about them."

She looked confused. "What? What about them?"

"How were they dressed? What did they order? How did they act?"

"Uh, I, umm …."

I had gone too fast for her. "One thing at a time. What were they wearing?"

That helped. "Oh. The Japanese men all wore suits and ties. Kind of formal."

"And Mr. Fontaine and Mr. McKenna?"

"Well, the red-haired guy—"

"That's McKenna."

"Okay. He was the most casual—khakis and a polo shirt. The other white guy—" She caught herself using the word "white" and looked at me, embarrassed.

"That's all right. I know what you mean—the other man who wasn't Asian."

"Yes." She looked relieved. "I didn't mean to be ... insulting."

I smiled to get her to relax. "You weren't. Some people are white, some are black or brown, and some, like me, are Asian. No big deal. Now what was Mr. Fontaine wearing?"

"Uh, he had on a jacket—you know, a sport coat—but no tie. Sort of between the red-haired guy and the Japanese."

"Good." I jotted on the pad. "What did they order?"

"That's easy. Everyone had steak. I remember because Louise—she was their server—commented on that as we were closing up. She said, 'Most people come here for seafood, but everyone at that table wanted steak.'"

That tallied with Fontaine's story—what there was of it. "Okay, let's keep going. What about drinks?"

"Scotch, I think. Whiskey anyway. And lots of it. Lots. Especially for Mr. Fontaine."

"He was drinking a lot?"

"Well, they all were. But he showed it more. He got ...."

She paused, apparently reluctant to say anything bad about a patron of the restaurant.

"What? What did he do?"

"Well, he got kind of loud. And he started arguing with, uh, Mr.—"

"McKenna."

"Right."

"When was that?"

"Oh, late. The place had pretty much emptied out by then. We were starting to clean up, wishing they'd finish and go home."

"What were they arguing about?"

"I don't know, really. Louise said Mr. Fontaine was accusing Mr. McKenna of things, things to do with their business. But I don't know what exactly."

"What's Louise's last name?"

"Rossi." She watched me write it down. "Do you need mine too?"

"Yes."

"Okay. It's Wagenaar." She spelled it for me.

"Thanks. So when did they leave?"

"A little after eleven. We stop serving food at nine-thirty, but the bar stays open until eleven. That night we had to turn the lights on and tell those guys we were closing."

"Did they all leave together?"

She thought a moment, frowning. "Yes, all but Mr. Fontaine. He'd already left."

"When?"

"Oh, maybe half an hour earlier. Like I said, he'd been arguing with that Mr. McKenna, and he got very angry. He started waving his car key around—I guess Mr. McKenna had told him he was too drunk to drive. And he sure looked that way to me."

"Did McKenna take his keys?"

"No. Mr. Fontaine pushed him—really hard, he almost fell—and then walked out. Well, right after …."

"Right after what?"

"After he told Mr. McKenna to go … fuck himself." She blushed at saying a word that as a cop I'd had to listen to about once a minute. "Everyone heard it. The hostess started over there to talk to him, but he walked out with Mr. McKenna right behind him."

"Did McKenna come back?"

"Yes, about five minutes later. He was shaking his head, so I guess he didn't keep Mr. Fontaine from driving."

I remembered what Marcus had told me about that night—how Fontaine's car was at his house when the police got there. "Apparently not. So the group left a little later?"

"Yes. Mr. McKenna paid the bill—Louise said he wasn't a good tipper—and they went out together. We closed right after that."

I was silent as I made some notes. What she'd told me was consistent with what the others had said about the case, including Fontaine himself. So I didn't see any alibi shaping up for him.

"Is there anything else you can tell me?"

"Like what?"

"Oh, anything that struck you at the time. Anything unusual about any of the men. How they looked or acted."

She thought for a moment. "No, not really. But maybe Louise could."

"Okay, do you have a phone number for her? And I'd like to get yours in case I have any follow-up questions."

"Sure." She gave me her mobile number and then read Louise's to me off her phone.

I put my notepad and pen away, stood, and held out my hand. "Thanks a lot. I really appreciate your taking time to talk to me."

She smiled, pleased at having helped with a murder case. "You're quite welcome," she said, giving me a shake made firmer than most by all the physical labor she did. "Good luck with your investigation."

"Thanks for that too." I tried to smile back, but my effort wasn't as successful as hers. "I think I'm going to need it."

CHAPTER ELEVEN

I sat in my car again—I probably spent more time in it than in my cubbyhole of an office—and thought about what Judy Wagenaar had told me. She'd basically confirmed everything I'd already known about the dinner. That seemed to eliminate some possibilities, but it didn't help to clear Fontaine. Well, maybe there wasn't a way to clear him. Maybe he had killed his wife—he certainly wouldn't be the first. In my cop days I'd met some of the others.

Thinking about my time on the force made me realize I still needed to look at the crime scene photos. I didn't think they'd tell me much, but due diligence required that I review them.

I phoned the Homicide Section and asked for Sergeant Connolly. The officer who answered the phone—his name a complex string of hard syllables—said Connolly wasn't there but would probably be back around 5:30. I told him I'd come to see Connolly then.

That left me three hours to kill, and I noted the irony of the expression as I thought about the best way to use that time. What theme, if any, was there to what I'd learned so far? That both Fontaine and his wife had had several affairs. But apparently that had been going on for a long time without resulting in murder. That Fontaine and McKenna argued over business, and it seemed to be getting worse. But how could that result in Susan Fontaine's death? She wasn't involved in their business, at least as far as I knew.

I decided to question Betty Partridge again. Maybe she wouldn't be as nervous the second time she talked to me, and I might learn something useful—maybe more about the apparently strained relationship between Fontaine and McKenna. And maybe more about those investors Fontaine seemed to want to have little to do with.

I called Fontaine-McKenna Associates and asked for Betty. The receptionist told me she wasn't in.

"Oh, that's too bad. I've got some things she needs to sign, some personal financial documents. I think she wants to get this process moving right away."

"Well, she'll probably be back tomorrow. She's home sick, but I was told it's nothing serious."

"Okay, thanks."

I clicked off. Something didn't seem quite right. Betty had appeared perfectly fine yesterday or at least not ill beneath her nervousness. And if she'd called in sick, why hadn't she talked to the receptionist? Maybe she'd dialed an office manager directly. Still, it seemed odd.

I don't make a habit of bothering sick people, but I decided to swing by Betty's house. Maybe she wasn't too sick to talk to me. Maybe she wasn't ill at all, just taking a "mental health day." In that case she'd be embarrassed—especially if I didn't call to let her know I was coming—and might say more than she would otherwise.

So many maybes. My whole life was full of them. Well, I thought, at least it made things interesting.

I used my phone to search for Betty's home address and found it easily. She lived in Virginia Beach about twenty minutes away from where I was. I started the car and pulled out of the restaurant's parking lot.

It was a nondescript ranch house, smaller than most of the thousands of others in "Vah-Beach" and lacking the usual garage. The yard was neatly but not fussily kept and had a beautiful magnolia tree as its centerpiece. Not a Southern magnolia, a tree I could recognize, but some smaller variety.

I pulled into the narrow driveway behind the single car parked there and got out. The hood of Betty's car, a small, oldish Ford, wasn't warm to the touch, so apparently she was home sick or at least at home.

I rang the bell and waited. I didn't hear a sound from inside the house. I rang again and still heard nothing, not even when I put my ear to the door. She'd been at work the day before, so she couldn't be deathly ill. Even if she wasn't going to talk to me, she probably would have come to the door and looked through the peephole to see who was ringing her doorbell. The back of my neck tingled, and I sensed that there was something odd about the whole scene. I tried the knob, but the door was locked.

I glanced up and down the quiet residential street and didn't see anyone. I went to the side of the house, through the gate in the picket fence, and into the back yard. The back was kept like the front but included a birdbath and a small vegetable garden. My steps disturbed a rabbit having a late lunch on some of Betty's produce, and the rabbit scampered away. That should have seemed funny to me, but for some reason it didn't.

Through the windows I could see that the kitchen was at this end of the house, so the bedrooms were probably at the other. I walked onto the concrete patio and weaved around its weathered table and chairs to try the back door. It, too, was locked.

Then I went to the corner window at the far end. I eased carefully through the low bushes to look inside.

The curtains were closed, but through the narrow gap between them I saw an unmade bed. Betty, wearing a nightgown, was lying on the bed, but she wasn't sick. She'd never be sick again. From the blood and brains that had crimsoned the pillow behind her, I knew she was dead.

My stomach roiled, and I almost threw up in the shrubbery. Almost, but I managed to keep my lunch down, and after a few deep breaths I forced myself to look through the window again. The view was just as gruesome, but now I was able to focus on the small pistol in Betty's right hand.

Apparently she'd killed herself. But why? And why this way? She was a woman who lived alone, sure, but nevertheless she didn't seem like the sort of person who'd own a gun. And if she'd decided to commit suicide she'd almost certainly have done it some other way, most likely with pills.

Still, there she was, dead with a gun in her hand. And here I was, having found her. So that I could stay focused on my investigation, I wanted to wipe my fingerprints off the two doorknobs and the gate and just leave, but I couldn't do that.

I called the police.

□ □ □

Two hours later they were finally done with me. After the ambulance and the police car arrived, a patrolman asked me questions while his partner broke into the house and confirmed that Betty was dead. Then when two detectives and a medical examiner arrived, one detective asked me essentially the same questions while her partner and the ME investigated what homicide courses refer to as "the death scene."

Of course one of the questions was why was I at Betty's house, and another was why was I peering through her windows. I showed my PI identification and explained that my agency was working for Whitaker Fontaine's defense counsel. I told the detective, a short African American woman who was built like a boxer and, despite wearing a stylish suit, looked tough enough to be one, that Sergeant Connolly could verify my story.

She gave me a searching look that told me nothing and walked far enough away that I couldn't make out what she was saying while she phoned Connolly. After a short conversation she slid her phone back in a jacket pocket and stepped over to me.

"Okay, he vouched for you. Said you're legit if inexperienced. I guess the inexperienced part explains why you were crawling around in the dead woman's shrubs and doing a peeping-tom routine."

"I wasn't crawling, and if I hadn't looked in her windows, no one would know she was dead. Not yet anyway."

"You think a PI license gives you the right to invade people's privacy like that?"

"No, but in this instance I think I did the right thing." I didn't want to call it intuition, but something had made me suspicious about Betty's sudden illness.

"Getting a good result doesn't justify improper procedure. Sergeant Connolly said you used to be a cop, so you should know that."

"I was. But now I'm a private detective, and the rules are different."

"Is that so? Well, my rules will let me take you to the station and keep you there while we ask you more questions."

"Or the same ones, over and over,"

"That too." She gave me another long look. "Do I need to do that?"

"I think it would be a waste of your time. I've told you all I know about this situation. I don't know why this woman apparently committed suicide. And if it wasn't suicide, I have no idea who might have killed her."

"You probably don't know who killed Susan Fontaine either." Although the detective didn't change her tone, the sarcasm still came through, mostly in her eyes. I wanted to snap back at her but managed not to. "No, I don't. But my client isn't guilty of murder unless the law says he is."

"Yeah," she said, drawing the word out, "that's how it works. But I'm pretty sure what the law's gonna say."

I held my tongue again and just looked at her, trying to keep my expression neutral. She waited to see if I'd say anything else, and when I didn't, she shrugged and said, "Okay, you're free to go. But don't leave town—we may have more questions."

"Thanks." I managed not to sound sarcastic myself but just barely.

The detective made a dismissive gesture, and I drove away before she could change her mind. I called Marcus and told him what had happened.

"Definitely suicide?"

"Looks like it. The house was locked, and no one else was in it."

"Did she leave a note?"

"I don't know. They didn't let me go inside."

"See if you can find out."

"Okay."

He was silent for a moment. Then he said, "The timing seems odd, considering the recent murder of her boss's wife."

"Yes, it does—quite odd. Still, she told me she under a strain. She said it didn't have anything to do with her job, so she could have been depressed about something we have no knowledge of."

"Maybe. Or maybe she was killed by someone close to her, someone close enough to have a key to her house"

"Right, another maybe. We have lots of those—too many."

He chuckled. "That's the name of the game, Wendy. It's also why they pay us the big bucks."

"Yeah, right. I always knew I'd get rich in this job."

"You'll be rich in knowledge, young lady, intimate knowledge of human nature."

"Of the dark side of human nature. I already have as much of that as I want." I said it partly as a joke, but as with most humor, there was truth in it.

I thought he might laugh but he didn't. After a long pause he said, "Well, I'm afraid you're going to get some more."

There was nothing to say to that. I knew he was right.

I told Marcus where I was headed next, ended the call, and went to meet Connolly.

CHAPTER TWELVE

I drove to Norfolk's Police Operations Center, the same place they'd questioned Fontaine after they arrested him. I'd been there many times, both as a police officer and as a private investigator. But it seemed different this time—or maybe I was different somehow.

When I checked in at the front desk, the duty officer said, "Yeah, Corporal Kaczkowski said you'd be coming by. He's back there in Homicide—you know where that is?"

"No."

He told me, and I followed his directions to a large room with cubicles around the walls and a large table in the center. I could see three detectives and one patrol officer sitting in the cubicles and working at computer screens or talking on the phone. A wiry, bespectacled man in plain clothes was getting a cup of coffee at the beverage station in a corner. When he saw standing in the doorway, he said, "You must be Wendy Lu."

I wondered if Connolly had said something to him about the "Chinese chick working the Fontaine case." That's just how cops talk sometimes—tough, like the back streets and the people they meet there.

It's a defensive thing. I'd done it myself when I was on the force. And I knew that being a cop had hardened me, changed me in ways I'd never be able to reverse. Even assuming I wanted to, and I wasn't sure about that. Part of me would always be a police officer, and that's probably why I was a private investigator and not something more traditional.

"Yes, I am." I walked over to him. "We spoke on the phone?"

"Right. I'm Corporal Kaczkowski—'Corporal K' is fine. You want to see Sergeant Connolly."

"Yes."

"Well, he's not back yet, but I called him after I talked to you, and he said he wants to see you. He volunteered to take this case—high profile and all that—and treats it like his baby. He should be here soon."

"Okay. Mind if I get some coffee?"

"Sure, help yourself." He picked up his Washington Nationals cup and stepped back to give me room.

There were some City of Norfolk Police Department cups in the drying rack, but I choose a plain white cup, poured it half full of coffee, and added some sweetener. Kaczkowski watched me, sipping from his own cup.

"The sergeant said you used to be with the Virginia Beach police."

"That's right, but I've been off the force for about a year."

"Didn't like it?"

"No, I liked the work and the people. But … it was time to move on."

"Uh-huh." He said it in a way that made me think he might know why I'd left. Maybe Connolly had told him. Or maybe someone else had. Well, it didn't matter. I couldn't undo the past.

Kaczkowski took another sip of coffee and stared into his cup for a moment. "It can get to you," he said, more to himself than to me. "I know—it gets to me sometimes."

He seemed embarrassed at what he'd said. He cleared his throat loudly and motioned with his head. "Come on. You can sit over here."

He led me to the table and pulled out a chair. "Sergeant Connolly should be along any minute."

I nodded, sat, and watched him go to one of the cubicles. I hoped Connolly was keeping an eye on him. Too many cops have let the job get to them, and some of them have seen suicide as the only way out. I'd heard it referred to as "eating the gun." More defensiveness disguised as black humor.

As I waited, I read over my notes, hoping they'd tell me something they hadn't before. They didn't, and I got another cup of the strong cop coffee. I had just returned to my chair when Connolly came in. He noticed me immediately and came over to the table, laying his briefcase on it. I stood, neither of us offering to shake hands.

"Hello, Sergeant."

"Hi. "How's the investigation going?"

I thought he seemed tired and a little irritable. I knew exactly how that felt. "Well, I'm asking a lot of questions."

"And I'll bet not learning much—at least not much helpful to Fontaine."

"Maybe not, but it's early yet. If he gets out on bail tomorrow, I can talk to him at length, and that may turn up something."

"Don't count on it." When I didn't reply, he added in a low voice, "I guess you want to see the photos."

"Yes, I do."

One of the detectives came out of his cubicle, pulled something off the printer, and went back to his desk. Connolly moved close to me and said in that same low voice, "You know I'm not supposed to show them to you. The prosecutor will give copies to Cushman when she's ready."

"I know." I waited, looking him in the eye.

He sighed. "Okay, I'll bend the rules. The prosecutor won't like it if she finds out, but maybe seeing the photos will convince you that you're chasing your tail. Come over here."

He picked up his briefcase and led the way to an empty cubicle. He sat in the desk chair and pulled a laptop from the briefcase. I took the chair beside the desk and watched as he clicked the laptop's keys, muttering to himself, until he found the file folder he wanted.

"Here." He turned the screen toward me. "Let's go through them."

He brought up the first picture, a wide-angle shot that showed the bedroom from the door. I could see Mrs. Fontaine's bare feet, soles facing me, on the carpet past the bed. The photographer had taken the next several pictures going closer to the body and narrowing the angle. Finally I was looking down at Mrs. Fontaine.

She appeared as Connolly had described her: lying on her side, dressed in a pale-blue nightgown, and wearing little jewelry. The photographer had taken some pictures of her face, and framed by her swirl of frosted blonde hair, her blue eyes were open, staring at eternity.

Or at her killer, I thought. In that last second she must have known that's what he was if not who he was. I noticed my use of "he" and had to remind myself that Maxine Walters was very much a suspect.

Connolly left that picture on the screen until I glanced at him and nodded. Then he moved on to close-ups of the gunshot wounds. They weren't pleasant to look at, but I've seen worse, and it was easier to look at them than at those staring eyes. I was pretty sure I was going to see those eyes in my dreams at some point.

"That's it," Connolly said when the screen went blank.

I was silent for a moment, thinking about what I'd just seen. Then I remembered they'd found her husband next to her body. "Where's Fontaine? How come no pictures of him?"

"We'd arrested him and taken him out of there by the time the photographer arrived. But the two guys who checked the house took these."

He searched for another folder, opened it, and then clicked the first file. A picture opened that wasn't as sharp or as well composed as the ones I'd seen earlier, but it clearly showed Fontaine lying on his back about three feet from his wife. He was dressed as Connolly had described and had one arm close to his body and the other almost perpendicular to it. A pistol lay just beyond the fingers of his outstretched hand. There were two more pictures from slightly different angles, but all three showed essentially the same thing.

Something about the photos of Fontaine bothered me, but I didn't know what.

"That's the lot," Connolly said, closing the last image. "I didn't think they'd tell you anything you didn't already know."

"Wait a minute. Let me think."

Connolly frowned at my telling him to wait, but he didn't say anything. After another moment I had it.

"The gun is near Fontaine's left hand."

Connolly clicked the last image open again. "Sure. That's natural—he's left-handed. We checked early on."

"Oh."

Seeing my disappointed expression, Connolly said, "Hey, that was a good catch. Most people are right-handed, and you had no way of knowing exactly where the gun was until you saw these pictures."

"I could have asked him."

"Why would you? Before now, I mean."

That made me feel a little better but not much. Then I remembered the gun in Betty Partridge's right hand. Which hand had she used to take my card? I replayed the scene in my mind. She had reached out with ... that hand. Yes, her right. So maybe it had been suicide.

When I didn't answer him, Connolly continued. "Anyway, he might have told you which is his dominant hand—a lie about that would be easy to prove—but I'll bet he said he doesn't remember anything about the shooting. Right? At least that's what he told us before he asked for a lawyer and then shut up."

Fontaine had told me the same thing. Because I was working for Scott and Jackie, what Fontaine had said to me was covered by the attorney-client privilege, so I couldn't tell Connolly that at least Fontaine's story was consistent. Anyway, Connolly would just have called it consistent lying.

I covered my silence by making notes about the position of the gun and the fact was Fontaine was left-handed. I noticed Connolly watching me—no, studying me—while I did it.

"I'll bet you were a good cop, Lu."

"Not really, but thanks for thinking so." I put away my notebook and pen, and Connolly closed the laptop. Seeing him do that jogged my memory—Marcus had mentioned asking about Fontaine's computer. "Do you have Fontaine's laptop?"

"Yep, two of them—one from his house and one from his office."

"Have you found anything on them?"

He knew what I meant. "No, not yet. Nothing that seems relevant to the case. But I'll let you know if we find anything incriminating—then you can quit wasting your time."

That crack about my wasting my time was just cop posturing—I'd done it myself on a few occasions. I couldn't think of anything else to ask him right then, so I stood to go.

"Thanks, Sergeant. I appreciate your taking time to go through the photos with me. I know you're busy."

"Just doing my job—or trying to." He glanced at the big wall clock that seems to hang in every cop shop. "I'm off duty in five minutes. Want to get a beer at Mickey's?"

Mickey Finn's bar was a dark, dingy place a few blocks from the Operations Center. The owner was a retired police officer named Mike Franklin, and he wasn't Irish at all. Still, I could see why he liked the sound and connotation of the name he'd chosen for his bar.

Not many people went there except cops—active and retired—and people who liked to hang around with them. Including women who wanted to date cops. I knew because I'd been there a few times with Bobby, sometimes the only female officer in the place, the other women checking Bobby out but giving me looks that weren't exactly welcoming.

When I hesitated, Connolly said, "Don't worry—I'm not coming on to you. I just thought you might want to talk to someone, someone who knows what it's like to wear the badge."

I looked at his face. He seemed sincere. "Okay."

"Good. I'll meet you there."

"Fine." I walked out, sensing that he watched me go.

I went to my car and drove through the tail end of rush-hour traffic over to Mickey's. People in Hampton Roads often complain about the traffic, but I've been in Washington, D.C., a few times, mostly for the Navy, and the traffic there makes ours seem light in comparison. Of course people tend to focus on what's right in front of them.

At Mickey's I parked where I could see the front door. I waited in my car, not playing music or even an audio book and not really thinking either. Just letting my mind drift.

I felt tired, mentally and physically. Maybe the job was getting to me. Or maybe it was just having to look at those pictures of the Fontaines. I was beginning to believe that Connolly was right: all the evidence did point to Whit. Well, that would make sense if he were the murderer.

If ....

It was my job to get past that "if" somehow, and I wasn't sure I could do it. I appreciated the confidence that Marcus had in me, but I wished I had more in myself.

I closed my eyes and tried to blank out all thought—something that never works, at least not for me. Suddenly it occurred to me that having a drink with Connolly would be the first time I'd been with a man socially since Bobby died. Not counting my father and Marcus and Larry, of course.

It was ironic that I was meeting with a cop. A police officer just like Bobby even if they didn't look alike. But I'm sure they were alike in other ways. Like the way Connolly had looked at me, studying me. Bobby had done that sometimes too.

I'd asked him about it once, and he'd said that it was hard for him to tell what I was thinking. Raising himself on an elbow as we lay in bed, the breeze from the ceiling fan cool on our bare skin, drying the sweat we'd worked up a few minutes before.

I'd smiled at Bobby, so happy to have him there with me. Then I'd laughed and said it was just one of the "mysteries of the East." He'd looked puzzled but only for a moment, as I'd reached up to pull him to me.

"Here," I'd murmured, "have another taste of Asia." Then I'd kissed him—kissed him so that he'd never forget it.

I felt my eyes grow hot, and I wiped them with my fingers. When I opened them I saw Connolly going up to the door of the bar.

I got out and walked inside right behind him.

CHAPTER THIRTEEN

As Connolly stood inside the doorway, looking around for me, I tapped him on the shoulder.

"Hey. I waited for you outside."

He turned to look at me and then smiled, the first time I'd seen him do it. "Did you think I wouldn't show?"

"No, I thought you'd be here, but I didn't want to go in by myself."

"Tough girl like you? A big, bad PI? I'm surprised."

I liked his teasing me. It had been a while since anyone had done that. "I didn't want it to look like …." I stopped, embarrassed.

"Like what?"

"Well, like I'm one of those women who comes here to meet cops."

He kept looking at me but didn't reply. Then he scanned the place and gestured toward a couple of empty stools at the bar. "We can sit there."

When I didn't say anything, he added, "Or maybe you'd like more privacy. In a booth maybe."

I didn't know what we might talk about it, but keeping it private seemed like a good idea. "Yes, if that's okay."

"Sure."

He led the way to a booth and let me slide in before he sat across from me. A tired-looking server appeared, her brassy hair no color known in nature. She smiled at Connolly, gave me about a quarter of what she'd given him, and then turned back his way.

"Hi, Ryan. Haven't seen you in a while."

Ryan? I felt foolish because I hadn't thought to find out his first name. Ryan. I liked it—it certainly went with his last name and his Black Irish looks, his hair and eyes being as dark as mine.

He nodded once to acknowledge their acquaintance. I sensed that he'd probably have been friendlier to her if I hadn't been there, and I wondered how close their acquaintance was. I thought I could probably make a good guess.

"The job, Gina. You know how it is."

"Yeah, don't I though."

I could relate to that. "The job" was the excuse a couple of cops had given me when they didn't want to take things further after a few dates. Come to think of it, I'd used the same excuse once or twice myself. Just "the job," which said it all to someone who knew about police work.

She gave us a questioning look. "Menus?"

Connolly glanced at me, and I shook my head. "No, we're just having drinks," he said. "Maker's Mark and a splash of water for me. What's yours?"

I'd been going to order a glass of wine, but whiskey sounded better. Just one, I said to myself. "I'll have the same."

"Got it."

As she went to the service area at the end of the bar, Connolly looked at me again. "I'm surprised. Not to stereotype or anything, but I didn't think Asian women drank much."

"Most don't. For cultural reasons as well as the fact that many of us don't metabolize alcohol the same way as other people. We can get 'Asian flush' when we drink."

"You turn red?"

"I don't, but many East Asians do. Of course, if someone has it, that person probably won't drink much, maybe not at all." I thought about that a moment. "I guess it's a good thing if it keeps you from drinking too much."

Gina arrived with our drinks, put Connolly's down first, then mine. She glanced at him, gave me an appraising look, and left. When she was gone, Connolly picked up his glass and softly clinked mine. "Here's to better days."

"And may they come soon." I took a sip. The drink was perfect—the whiskey tasted strong but not overpowering, and there was enough ice but not so much that you got a glass of ice water with a little whiskey in it. Well, you'd figure they'd make a good drink in a cop bar.

Connolly also took a moment to savor the first taste. Then he said, "That Asian flush thing is interesting. I've never heard of it."

"We consider it a weakness, and we generally don't talk about our weaknesses."

"You don't want to lose face, right?"

"That's one way to put it. The Chinese call it miànzi—being respected, avoiding shame. In Chinese culture what others think of you is really important."

"Do you believe that? I mean, why should you care what other people think?"

I had some more of my drink. I put the glass down and stared into it as though the pattern of ice and liquid would tell me something—I wasn't sure what. "Sometimes I don't know what I believe."

When I looked up, Connolly was studying me again. "That's okay.

Sometimes I don't either."

"Yes, but you know who you are, don't you?"

"I guess. Don't you?"

"Not always."

"Well, you're still young. When you're over forty, like me, things may seem clearer."

I took my turn to study him. "You look younger. I've always heard the job ages you."

"Thanks. And it does age you—mostly inside."

I thought he might elaborate on that, but he didn't. He had some of his drink, and I did likewise. Neither of us spoke for a while, but he seemed comfortable with the silence. Not that the bar was silent—there was music and the sound of several simultaneous conversations—but between us there was a pause. Maybe to think about what we'd already said.

After a couple of minutes Connolly said, "I'd like to hear why you left the force."

That surprised me. "What difference does it make? And why would you care?"

"I've heard you were doing well, had a promising future. Then something went wrong."

"Did you hear what it was?"

"Yes, but the story is probably wrong. At least parts of it. I'd like to hear it from you." When I didn't say anything, he added, "That is, if you don't mind talking about it. To me."

I finished my drink, thinking that I'd had my one and should go. That I should leave before I told him, a man I hardly knew, some things I'd never told anyone. But something in Connolly's face made me trust him.

And I had to admit that I liked him. I liked that face, the square jaw, the not-quite-straight nose that looked as if it had been broken at least once, the wide-set eyes with faint lines radiating from the outside corners. I also liked the way he looked at me, looked into my eyes as though he could read something there and wanted to read more.

"Okay. Maybe it will do me some good to tell it. I'm sure tired of carrying it around inside."

"Good. I'm going to have another drink. Want one?"

I hesitated a moment before I said, "All right. I'll probably need it for this."

He caught Gina's attention and made a circular motion with an index finger. Then he turned back to me. "Go ahead—I'm listening."

I took a deep breath and began. First I told him how I met Bobby, a slightly older and more experienced police officer, not long after I graduated from the academy. For a long time he was just someone I knew, a fellow cop with a big grin and a way of making everyone laugh. He was said to be a good officer, a careful man who went by the book but was fair and reasonable about enforcing the law. I found him attractive, but I noticed his wedding ring and made sure our occasional teasing of each other never got flirtatious.

Gina brought our drinks, and I had some of mine while I thought about how to tell Connolly the next part of the story.

"Then we are assigned to patrol together. You know how it is—when you spend that much with someone, you get to know the other person very well, warts and all."

Connolly nodded. "Yep, been there, done that. But I'm guessing you two made a good team."

"I think so. Until—well, I'm getting ahead of myself."

Then I told Connolly how I'd talked to Bobby about my feeling that I was a misfit in my own family. Bobby had listened attentively but hadn't tried to give me advice. He'd seemed genuinely interested in my struggle to put my life into some sort of order, to find some path that made sense to me and would earn at least grudging respect from my family.

"We all need a sympathetic ear from time to time," Connolly said. "But I have an idea where this is going."

I blushed but not from the booze. "Yes, you're right. That's where it went. Not right away—in fact, not for quite a while. But I could sense that he wasn't happy in his marriage, and finally he told me about it."

I paused, remembering. "His wife, Nicole, was—is—an assistant manager at one of the big resort hotels on the oceanfront. All caught up in her job, working crazy hours, not home much, at least not when Bobby was. He told me he wanted her to find something else, something that would allow them to start a family."

"And she didn't?"

"I guess not. At least they never had a child. And he told me they'd basically stopped having sex. Whenever they were home at the same time, she was too tired or not in the mood or had brought work home that she had to finish. Always some excuse."

"Did you believe that? I mean, that's what a married man would say who wanted to go to bed with you."

"Maybe so, but I think he was telling the truth. I met his wife once, at a party one of the guys had at his house, and she didn't seem all that close to Bobby. She acted like she didn't want to be there."

"She probably didn't. You know—civilians mixing with us pigs."

He said it lightly, but I noticed he drank some whiskey right after, and I thought that maybe someone had called him that before. I'd never heard it as a cop, but I knew others who had.

"Well, anyway, she went out of town on business, and Bobby invited me to dinner. I thought that's all it would be—dinner—but somehow we ended up back at my place, and he spent the night. That's how it started."

I had some of my drink then, remembering. How we'd tried to meet whenever we could, have a meal or a drink. Sometimes just go right to bed, sometimes just sit on the couch and talk. Bobby had told me about his lousy childhood just as I'd told him about my confused one. We'd gotten very close, and I thought there might be a future for us.

"I'll bet he told you he was going to divorce his wife."

"Yes, he did."

"And you believed him."

"Yes, I believed that too—and still believe it." I paused, looking at Connolly. "You sound rather accusatory. Any particular reason? You didn't know Officer Robert C. Blanchard, did you?"

Connolly looked down at his glass, moving it in little circles in the condensation it had produced. It struck me that Vanessa had the same habit, and I wondered whether she'd like Connolly. Then I mentally kicked myself for having such a premature thought.

"No, I didn't know your Bobby. But I knew one like him." He stopped toying with the glass and looked at me. "So did Sarah, my wife. My ex-wife, I mean."

I let that sink in for a moment. "You mean she left you for ...."

"Yeah, another cop. A guy I knew pretty well. Recommended him for promotion, in fact. I didn't know what he was promoting at my house when I wasn't around."

"I'm sorry." I didn't know what else to say.

"Sure, so am I. But it happened. We got divorced, Sarah married him, and I'm over it."

Really? You don't sound very over it, I thought. "Any kids?"

"Two, a boy and a girl. They stay with their mother. The girl's only seven, so I don't see her much. My son is a few years older, so I get him some weekends—if I'm not working."

"I'll bet he wants to be a police officer when he grows up."

"Naturally—his father and stepfather both cops. But I've told him to be a doctor or lawyer or anything but somebody wearing a badge."

"Good advice. My parents told me essentially the same thing."

"I can see it took."

"Sure it did."

I finished my drink. Connolly's glass was already empty, and without his asking me, he motioned for Gina.

"Another round," he said to her.

"Not for me." I handed her my glass. "Any chance of some coffee? Or maybe hot tea?"

"We have both. Although with this crowd we don't get much call for either one."

"Hot tea, then."

"Sure, honey." She picked up Connolly's glass, and for an instant I could see what she'd looked like when she was my age or even younger. I wondered whether, when or if I was ten or fifteen years older, time would show in my face as it did in hers. Probably, the way I was going.

I figured Connolly wouldn't have ordered another drink if he hadn't wanted to continue our conversation, but he didn't say anything while we waited for her to return. I didn't say anything either and tried to be as comfortable with the silence as he seemed to be. Then, after Gina returned with his drink and my hot water and tea bag, I busied myself with brewing the tea, enjoying the familiar floral scent as the leaves steeped.

After I had my first sip and put down the cup, Connolly said, "So what happened then? Between you and Bobby?"

"Nothing happened to us—something happened to him. Something bad."

"On the job?"

"Yes."

Connolly waited until I finally forced myself to say it. "He was killed. My fault—I got him killed."

CHAPTER FOURTEEN

Connolly picked up his glass and drank some whiskey. He put the glass down and looked at me. "You say you got him killed—how?"

At first I thought I didn't want to tell him that part of it—the awful part. I'd never told the details to anyone but the officers who investigated Bobby's death. But then I realized I did want to tell Connolly, a fellow professional who must have been in bad situations himself. I guess what I really wanted was for him to hear the story and pass judgment on me.

"It was a Saturday night, a hot, humid night, the kind where you can't seem to stop sweating. We were working a bad part of Virginia Beach—neighborhoods where you get a lot of domestic violence calls."

"Like Norfolk's Texas streets."

I'd heard cops talk about the Texas streets—Fort Worth Avenue, San Antonio Boulevard. And, of course, Dallas Street itself. Dilapidated housing, junky cars, mean dogs. Some mean people too. Not that many, really, but enough to make the rest of the residents nervous and, on occasion, afraid. Police officers don't like to go there but have to—often.

"Yeah, like that. Anyway, we got a call about a man threatening his woman with a knife. Yelling so loud a neighbor phoned us. We rolled in on it, and there he was. Standing in the front room, in boxers and an undershirt, weaving, waving that knife around. Cursing the woman and saying he'd cut her."

"Sometimes talking like that means they won't actually do it."

"Sure, but you how can you predict?"

Connolly lifted his glass again. "You can't."

"Exactly. There were empty liquor bottles on the floor, and the guy certainly seemed drunk. Or high."

"Probably both."

"Yep, and the woman looked about as wasted as he was. Anyway, it was my turn to take the lead, so I went in to try to calm the guy down. Bobby went to talk to the woman, maybe get her to go into another room."

I paused, remembering. "But she wouldn't cooperate. She cursed the man back—called him a motherfucker several times—and yelled that he'd better stop screwing her sister. That set the guy off even more. He lunged at her with the knife, and I tried to stop him."

"With your bare hands?"

"Yes. I should've had my baton ready, but I didn't. Dumb mistake. He cut my arm—not that bad really, but it started to bleed pretty heavily. Then while I was putting pressure on the cut, somehow he managed to kick my legs out from under me. I hit the floor, and that made Bobby turn his back to the woman and move to help me."

"Instead of calling for backup."

"Right. He pulled his baton, knocked the knife out of the guy's hand, and backed him up against the wall. Then Bobby drew his pistol and shouted that he'd shoot. He was just trying to intimidate the man, get him to give up the fight, but the woman must have thought Bobby was a trigger-happy cop. She screamed and grabbed a gun from somewhere. I hadn't been watching her, which was another dumb mistake."

"I'm surprised she didn't get that gun out when the man threatened her."

"Well, neither of them was thinking too clearly. And maybe she wasn't that scared before we got there—the guy might have acted like that previously, and she figured it was just nasty talk. Anyway, once she had that gun in her hand, she shot Bobby twice."

"In the back?"

"Yes. He pitched forward onto the man, and they collapsed to the floor. I drew my own pistol and radioed for help. I held my gun on the man and woman until I passed out, and then they ran away. When I woke up in the hospital, they told me that Bobby was dead. They caught the woman the next day. The man is still at large."

I trailed off then. That was almost all of the story. I didn't want to think about the ending that was left.

Connolly didn't speak for a minute. Then he said, "I'm sorry. I—well, what a godawful thing. I remember now—it was in the news for a day or two."

"Yes. Not long—the department hushed things up as best they could. They don't like to highlight cops' mistakes."

"No department does. That's understandable."

"I guess. But I still knew it was all my fault. If I hadn't gotten romantically involved with Bobby, maybe he wouldn't have compounded my mistake with one of his own. I know he was just trying to protect me."

"He would've done that in any case."

"Yes, but maybe he would've smarter about it. And maybe if I'd been more objective myself, thinking of it as being there with my patrol partner, not the man I was in love with, I would've been smarter too. At least gone by the book."

"That's a lot of maybes. You can't know things would've been different."

"No, but I'll always wonder if they might have been. And I'll always remember the funeral. Lots of police officers—all of us in dress uniform. Some of them wouldn't look at me. But there was one person who did."

Connolly just waited. He probably knew what I was going to say.

"Bobby's wife. That's when I realized she knew about us. I don't know how, but she did. She stared at me from across the grave, and I could feel how much she hated me. She must've thought I'd been trying to take Bobby away from her."

"Well, perhaps. I guess that's understandable."

Connolly must have felt that way about the guy who seduced his wife, I thought. I couldn't blame him for making the comparison. "Yes, but I wasn't trying to do that. I never asked Bobby to divorce her. I thought he'd be happier if he did, that's all."

Connolly nodded and finished his drink. I had some more tea, but it had cooled to lukewarm, and I put the cup down.

"Sorry for telling you such a sad story."

"No need to apologize—I asked you to tell it. And I'm glad you did."

"Thanks. It felt good to tell someone who ... well, someone who understands."

"We're all human, and we all make mistakes. Maybe you should stop blaming yourself so much for yours."

The therapist had told me the same thing, but it was easier to say than do. Still, I knew I should try.

"I hope I can someday. But I'm not there yet."

"Healing takes time. But I guess the situation was bad enough for you to leave the force?"

"Yes. I wasn't forced to leave, but they didn't beg me to stay either. The word got around about Bobby and me, and I think a lot of the guys believed I'd acted badly—at least foolishly—and contributed to Bobby's death. I couldn't blame them—I felt the same way."

"So that's when you became a PI?"

"No, that's when I started drinking. I had some savings, so for about six months I didn't do much but drink and sleep. I sobered up for my Navy Reserve drill weekend once a month, and I went to the store when I had to and to the gym when I couldn't stand the inactivity anymore. But mostly I hid from the world."

"How did your family take it?"

"They were worried about me. I went to my parents' house for dinner only a few times, and it was always awkward. My father had talked to one of my friends on the force and found out about Bobby and me. I know he was disappointed, and my mother was actually shocked. She didn't think

I'd ever do anything like that."

"You're hardly the first."

"No, I'm not, but my parents always set high standards for us kids, and I let them down. I don't know what I would have done if Marcus hadn't offered me a job when my money was about to run out. I thought it would just be a way to make a living while I figured out what to do with the rest of my life. But now I've found that I kind of like it."

"You seem to be good at it. That's not surprising, given that you were a good cop."

"Except for when I wasn't."

"Well, I think this is a good job for you."

"Let's see how I do on the Fontaine case."

Connolly nodded. "Okay." He put some money on the table for the drinks—leaving a generous tip for Gina—and stood to go. "We will."

He walked me to my car, a courtesy I appreciated, especially after dark. I unlocked the door but didn't open it. I turned to face him, and he looked into my eyes.

He didn't say anything, and I didn't either. The night air felt humid and heavy as though a thunderstorm might be on the way. I imagined lightning flashing, freezing the world for a moment like an old black-and-white photo.

Connolly moved closer to me, his six-foot frame looming over my shorter one. I thought he might try to kiss me, and I wondered what that would be like. No, more than that, I wanted to find out what it would be like. I turned my head up and waited.

"You need to be careful, Wendy."

That was the first time he'd called me that, and I liked the way it sounded coming from him. I wanted to hear him say it again.

I wasn't sure what he meant by telling me to be careful. Careful of what? How I investigated this case? The people I talked to about the murder? Or careful of him?

"I try to be." I spoke softly, as he had even though no one was near us. "Always."

"Good."

"But why do you think there's some special need for me to be careful? Even if Whit Fontaine did kill his wife, I'm trying to clear him, so he's got no motive to try to hurt me."

Connolly frowned. "He killed her all right."

"Well, let's say he did. Then no one else has any such motive either."

"Maybe not with respect to his wife's death. But if you go around asking people a lot of questions, trying to prove something that can't be proved—Fontaine's innocence—you may learn some things people don't want you to know."

"Why do you say that?"

He paused before answering. "Everyone has secrets, Wendy. We told each other a couple of ours tonight."

Yes, I thought, we did. I hadn't planned to, but I found Connolly—for some reason I had a hard time thinking of him as "Ryan"—easy to talk to. Maybe it was our shared police background. Or maybe—and this I almost didn't permit myself to say—we just clicked. The thought of that excited me and scared me at the same time.

When I didn't answer, he continued. "All I'm saying is that you need to be careful not to disturb the skeletons in people's closets."

"What if the skeletons need to be disturbed?" I said it lightly, but I couldn't keep a touch of seriousness out of my voice.

"If they don't have anything to do with your investigation, then leave them alone."

"Is that what you do when you investigate a murder?"

"Yes. That's what a good cop should do."

"And you're a good cop."

"I try to be. And you should too—a good private cop."

"All right, I will."

There was silence then, but the short space between us was like a magnetic field, and I could feel myself being pulled toward him. Then his arms were around me and we were kissing.

It was as good as I'd hoped. I wanted it to go on for a long time, but after a few moments he pulled his head away to look at me.

"Sorry—I guess I got carried away. It must be this night air ... or something."

I wished he hadn't felt a need to apologize even though I knew he meant well. "Oh, that's all right. I was a bit carried away myself. But it's fine."

I took a step back and smiled at him. "I enjoyed talking to you ... Ryan. It's been a while since I said so much to anyone." Especially about the past, I thought. And never about Bobby.

"I'm glad you did." He paused again, seeming to weigh what he said next. "Now I'll follow you home."

When I didn't reply, he added, "Just to make sure you get there safety, especially after a couple of drinks."

"Okay." I don't know what I would have said if he'd suggested going home with me or perhaps going to his place. Maybe I would have agreed. But it was a moot point because he didn't seem to have that in mind. Although I barely knew the man, I felt vaguely disappointed, as if I'd been denied something I hadn't really known I wanted.

I opened the door and got into the car. Before I closed it I looked up at him and said, "Thanks for the drinks. And for listening. Also for making sure I get home all right."

"You're welcome. I enjoyed spending time with you. You're an interesting person, Wendy."

Just what every girl wants to hear, I thought. You're *interesting*. Well, maybe that was better than being thought of only as a bedtime playmate.

I started the car and waited while he went to his, got in, and turned on his lights. Then I pulled of the parking lot slowly, giving him plenty of time to follow me.

I drove home fairly slowly too. Not because I thought I might lose him—he was surely an expert at trailing another car—but because I remembered what he'd said about the drinks and about being careful. He was right on both counts.

When I got to my apartment building, I parked in my reserved spot and then walked back to the curb where Connolly had pulled up. As I approached his car, he let down the window.

"Thanks again." I waited to see what he'd say.

"You're welcome again. And let's get together again. When both of us have more time to enjoy it."

"I'd like that."

"Well, goodnight, Wendy."

"Goodnight, Ryan."

He gave me a little wave and drove away. I watched his taillights as they faded into the night.

Then I looked around for the black Lexus but didn't see it. That didn't mean much, I told myself. The driver could be parked somewhere not too far away, watching me through binoculars or even night-vision goggles.

I wondered if I was simply being paranoid. Why would anyone be conducting surveillance on me? I wasn't a threat to anyone. And I wasn't the kind of woman who might attract a stalker—at least I didn't think so.

I tried but couldn't quite convince myself. So I decided I'd better start carrying my pistol in my briefcase. If someone was after me and made a move, at least I'd be armed.

I went upstairs and ordered some delivery from my usual place. It's not the best Chinese restaurant in Hampton Roads, but the food is good and it's close by. Before I placed my order, I answered in Mandarin the owner's polite inquiries about my health and that of my family members.

Then I phoned Marcus and told him what I'd learned at the Lynnhaven Dock House. I also told him I'd looked at the crime-scene photos, but I didn't mention meeting Connolly at the bar. I told myself it was because having drinks with Connolly was personal, not business, but I knew the real reasons were that, first, Marcus might ask me what we talked about and, second, he might disapprove. Not of Connolly per se but of my spending time with him while we were working opposite ends of the Fontaine murder.

And he'd probably be right, I thought, after I'd hung up and was jotting down the details Marcus had given me about Fontaine's bond hearing the next day.

After the food arrived, I ate in front of the TV, watching the news and then half of a movie. It was a modern PI flick, not very good, and I amused myself by noting the things they'd gotten wrong. The food or the movie or both made me sleepy, and I went to bed early. When I did, I put my gun on top of the nightstand so I could grab it quickly if I needed to.

I closed my eyes, remembering that kiss, and it was a long time before I dropped off to sleep.

CHAPTER FIFTEEN

For once I didn't have bad dreams—maybe because I'd confessed my sins to Connolly. If he hadn't become a police officer, he'd have made a good priest, I thought. As I made the bed, I decided to tell him that the next time I saw him. I wanted to see his reaction.

In Norfolk the Juvenile and Domestic Relations District Court has jurisdiction over domestic assault cases such as Whit Fontaine's. Bond hearings are the first thing on the court docket every Friday, and I made sure to be at the courthouse early. I went to the courtroom Marcus had specified and sat as close to the defense counsel's table as I could. I was the first person there, but Marcus came in soon after and sat next to me.

He was wearing a gray suit, a crisp white shirt, and a mostly-red tie that complemented the suit so well that I thought Simone had probably picked it out for him. He looked at my navy-blue pantsuit and minimal jewelry. "Well, well, you sure do clean up good. Nothing like a little 'courtroom attire' once in a while, is there?"

"I'm just glad I don't have to doll up every day."

"That's the cop in you, Wendy. Hard to chase bad guys in stiletto kicks."

"Don't I know it." I glanced at the people who were coming in and taking seats in the rows of benches that took up about two-thirds of the room. "Where are Scott and Jackie?"

"Oh, they'll be here. But not too early—they don't want to look like they have nothing else to do."

He was right—they came in about five minutes before nine and sat in the bench reserved for defense counsel. When they saw us, Scott mouthed a silent "hi" and Jackie did the same.

After they were seated, Scott turned around and smiled at me. "Good to see you, Wendy," he said, keeping his voice low. "Marcus has been keeping us up to date on your progress. Sounds like you're covering a lot of ground."

"Yes, without much in the way of results so far."

"Well, it's still early. Give yourself time. By the way, you look very nice this morning."

The bailiff came in, and Jackie elbowed Scott in the ribs. I wasn't sure whether she was reacting to the bailiff's entrance or Scott's comment. Maybe both.

The bailiff went to his desk, clicked the computer keys for a few moments, and then checked the time. At exactly nine a.m. he stood and said, "All rise."

We stood while the bailiff announced that court was in session and named the judge, the Honorable Winston H. Chambers, who was presiding over the bond hearings that day. Although there were obviously a lot of jokes about his name—"Chambers in his chambers," things like that—he was said to be a fair judge, and his even-handedness might help our client.

Fontaine's bond hearing was the third one on the docket. The first two took about forty-five minutes. Chambers granted bond in one case—a scared-looking nineteen-year-old charged with robbing a gas station—and denied it in the other—an older man, charged with aggravated sexual assault, who had several prior convictions and a couple of prison sentences in his record.

As the older man's lawyer and the prosecutor sparred over whether he deserved bond, the judge listening impassively, the accused man stared at the people in the courtroom. As his gaze lingered on me, his mouth twitched, and I thought he was forcing himself not to smile. I knew that if he'd been alone with me, he would have leered and said something dirty. Even though I'd have told him to go to hell, I was glad when the judge ruled that the man was likely to flee or commit another crime and denied him bond.

As two sheriff's deputies led him away, the man looked at me again and winked. I felt as though he'd put his hands on me, and I wanted to punch him in the face.

Then they brought Fontaine in, and the judge, although continuing to keep his expression impassive, sat up a bit straighter. He had to know who Fontaine was—they probably moved in the same, that is, "moneyed," circles, and both of them might even belong to the Tidewater Yacht and Country Club.

Still dressed in an orange jumpsuit, Fontaine looked more tired and pale than when I'd seen him on Wednesday. As they led him toward the defense counsel's table, he glanced at the spectators in the courtroom. When he saw me, he nodded once, and I gave him what I hoped was a reassuring smile. He didn't smile back as he sank into a chair next to Scott and Jackie, who had gone to the table and were busy getting papers out of their briefcases.

The bailiff called the case, and the judge asked the prosecutor if she was ready. A tall, thin brunette in her late thirties or early forties, she had hard eyes and looked as though she'd been in the job a while.

"Yes, Your Honor."

"Then you may proceed."

She described the charges against Fontaine and asked that, in view of the seriousness of his alleged crimes, he be denied bond and kept in jail while his trial was pending. She stuck to the facts, describing the murder scene in detail but avoiding language that might have drawn an objection—"brutal murder," for example. Still, she made clear that she thought there was little doubt of Fontaine's guilt.

When she finished, the judge said, "Do you consider this man a flight risk?"

"Yes, Your Honor. Murder defendants are almost always a flight risk."

"Hmm, well, yes, but 'almost always' isn't 'always'. Mr. Cushman, your rebuttal?"

Scott rose to address the judge. In his custom-tailored pinstripe suit and with his salon-styled touch-of-gray hair, he looked like someone who played a lawyer on TV. Or maybe the TV lawyers were simply supposed to look like him. At any rate, he looked impressive.

And he gave a well-prepared argument. Jackie had probably drafted it—she was the better writer of the two—but Scott delivered it beautifully, his rich voice with a trace of Tidewater accent rolling into every corner of the courtroom.

He began by claiming that the evidence against Fontaine was not nearly as strong as the prosecutor had said. He pointed out that there were no witnesses, there had been no gunpowder residue on Fontaine's hands, and given his fortunate situation in life, Fontaine had no motive for murder strong enough to lead him to kill Mrs. Fontaine.

The prosecutor hadn't focused on a possible motive for the murder, probably thinking that the circumstantial evidence was so damning that she didn't need to. But as Scott unspooled his argument, she shook her head and furiously took notes, perhaps to help her if the judge gave her, as the lawyers like to say, "another bite at the apple."

Scott took more time than the prosecutor had, but he was careful not to try the judge's patience by going on too long. He soon turned to the main point of contention in the bond hearing.

"Your Honor, Whitaker Fontaine is not a flight risk, much less a murderer. He is a native of Norfolk with strong ties to the community. He went to kindergarten, elementary, and secondary school here. His home and his business are here. In fact, your Honor"—at this point, Scott, a good actor in the courtroom, put a little catch in his sonorous voice—"both of his parents are buried here."

He paused to let that sink in. Then he continued. "Mr. Fontaine has never before been charged with a crime, much less convicted of one. Moreover, not only is there no reason to keep him incarcerated, there is a very good reason not to: Mr. Fontaine needs to be free to work with his legal team and our private investigators to clear his good name. Thus, justice requires that this court grant him bond."

For a moment I thought that perhaps Scott had gone too far. Judges don't like to be told what they're "required" to do. But Judge Chambers didn't seem to take offense. He was silent for a moment, probably thinking about each of the lawyers had said. Maybe he was also thinking about how much he and Fontaine had in common, how he'd feel if he were Fontaine standing there in that orange jumpsuit, possibly, although certainly not probably, innocent.

The prosecutor watched the judge expectantly, undoubtedly hoping that he'd give her a chance to refute some of Scott's claims. But he didn't. He looked at Fontaine and said, "I'm going to grant Mr. Fontaine's motion for bond and set the amount at three hundred thousand dollars. Mr. Fontaine, you understand that if you fail to show up for your trial, you will forfeit the bond?"

Jackie nudged Fontaine, and he stood, clearly relieved. "Yes, Your Honor, I understand."

"Good." The judge banged his gavel. "Next case."

The amount of the bond was unusually high, but as the courtroom doors closed behind us, Scott, clearly elated by the ruling, noted the obvious that all Fontaine had to do was pay a fee to a bail agent—a lot of money but nothing he couldn't afford—and pledge collateral equal to the bond. With his usual confidence Scott had already discussed the logistics with Fontaine, so he and Jackie left to make arrangements with the agent.

"Well," Marcus said, loosening his tie, "at least he'll be out—for a while."

"Yes, for a while."

Marcus looked at me. "You think we can keep him out?"

"I don't know. Maybe. But I'll have to find something I haven't found yet."

"Keep looking."

"Of course. I'll wait for Fontaine and take him home. Or wherever else he'd like to go. I need to talk to him anyway."

"Good. Call me with any news."

"I will."

Marcus left then, and after retrieving my phone from the car, I went to the jail. For two hours I sat in a dreary waiting area, surrounded by sad-looking people, almost all women who, like me, were waiting for a man to be released. I tried to read a Daniel Woodrell novel on my phone, but the depressing atmosphere of the place made it hard to concentrate.

Eventually Scott and Jackie paid the bail agent on Fontaine's behalf, the agent posted the bond, and the deputies processed Fontaine for release.

Finally he came out, dressed in ordinary clothing. I gave him a wave, and he walked toward me. He still looked tired and pale, but there was more light in his eyes than when he'd been in court in that jumpsuit.

"Hi, Mr. Fontaine. Congratulations on being bailed out. We weren't sure the judge would allow bond in your case."

"That's what Scott said. I guess I got lucky. And please call me 'Whit'."

"All right ... Whit. I've got my car. May I give you a ride somewhere?"

"Thanks. I want to go home, lie in my own bed. I didn't get much sleep in there."

"I understand."

"But first I want to get something to eat. The jail food is awful."

"That's what I've heard. Where would you like to go?"

"How about The Captain's Table?"

"In Ocean View?"

"Yes. We helped to build that place. And a lot of other places along there."

Not so long ago Ocean View—which actually has a view of the Chesapeake Bay, not the Atlantic Ocean—had been a rough place known for sleazy motels and decrepit houses inhabited partially by career criminals, drug dealers, and hookers. There had also been some honest, hard-working folks who'd had to put up with their disreputable neighbors, but formerly the whole area had a reputation as a place one should try to stay out of, especially at night.

But then developers like Fontaine-McKenna Associates and some enterprising real-estate agents "discovered" Ocean View and started to transform it into a desirable area with trendy restaurants, boutiques, and other small businesses and neighborhoods with new but vintage-looking houses. They'd made a lot of money in the process.

Although I sometimes missed the raffish charm of the old Ocean View—for example, the colorful painted flamingoes that had paraded across the concrete-block wall of one now-razed building—I was practical enough to recognize that the transformation had been good for Norfolk. The Captain's Table, the place Fontaine had suggested, was a popular seafood place right on the bay in a spot formerly occupied by a motel so seedy that Larry would have hesitated to conduct surveillance there.

"Sure, that's fine. I've heard it has good food."

"You haven't been there?"

"It's a bit out of my price range." Like most upscale restaurants, I mentally added.

"Well, then you're in for a treat—my treat." He managed a slight smile, which I took as a good sign for a man just released from jail. Especially one accused of murder.

Because this was a working lunch, I would have put the tab on my expense report, and he ultimately would have paid for it anyway, but it was nice of him to offer to be the host. My parents tried hard—unfortunately with mixed success—to instill good manners in me, and I appreciated good manners in others.

"Okay, thanks."

It was a short walk to the city garage where I'd parked, and we made it in silence. Fontaine—despite his asking me to use his first name, I was still having a hard time thinking of him as "Whit"—seemed preoccupied or maybe he was just too tired and emotionally exhausted to talk. He was the client, so I followed his lead and didn't try to chat.

He was almost as silent in the car. Mentally reviewing my notes, I remembered Marcus's question about Fontaine's Navy service.

"Say, when you were in the Navy, did you qualify on the pistol range?"

"Sure, almost everyone does. Why? Oh—I see."

I was glad I didn't have to explain it. "Have you practicing shooting since then?"

"Not much. I went to the range a couple of times right after I bought my pistol. But that was a few years ago ... ." He paused, seeming pensive. "I haven't done any more boxing either."

"Boxing?"

"Yeah, I was pretty good at it when I was in the Navy. We used to have boxing matches once in a while—just something to do out at sea. But I haven't put on the gloves in years."

Then he made me talk. He asked what I'd found so far, and I gave him the rundown. He threw in a couple of questions, but mostly he just sat and listened, nodding once or twice.

When I finished, he looked over at me and said, "Obviously you've been busy."

"Yes, but unfortunately I haven't found anything that will help us much."

"Maybe not yet, but the evidence is out there. It's got to be."

He sounded sincere, and I wondered if maybe he really was innocent. If he was guilty, he was certainly putting on a good act. But people do that sometimes—I'd seen it often enough, both as a cop and as a PI.

And, I thought, remembering how Bobby and I had acted around other cops, I'd done it often enough too.

CHAPTER SIXTEEN

Because of our late start and the traffic and lights on Shore Drive, we didn't get to the restaurant until almost two o'clock. The lunch crowd had thinned out, and the hostess gave us a good seat by a window. The day was sunny, and the waves of the Chesapeake Bay to the north sparkled in the bright light. So did the bigger waves of the Atlantic Ocean that I could just barely see far to the northeast. The view was beautiful and a lot more peaceful than I felt.

Fontaine glanced through the menu and decided quickly. I took more time and was still considering when the server arrived—a young African American woman with "Victoria" on her name tag.

"Want a drink?" Fontaine asked me as he handed her the menu, cutting off her usual introduction.

"Just hot tea."

"I'll have a double bourbon—Blanton's. For lunch, grilled salmon with rice and a house salad, oil and vinegar dressing."

I thought his abrupt manner might annoy the server, but she'd probably experienced worse, because she merely nodded and jotted on her pad.

"I'll have the Caesar salad with chicken."

She made another note and gave me a brief smile—maybe she could tell I was working too. Then she went away.

Fontaine didn't say anything until our drinks arrived. He just sat staring out at the expanse of blue. I wondered if he was trying to memorize the view so that he'd have it with him if he had to go back inside. I knew he'd been though a lot in the past few days, so I didn't try to distract him with small talk.

Victoria brought the drinks quickly, setting the whiskey in front of Fontaine—she could probably tell he needed it—and a saucer, cup, and small pitcher of hot water by me. Then she opened a wooden box to let me select a tea bag.

While I was doing that, Fontaine had about half of his drink, first one big swallow and then two smaller ones. Then he put the glass on the table and looked at me. "I've missed that. The taste, the calming effect. I always enjoy a cocktail or two in the evening. Know what I mean?"

"Yes." All too well, I thought. But I'd been doing better lately and wanted to continue—staying, if not on the wagon, at least out of that deep ditch next to it.

Fontaine had more whiskey. "I hate prison. I'm not sure I can take any more of it."

I didn't tell him that an actual prison—a penitentiary—would be a lot worse than the city jail. He'd find that out for himself if he had to go. More likely *when* he had to go.

"Well, maybe you won't have to." I checked my tea and decided to let it steep a bit longer. "Let's talk about who might have had a reason to frame you for murder."

He looked annoyed. "I already told you: I can't think of anyone."

"You've got to try. And try really hard. Otherwise, there's nothing we can do for you."

"Goddamnit! Don't you think I would if I could?"

I paused to give him time to calm down. "Yes, I do. What about Maxine Walters?"

"Well, what about her?"

"Could she have killed your wife? So she could have you all to herself?"

The question seemed to surprise him. "Uh, no, I don't think so. Maxine isn't that kind of person. I mean, she can be a little bitchy at times, but she wouldn't kill anyone."

"You never know. I've seen what some women can do with a knife or a gun. Or even their bare hands."

"Maxine's not that way. Besides, she doesn't want to marry me."

"How can you be certain? Did she ever say that?"

The questions seemed to confuse him. "Well, not in so many words. But she told me she's independent, has a career, lives her own life."

"Sure she does. But I'll bet she was willing to accept gifts from you—probably expensive gifts from time to time." I pictured that gold necklace she'd called gaudy.

"Yes, but she never asked for them."

"She didn't have to. She knew you'd want to give her nice things to compensate her for … being the other woman." I paused. "For spending most nights alone. And every holiday."

"Well, so what?"

"So I doubt she's quite as happy on her own as she pretends. In fact, she told me she wants to marry you."

"She did? Really?"

His surprise was clearly genuine. Probably to give himself time to think, he raised his glass again.

Victoria arrived with our food, and he had more time to think while she rearranged things slightly on our table and distributed our dishes. Neither of us said anything but "thank you" until she left, giving me a curious glance as she walked away. Maybe she'd overheard part of the conversation.

I kept my voice low as I said, "So she had a motive. I think she knew where you kept your gun—that was the means. And she knew about your business dinner that night. That was her opportunity."

He picked up his knife and fork, looked at his plate for a moment, then put them down again. "Do you think she did it?"

"Maybe. It's certainly possible." I took a bite of my salad. They'd cooked the chicken perfectly—something I seldom do. "Raising that possibility might be enough to create reasonable doubt in the minds of the jury."

"But putting our relationship out in public … it would ruin our reputations."

"I hate to be the one to tell you, Whit, but your reputation is already ruined. Even if you're acquitted, some people—maybe a lot of people—will always think you did it."

"And if I point a finger at Maxine …."

"Some people will always think she did it. Whether she did or not. But we don't have to prove she's guilty—we just have to make a plausible suggestion that you're not."

"I don't want to do it. At least not unless there's some evidence that she really did kill Susan. Do you have any?"

"No, not yet."

He ate some of his lunch, chewing with a thoughtful expression. "There must be someone else."

"Okay, who?"

"Maybe somebody who thinks he got a raw deal from our firm."

"Do you have a name?"

"A name? Hell, I could give you twenty." He drained his glass and held it up until he caught Victoria's eye. "But to kill a man's wife because you think his company shaded you in a business deal … that seems like a stretch."

I agreed, but we had to keep trying. I pulled my notebook and a pen out of my briefcase. "Give me the names of the top three candidates, and I'll start with those."

I jotted down what he told me. "And I need the names of Susan's best female friends—say, her top two or three."

"Why would you want to talk to them? They certainly didn't kill her."

"No, but they might know something useful. A woman will tell another woman things she would never tell a man—even her husband."

"I know, but I've never understood that."

"Just like I've never understood why men talk about sports so they won't have to talk about anything personal." I paused, remembering how hard it had been to get Bobby to open up to me, even as close as we were. "I guess there are things about each gender the other will never understand."

"I guess you're right. Well, her best friend by far was Liz Hutton. They were roommates in college and stayed close after that. I think they talked three or four times a week right up until ...."

Until Susan died, I mentally finished for him. "Where does this Liz Hutton live?"

"Oh, here in Norfolk. Her husband's a banker, quite successful. Susan and Liz did a lot of volunteer work together. Susan was like an aunt to their kids—when they were little of course."

"Do you have a phone number for her?"

"No. I'm not especially close to her or her husband, but it shouldn't be hard to find. They live in Edgewater."

That was an upscale neighborhood on the other side of the Lafayette River from Lochhaven.

"Okay." I made a note. "Did she have other close women friends?"

"If Liz doesn't know whatever it is you want to know about Susan, no one else will either."

Liz Hutton might not have anything helpful to tell me, but it sounded as though I should talk to her. "All right. I'll see if she knows anything about Susan that could help with the case."

He nodded and had some more salmon. I took another bite of my salad, thinking about who else might be a suspect. "What about Tom McKenna?"

Fontaine put down his fork again. "Tom? You can't be serious. Besides, he was at the dinner with me."

"Well, you don't remember anything after a certain point. He could have killed her."

"Okay, I guess it's a theoretical possibility. But why? I mean, what motive would he have?"

"He's your partner. You tell me."

Fontaine said nothing, but he seemed to be thinking about it. Victoria arrived with his fresh drink, and he thanked her absently. She looked at me and raised her eyebrows, but I shook my head that, no, I didn't need anything.

I had a couple more bites of the salad, giving him a few more moments. Then I said, "What was McKenna's relationship with your wife?"

That brought him around. "What do you mean?"

"Did they get along?"

"Sure, they got along fine. Not that they saw each other all that often, but they always seemed cordial toward one another."

"Did you wife ask about him often?"

"No. Well, she brought his name up once in a while, but not so often that I noticed it."

"McKenna's single, isn't he?"

"Divorced. About five or six years now."

"No children?"

"No, no kids. Just like Susan and me." He looked at me. "Do you have children?"

The question made me a bit uncomfortable, but I needed to have a good relationship with Fontaine, so I decided to answer it. "No, not yet and maybe never. Two nephews though. And another baby on the way."

"I'll bet you're a good aunt."

"I try to be." I cleared my throat. "Okay, getting back to your case, is McKenna seeing anyone?"

"You mean romantically?"

I nodded.

"I don't know. Probably. He mentions different women from time to time. But he's practically married to the job, so that doesn't leave him much time for socializing."

"You said he was the one who set up the dinner with the Japanese businessmen?"

"Yeah, that was his baby." He paused to sip his drink. "Investors around here have gotten a little gun-shy about commercial real estate—too many projects have gone belly-up or not made enough money. Hell, no money in some cases. So Tom came up with the idea to look for some foreign capital."

"What do you know about them?"

He shifted in his chair, "Hmm, not much really. As I said, Tom set it up. I was there just to smile and shake hands."

"Do you have their names?"

"I don't remember any. Everything they said sounded the same to me."

"Any business cards?"

"Maybe in the blazer I was wearing. The police still have it, but Tom could tell you who they were."

"Okay." I wanted him to be as relaxed as possible so I wasn't writing any of that part down, but I made a mental note. I doubted that this particular trail would lead anywhere, but I wanted to check every possibility.

I knew what Marcus would say: "You're reaching, girl." And he'd be right, but I was determined to show him that I could handle this case.

"So what's the deal? You want them to back one of your development projects?"

"Yes, and they seem interested. At least they did that night." He had another bite of salmon. "Of course Tom and I haven't yet agreed on what sort of project would be most suitable."

"What are the options?"

"Oh, the usual. A strip mall or an office building. Maybe even an office park. But Tom wants to try something else."

"Like what?" I didn't think this line of investigation was going anywhere, but I couldn't seem to stop asking questions.

Fontaine put down his fork and looked at me. "He wants to build an Indian casino. Sorry—a Native American casino. He says we'll make a lot more money that way. And he may be right, but it seems too risky to me."

"Here in Hampton Roads?"

He smiled. It was faint, but I was glad to see that he was beginning to feel better. The food probably helped—and of course the whiskey.

"No, ma'am." He put on a fake Southern accent that reminded me of a pompous rooster I'd seen in a TV cartoon a long time ago. "The great Commonwealth of Virginia will not sully itself by allowing casino gambling within its stately borders."

He paused, then continued in his normal voice. "Pun intended. That could change—one or more of our local tribes may eventually get permission. And there's the notable exception of the state itself promoting gambling in the form of a lottery—a tax on poor people."

"You've got a point, but there's no law against hypocrisy."

"No, or we'd all be in jail. Unless you're an exception to the rule."

"Afraid not." I had a last bite of the salad and put my knife and fork on the plate. "I can be as hypocritical as anyone else when the occasion calls for it."

He studied me for a few seconds. "You're a puzzling young woman, Wendy. How did you end up as a private eye?"

So Connolly thought I was interesting and now Fontaine thought I was puzzling. Well, I supposed there were worse things. "It's a long story."

"I'd like to hear it."

"Maybe another time. Getting back to your partner's plans for a casino, where would he build it?"

"In North Carolina *if* he—we, rather—could build it. They allow Native American casinos there, and Tom took an option on some raw land not far from the Virginia-North Carolina border. But I haven't agreed to his plan, and it would take a lot of money. Which the Japanese haven't promised to lend us."

"At least not yet."

"Right."

"How did you and Mr. McKenna leave it with them that night?"

"What do you mean?"

"What was going to be the next step?"

He flushed slightly. "Frankly, I don't remember. And since then I've been ... focused on other things."

I nodded. "Sure. Well, I'll check with your partner, see what he says."

"But that project can't have anything to do with the murder."

"Probably not. But I've got to check every possibility. I'll be frank too: we've got to come up with something or you'll be going to prison for a long, long time."

He said nothing for a moment, letting my remark sink in. Then he said, "I don't think I could handle that. I'd rather have them stick a needle in my arm and get it over with."

"Maybe you would, but you're not going to get the death penalty. A rich guy like you wouldn't have gotten that even before Virginia abolished it."

He didn't argue the point, and I liked him a little better for it. Victoria's arrival kept either of us from saying anything else just then. After clearing the plates quietly and efficiently, she said, "Would you like dessert? Coffee?"

"Nothing for me, thanks," I said. Fontaine looked at her and shook his head. When she put the check in the middle of the table, Fontaine glanced at it, took an American Express Platinum Card out of his wallet—I'd never seen one before—and laid it on the check.

We remained silent in the short time it took her to return with his credit card and the charge slips and leave them on the table. Fontaine scribbled on the restaurant's copy, picked up his card, and excused himself to go to the restroom. "Head," he called it, as I usually did myself. It occurred to me then that we had Navy service in common if little else.

I glanced at the charge slip, saw that he'd inserted an adequate but not generous tip, and added enough cash to bring the total to twenty percent.

When Fontaine returned, I stood and said, "Thanks for lunch. Want me to drop you at your place?"

"I guess. I mean, if ...."

"The police are finished with it. You can stay there if you like." Then I remembered the bloodstain that was still on the bedroom floor. "Although maybe you'd prefer a hotel, at least until you can have the place … cleaned."

"No, I've got to face things eventually. Let's go."

Fontaine didn't say much as we drove to his house—just his now—and I made only minimal replies. I pulled into the driveway and he got out.

"We'll be in touch," I said. I scribbled my mobile number on one of my cards and handed it to him. "Call me if you think of anything that might be useful."

"Okay." He hesitated a minute. "Want to come in? Maybe have a drink?"

Perhaps he was hitting on me, but I didn't think so. I thought he just wanted some company walking into that house. There's nothing lonelier than an empty house with the aura of death still in it.

"Thanks, but I need to get back to the office." I saw disappointment flicker across his face, so I added, "Maybe some other time."

"Okay," he said again. "Well, see you."

I waited until he got to the front door and unlocked it. He opened the door and turned to look at me. I gave him a little wave too and backed the car down the driveway.

Before I drove away I turned to look at the house. Fontaine was all alone in there, in that big, cold place with its gleaming floors, expensive furniture, and original artwork. He'd probably felt lucky to live there, a successful man married to a bright and beautiful woman, both of them cushioned by money. Yes, he had been lucky.

But now it was beginning to appear that his luck had run out.

CHAPTER SEVENTEEN

It wasn't quite three-thirty and I was close to Edgewater, so I decided to squeeze in an interview with Liz Hutton if she was home. I parked and ran a Google search for Huttons in Edgewater but didn't find anything. I called Simone and asked her to see what she could do.

Then I closed my eyes and tried to think about nothing for a few minutes. My father taught me that technique for uncluttering one's mind, but I'd never gotten as good at it as he was. It didn't work completely this time, but it did help to reduce the jumble of thoughts in my head and allow me to think more clearly. Unfortunately for our client, my clear thinking led me to the same conclusion Connolly had drawn: Whit Fontaine had probably killed his wife.

Well, maybe so. But I was still on the clock and still wanted to earn my paycheck if I could. So I was pleased when Simone called back with the Hutton's home address and phone number.

"The number's unlisted, Wendy, so it would be better just to go over there and ring the doorbell. That way they won't wonder how you were able to call them."

Simone had probably gotten the number by calling our "friend" at the phone company who would provide unlisted numbers for the right price, which wasn't high but provided some nice extra income for him. Especially when you considered that he was almost certainly doing the same thing for other people.

"Sure, Simone. Thanks. Please tell Marcus that I'll swing by the office later."

We said goodbye, and I drove slowly through the streets of Edgewater, looking for the right house. I soon found it—a big house more traditional than the Fontaine place but with the same carefully tended emerald lawn. The back yard sloped down to a wooden dock that had a large, expensive-looking power boat tied to it.

There was a late-model Mercedes in the driveway, so I thought the Hutton woman might be home. I rang the bell, waited, and was about to ring again when a slim, attractive woman with beautifully cut blonde hair opened the door.

"Yes, may I help you?"

"Liz Hutton?"

"Yes. How may I help you?"

"I'm Wendy Lu, a private investigator looking into the death of Susan Fontaine." I gave her my card. "I understand that you and Susan were close friends."

She looked up from the card, studying me. "Who told you that?"

"Whit Fontaine. His lawyers have engaged our agency to find out who killed her."

She let out a short, bitter laugh. "Whit killed her. Everyone knows that."

"He's innocent until proven guilty, and people have been framed before."

"You can't be serious."

"Yes, ma'am, I'm quite serious. It's my job to find out if someone else could have done it."

"Well, good luck with that—you'll need it."

"Probably, but I think talking to you might also help."

"How?"

"Maybe you can tell me something about Susan that suggests a motive for murdering her."

"Whit had plenty of motive—her money."

"Money he won't get if he's convicted of her murder. That's the 'slayer rule'—a murderer can't inherit property from his victim."

"Hmm, I didn't know that. But it makes sense."

"Just like it doesn't make sense that Whit would've staged a murder so clumsily. If he killed her, it had to be a crime of passion, not preplanned."

She pursed her lips, thinking. After a moment she said, "All right. Come inside and we'll talk."

The interior of her home was what I expected—beautifully decorated in a obviously expensive but classically tasteful way. She led the way to what everyone calls the "living room" even though it typically sees less living than any other room in the house.

We sat, she in a red armchair and I on the sofa, cream-colored with a delicate pattern of roses. The room made me feel smarter and richer than I actually was, and maybe that was the intent.

As I pulled out my notebook, she said, "Would you like something to drink? Perhaps some tea? Or a glass of wine?"

"I'm fine, thanks. I'll try not to take too much of your time."

"I have an hour or so. My husband's out playing golf, but we're meeting some people at the club later for drinks and dinner."

I wondered if I'd ever be able to toss off a reference to "the club" as easily as she did. Probably not.

"This shouldn't take too long. I understand that you and Susan met at UVA."

"Yes, we were roommates our first semester there. Sometimes roommates don't get along, but we clicked and became good friends. We even joined the same sorority. Sometimes people thought we were sisters—I mean real sisters, not just sorority sisters."

"She also met Whit there."

"Yes, when we were fourth years. He was charming, very handsome. And of course worldly from having been in the Navy and sailed all over the globe." She smiled to herself, remembering. "Honestly, I wanted to date him myself, but he preferred Susan. And we were careful never to compete for the same man."

"And you kept in touch after they married."

"Always. I was maid of honor at her wedding, and we were in Junior League together here in Norfolk. Whit and George—that's my husband—were never close, but Susan and I remained very good friends. She doted on my children—she never had any of her own, of course."

Liz paused. "I think that was a real tragedy. She wanted kids but couldn't have them, and Whit was so busy building up his business that he didn't have much time for her."

"So she found other ... interests."

She gave me a sharp look. "You mean affairs, don't you? Well, yes, she did, and unfortunately—for herself as well as Whit—she was never very discreet about it."

She shook her head. "I mean, my God, the tennis pro at the club. What was she thinking? That could have been a scandal, but the club hushed it up. They fired him, and Susan just didn't go there for a while."

"And there were others?"

"Yes, several. Sometimes she even thought she was in love with the man, but all of her affairs ended eventually. I learned not to regard them too seriously."

"Do you think any of her lovers might have killed her?"

"No. I mean, I can't think of anyone who'd do that. Why kill her? It wasn't like any of them would've inherited her money."

I thought about that. She was right, but maybe there was another angle.

"Can you think of anyone who would've killed her to frame Whit?"

"What?"

"Could someone have murdered Susan just to get at Whit—to have him sent to prison for killing her?"

"Do people really do things like that?"

"Yes. Not often, but it does happen." I knew of only one such case in Hampton Roads, but there had to be others. And maybe this case was one of them.

She frowned. "Well, it's hard to believe. In any event I can't think of anyone who'd do that either."

"Whit doesn't have any enemies? No one who hates him?"

"I can't think of any. I mean, I'm sure there are people who don't like him—in fact, I'm not overly fond of him now—but kill Susan over that? I just can't believe it."

Well, maybe there wasn't anyone. Or maybe she just didn't know of anyone.

"Okay, let's get back to Susan. What was she like?"

Liz's face brightened at the more congenial topic. "Oh, she was wonderful. Smart, accomplished, generous. A loving person and a loyal friend." She paused. "So loyal. You understand?"

I nodded, thinking of Vanessa Hoang. She'd always had my back just as I'd had hers. Yes, I understood.

"She sounds great. I know you'll miss her a lot. Anything else you can tell me about her?"

"I can do better than that—I can show you."

"Show me? How?"

"Come with me."

She rose, and I followed her out of the room. We went into the den, which was softer and more feminine than the Fontaine's, suggesting that the Huttons shared this space more than Whit and Susan had theirs.

She clicked on a DVD player and then the large TV next to it. She rummaged in a drawer of the low table the player and TV sat on and pulled out a DVD.

"We made this video as a gift for Susan's forty-fifth birthday. I kept a copy. I'm not sure why I did, but I'm glad to have it now. It's only about twenty minutes long, but it will give you some idea of who she was."

She put the disc into the player and clicked the start button. The TV came alive with some cheery music and a banner that read, "Happy Birthday, Susan! This is YOUR life!!" After a few seconds a series of photos of Susan began appearing interspersed with moving pictures of her taken from home movies and videos. The music continued to play as the images came and went.

I saw Susan as a baby, happy, smiling, in pictures posed and unposed. I saw her as a young girl, laughing as she played outside. I saw her at about age thirteen or fourteen, balanced precariously on the dividing line between being a child and becoming a young woman.

I saw her as an awkward young teen, with acne and braces, and then as a graceful older teen, her skin clear and her braces gone. There was video of her at that age, on the ice in a red skater's dress that showed off her impossibly long legs as she floated, flashed, and twirled across the rink. The next picture was of her, still wearing that dress, smiling into the camera as she held up the blue ribbon she'd won for her ice-dancing.

I saw her behind the wheel of a car, laughing and waving at whoever was behind the camera. Then there was a long series of photos of Susan at college, many of them also showing Liz. There was a photo that must have been from a spring break—Susan in a black bikini, looking tan and fit and happy.

She also looked happy on her wedding day, and there was video of her walking down the aisle, wearing that dazzling white dress I'd seen in a picture at the Fontaines' and escorted by a man who must have been her father. He didn't look nearly as happy as she did.

There were fewer pictures after that. Some of Susan and Whit at various social gatherings, many black-tie. Some just of Susan at those events, usually posed with other women, often including Liz. One of her and Tom McKenna, sweaty but grinning after they'd finished running a 10K race. And several of Susan painting or exhibiting her paintings in various galleries. I was no art expert, but it appeared that she'd had talent, perhaps considerable talent if she'd worked to develop it.

She always looked tasteful and elegant, nothing out of place. And she was smiling in the photos, but the smile seemed strained as the photos flickered by.

And near the end there was a photo of Susan, older but still lovely, seated at a metal table near a tennis court with a tennis racquet on the table and some sort of tall cocktail in front of her. The sun had been behind the camera, so she was holding a hand to her forehead, shielding her eyes from the glare.

Or from something else? The photo stayed on the screen for several seconds, and Susan wasn't smiling in it, so I wondered why Liz had included that particular picture. I gave her a questioning look.

"That's the last photo I took of her. We'd played tennis at the club that afternoon, and something just made me want to take her picture. I'm glad now that I did even though it's really not a very good one. But it is the last."

The video ended with a photo of Susan at about five or six smiling into the camera with the utter innocence of a child that age. The photo gradually enlarged until the entire screen was filled with an image of Susan's strikingly blue eyes, like twin pools of deep, still water.

Then "The End" flashed on the screen and after that it went dark.

"Well?" Liz said as she shut off the equipment.

I reflected on what I'd seen. I didn't think I'd learned anything specific about Susan Elizabeth Fontaine, née Blackledge, that would help me find her murderer, but I had a better sense of her, of who she'd been and how she'd lived. She'd obviously been a bright, beautiful, and talented woman who'd tried to create some art and also do some good in the world. That wasn't a bad legacy to leave behind.

"She was an impressive woman. I can see why you liked her."

"Yes," Liz said, resuming her seat. "And that video can't really show how full of life she was, how warm and giving, how ready to help others."

"I understand." I paused. "But—and please don't take this the wrong way—didn't she have any flaws? I mean, no one is perfect."

Liz waved a hand. "Of course she did—we all do. She had a quick temper, and she didn't suffer fools gladly. I don't myself. She could be—she *was* too blunt with people at times."

She paused. "Including with me, but she was my best friend, so I forgave her. And she could be single-minded, perhaps to a fault, about going after what she wanted."

"What did she want?"

She gave me another sharp look. "That's a foolish question, Ms. Lu. She wanted what we all want: to be happy. And she and Whit weren't happy together, not near the end. I think that was a great disappointment to her. Just like their not having children."

"I understand. What about Whit? What did he want?"

"I think he wanted out."

She almost spat the words, and I gave her a moment to collect herself before asking, "Out of the marriage?"

"Yes. I don't think he loved her anymore—assuming he ever had. And I think he wanted out of his … life. The business, the pressure, the worrying about whether he and Tom would be able to finance their next deal."

I made a note, one of the few I'd taken since the interview began. "What does he want to do instead—I mean, if he could get out, as you say?"

She paused again. "I'm not sure. I don't know him nearly as well as I knew Susan. But I think he'd like to buy a sailboat and just go away. Maybe to the South Pacific, maybe sail around the world. He told me once that he'd been happiest when he was in the Navy. He said he missed driving ships."

I pictured Whit Fontaine as he must have looked while a lieutenant standing watch on the bridge of a destroyer or cruiser, and I could see how that might have suited him better than the life he'd chosen. Well, he couldn't go back and undo that choice—none of us gets to do that—and I suspected that now he might never get a chance to sail into the sunset no matter how much he wanted to.

I rose and held out my hand. "Thank you, Ms. Hutton. You've been very helpful, and I appreciate your giving me so much of your time."

She took my hand, obviously trying to be more gracious than she felt toward someone trying to clear Fontaine. "You're welcome. I hope that now perhaps you understand Susan better."

"Yes, I think so. Seeing the video was particularly useful." And it had been—maybe not in terms of helping me find someone else who might have killed her, but now when I thought of her I wouldn't think only of how her bloody body had looked lying on the floor.

☐ ☐ ☐

Back in the office by five, I sat in front of my computer screen and spent almost an hour putting all the information I had into a consolidated report. I printed a copy and took it to Marcus. He waved me to a chair, and I sat while he read the report.

When he finished, he dropped the report on his desk and looked at me. "Not getting very far, are we?"

I tried not to take it personally, but still I felt my cheeks grow hot. "I'm doing all I can, Marcus. If you can think of any leads I haven't followed, I wish you'd let me know."

He rubbed a big hand over his dark face. "No, I can't think of any. The guy probably did it, so maybe we're stuck."

"What about Maxine Walters?"

"Doubtful. I can see Walters confronting the wife, telling her Fontaine didn't love her and wanted a divorce, but I can't see Walters pulling a trigger. Can you?"

"Stranger things have happened."

"Yeah, but not often. Well, if she's all you've got, you may have to lean on her. See if she cracks."

"You're better at that than I am."

"You got to learn, girl. It's part of the job—and this is your case, remember?"

How could I forget? I put the thought out of my mind and said, "Okay. She's probably working tomorrow, so I'll go see her."

"Good. Let me know how it goes."

"Sure."

"Now get out of here. Take a break from the case. Go on a date or something."

A date. I hadn't been on one of those in a while. "I'm having dinner with my family."

"Fine. Please tell your parents I said hello. Tell them I wish my kids would keep in touch the way you do."

"It's a Chinese thing."

"Where have I heard that before?" He gave me a smile. "Okay, see you later."

CHAPTER EIGHTEEN

I drove to my parents' house. Chong had already parked his large Nissan SUV, but the driveway was just wide enough that I could squeeze my car in next to his.

I went into the house and saw my mother and Nannan busy in the kitchen. We all said hello, and I offered to help. My sister-in-law is a smart and tactful woman, so she let my mother answer.

"No, thanks, Wen. There's not much more to do, and three of us might get in each other's way. Your father and brother are in the den."

Well, at least she hadn't commented on my rather meager cooking skills. Nannan and I exchanged sly smiles over the top of my mother's head, and I went out to the den.

My dad was busy being the doting grandfather to Chong and Nannan's two young boys, and my brother was watching, visibly pleased that they were—so far—behaving well. Dad spoke to them in Mandarin, and they answered in an exuberant mix of Mandarin and English. I knew that Chong and Nannan spoke mostly Mandarin to them at home, so the kids would grow up to be bilingual. I wondered idly if I would do the same with any children I might have—a highly theoretical proposition.

My brother noticed me standing in the doorway and gave me a wave. "Hi, Wen. It's good to see you."

"And I am glad to see you," I said, adding g ge, the Mandarin word for elder brother.

"Hello, Wen," my father said. "Can you believe how fast these boys are growing?"

They looked the same to me as when I'd last seen them two weeks ago. But to please my father, I said, "No, it's amazing."

I remembered how he had played with my brother and sister and me when we were that age. It seemed to me that he'd been more reserved then but perhaps that was just the difference between a parent and a grandparent.

"How's work?" I asked Chong.

"Fine. Busy, but things seem to be going well."

"That's good." I sat next to him on the sofa and looked around the room. Having little flair for decoration myself, I was always pleased by how well my mother balanced Western and Asian influences. In this room the walls were a soothing light blue with an elegant gray trim, and to give the room a splash of color, she'd hung artwork with the pink of cherry blossoms and the bright reds and rich purples of Asian flowers.

The furniture was mostly Western and bought new. Antiques could bring bad luck, especially if formerly owned by a bad person. However, there was a black lacquered cabinet she had inherited from a favorite aunt in China and—despite my father's pointedly noting the considerable expense—had the woman's son ship to her.

On top of the cabinet and flanked by bronze candlesticks she'd placed a small bronze Chinese dragon—one of the few things she'd been able to bring from China. Although she pretended not to believe in folklore, I knew she thought the dragon would bring the household good fortune.

"Your brother has been promoted," my father said. "He won't tell you, so I will." He looked at Chong. "We are all proud of you."

My brother ducked his head, embarrassed.

"So what's your new title?" I asked.

"Manager of Information Technology."

Chong, a computer science major in college, worked for a big health care company in Chesapeake. He had done well there, using "Charles" as his American name and rising rapidly through the ranks. He made enough money to allow Nannan—"Nancy" being her concession to English—to stay home with the boys. She'd told me she missed being in accounting though and probably would go back to it when they were older.

"That's great. Congratulations!"

"Thanks. And how about you? Dad said you're working on some big investigation now."

I didn't want to talk about the Fontaine case, but I felt I had to say something. "Well, I, uh—"

My sister's arrival saved me from having to say more. I heard her voice—high-pitched and always sounding a little breathless—in the kitchen. She said hello in Mandarin but quickly switched to English. Then she came into the den, and I scooted toward the far end of the sofa to make room for her. Meihua was petite like our mother, so this pregnancy, her first, had made her seem as round as a ball.

Her big, blond husband, Greg, trailed in her wake. He always reminded me of a Viking but one who'd never been especially fierce and now had been tamed by domesticity.

Both he and Meihua were teachers, Greg high school history and Meihua first grade. "Mary" had told her school's principal that she planned to take a year or two off after the baby came, and I imagined things would be tight financially unless my parents helped—which, of course, they would.

Greg and I once had a lively debate once about whether the Vikings or the Chinese had discovered the New World before Columbus. I thought the Chinese claim was rather weak, but I'd argued it as well as I could. My father had acted as referee and diplomatically called the debate a draw although later he'd privately commended me for holding my own.

My father liked Greg, partly because they were both teachers but also because they just got along well. But I think his physical size and booming voice intimidated my mother, and even if they hadn't, she could never get past the fact that he wasn't Chinese or even Asian.

Luckily for Meihua, my mother didn't allow her coolness toward her son-in-law to affect her favoritism. My mother not only forgave my little sister—my mèimei—for not speaking Mandarin well and for marrying a non-Asian man, she rarely criticized her and then only in the mildest terms.

Once at her house, when Greg was away at a conference and we'd both had a few glasses of wine, I'd pointed out to Meihua that she was Mom's favorite daughter. She'd bristled a bit but hadn't denied it. Then she'd countered by saying, "So what? Of the two of us, you're Dad's favorite and always have been. Even Chong knows it—he told me so."

That surprised me. I didn't consider myself anyone's favorite. Chong was a son any father would be proud of, and Meihua was just like my mother in so many ways, but what was I? Just the mixed-up middle child, neither an accomplished professional like Chong nor a happy wife and mother-to-be like Meihua.

My sister sat, clearly relieved to get off her feet for a while. She said hello to Chong and then turned to me. "Wen, I'm glad you could come to dinner. We haven't seen you in—what?—a couple of weeks at least."

"Just busy," I said. "Working. But how are you? Ready to have that baby?"

"Yes! There's nothing like being almost nine months' pregnant in the summer. You should try it sometime."

"Who knows? Maybe I will." I smiled and was pleased at the smile I got back.

"And how's the father holding up?" I looked at Greg, who'd sat in my mother's chair, perhaps not realizing it was reserved for her.

"Okay, I guess. We'll just be glad when the baby's here."

"We all will be," my father said. "I want to meet my new granddaughter."

"Yes, we meet soon," my mother from the doorway in her weak English. "Now come—dinner is ready."

We ate in the dining room, all of us but Nannan and the boys, who sat at the kitchen table. They were still learning to use chopsticks, and Nannan tried to keep them from making too much of a mess. I would have liked to be there with them—I enjoyed spending time with my nephews—but my mother wanted me in the dining room, so that's where I was.

There the walls were cream with light-gold trim, and the artwork was red and darker gold. My mother didn't get to use the dining room much, and she'd clearly wanted to make this meal special. She'd set the big mahogany table with her best placemats and china, dimmed the light fixture that hung over the table, and lit the candles.

The food was, not surprisingly, excellent although as usual Mom had made more than we could possibly eat. I knew she did that partly so she could send something home with each of her children, and I also knew I wouldn't mind having my share.

Although I can be talkative at times, that evening I was quiet, letting the conversation—in English except when my mother said something she could express only in Mandarin—and occasional laughter enfold me like a warm blanket.

Having seen me earlier in the week, Mom directed most of her questions and comments to Chong and Meihua. Chong, always reserved, answered politely, and Meihua, never reserved, bubbled with her usual flow of words. Greg limited himself to praising the food. At one point, when Mom was giving Meihua advice about taking care of the baby when it arrived, he caught my eye and winked. I just nodded slightly and kept busy with my chopsticks.

My father sat at the head of the table, smiling happily at having his family together and taking in the scene. He spoke only to deflect some of my mother's less diplomatic comments, and I realized that having to help the children wasn't the only reason Nannan was in the kitchen.

But he looked at me several times, and I could tell he was worried about me, probably because of the Fontaine case. It pained me to cause him and my mother any anxiety, but there was nothing I could do about it at that moment. I'd voluntarily entered the PI game, and I had to play the hand I'd been dealt. But it was good to be there with my family, to feel the affection in that room and also the strength—the determination to persevere.

As I ate and looked at the animated faces around the table, I thought about my parents' long and difficult road to this place. My mother became pregnant with my brother a few months after she married my father, and five years later I came along, violating the strict one-child policy. I'd always wondered whether I was an "accident," but I hadn't asked my very private mother that very personal question and knew I never would.

My mother might have aborted me or abandoned me at a hospital somewhere—those things often happened, and sometimes there was even infanticide. But she didn't, and for four years my parents put up with the negative consequences of having violated the policy. Then they decided they'd had enough and left for America.

I had only a few vague memories of China, my favorite being one of sitting on a blanket in a springtime garden bright with flowers while my mother sang softly to me. Sometimes, especially when I was tired, I could hear that song in my head.

Chong remembered China much better, having lived there for the first nine years of his life. Nannan had been born in China too, so they used Mandarin with each other and took the kids to the Hampton Roads Chinese School every Saturday afternoon during the school year.

My sister was definitely more American than Chinese, but my mother made an exception for her because Meihua had been born here, a gift for the family to celebrate its new life in America. Meihua had even married what the Chinese American community refers to as an "American" man, meaning someone born here who wasn't of Chinese descent. A person born here who was of Chinese descent wasn't just an American—he or she was an "ABC"—an American-born Chinese.

When you're an immigrant, things get complicated sometimes. But sitting there, looking around the table at my family members, I realized I had no real reason to complain. Things were much more complicated for my parents than for us children, and my nephews and niece wouldn't have to face those complications at all.

After we finished dinner, I insisted on helping to clean up, shooing Nannan off with her boys and telling my pregnant sister to go sit on the sofa. Both of them looked at me with relief. My father and Chong, both raised in the traditional Chinese way, didn't offer to help in the kitchen. Greg did offer, but I knew Meihau would want him nearby, so I recycled my mother's claim that the kitchen was too small for three people to work efficiently. It wasn't, but he didn't argue, and that left my mother and me alone.

After the first flurry of clearing the table, she said in Mandarin, "Are you all right, Wen? You were very quiet tonight."

"I'm fine. I was just listening to everyone else. I don't get to see my brother and sister often—or Greg—and I wanted to hear what they had to say."

"They might want to hear from you too." My mother paused, looking at me. "They worry about you sometimes—just as your father and I do."

"Oh, Mom." I gave her a quick half-hug, the only kind she was comfortable with. "Don't worry. Everything is all right."

"Everything is all right?" She went to the little table near the door where I'd left my briefcase. She picked it up and weighed it in her hand. "You're carrying a gun, Lu Wen. But you tell me that everything is all right."

I was amazed at her perception and also at how calm she was. But then it occurred to me that my mother had risked a lot, had become a criminal, simply to have me.

She'd told me once how she'd been questioned by the police—and not gently. She hadn't said so, but I was sure she'd seen some guns in her time, guns in the hands of people hostile to her. What else had she seen that she'd never told me about? Perhaps some things she didn't want to remember, much less reveal to others. Suddenly I was ashamed of the dismissive way I'd often thought of her even if I'd tried not to show it.

"That's just for work—a routine precaution." As soon as I said that, I realized it wouldn't help.

"Yes, I know. My elder daughter has a job where she has to carry a gun. And shoot someone if she has to … or, even worse, get shot …."

Herself. I finished the thought, struck by how concerned she was for me, her dà n 'ér, her older daughter, even if she and Meihua were obviously more alike.

"Mom, no one's been shooting at me. And I can take care of myself, you know that."

"Like you took care of yourself after that … bad thing happened when you worked for the police?"

There was nothing I could say to that. The long months after Bobby's death had been a bad time in my life, and I hadn't handled it very well. No, be honest, I thought. You wanted to crawl into a hole and die. And made an effort to do just that.

I busied myself putting things in the dishwasher. I ignored the hot wetness in my eyes as long as I could, but finally I had to dry them on a dish towel. My mother watched me silently, moving more slowly than she usually did when she put leftovers into containers.

"Wen, you are our daughter. Your father and I just want the best for you—we want you to be happy. And safe."

"I know." I wanted to say more, but I didn't trust myself to do it without crying, so I finished the job of loading the dishwasher.

By the time I was done, I was almost back to normal. I gave my mother a quick smile and said, "Thanks, Mom. I know you care, and it means a lot to me."

Then before she could say anything else I went into the den, where they were talking pleasantly together. Nannan was sitting at a table, playing a game with the boys.

I looked through the sliding glass doors that led to the flagstone patio. The ground-level accent lights were on, and I could see the water bubbling in the small but very pretty fountain in the center of the patio.

My parents liked to sit there after dinner—the patio had "good feng shui," my father said. According to the philosophy of feng shui, which means "wind-water," the sound of flowing water is a harmonious, positive thing, and having often sat on that patio myself, I knew the fountain had a calming influence.

"Excuse me," I said. "I think I'll sit outside for a minute."

I crossed the room, slid a door open, and walked out onto the patio. The summer night was warm and humid but not uncomfortable. I looked up at the few stars visible in the sky lit by the pervasive nighttime glow of Virginia Beach. I took a deep breath, smelling the rich, mixed odors of the flowers my mother had planted everywhere. Then I sank into one of the deep chairs near the fountain.

I imagined myself throwing a switch and turning off my brain just as I turned off my car. I knew it didn't work that way, but I wanted it to—badly. I was tired of thinking about death and guns and a strange man following me in a black car. I was tired—period. I had been ever since Bobby died.

I wondered what Marcus would say to that. What Connolly would say. Probably the same thing. They'd tell me to buck up, to get back into the fight. Just like my drill instructor had in boot camp.

Well, maybe they were right. But I didn't want to think about that—I didn't want to think at all. I closed my eyes and listened to the fountain gurgle.

Then I hear the door slide open again. I didn't have to look—I knew my father was coming out to join me.

He sat in the chair next to mine. I tensed myself for what he might say—perhaps he'd talked to my mother since I'd left the kitchen—but he didn't say anything. He patted my arm and leaned back in this chair.

We sat there for a long time. We sat there, saying nothing in the stillness of the night, listening to the fountain.

CHAPTER NINETEEN

As I drove home I watched for anyone following me. If someone was, I didn't spot him. But when I got to my neighborhood I saw a dark car parked on a side street near my apartment building. The car looked like the black Lexus I'd seen before.

I parked in my usual spot. I pulled the pistol from my briefcase and got out, locking the door behind me. I stuck the pistol in the waistband of my pants and pulled my shirt out to cover it.

Then I walked down the street toward the dark car. I couldn't tell for certain, but I thought there was someone in it. As I got closer, I could see a figure sitting behind the wheel. I couldn't make out any features, but the size and shape made me think it was a man. He—if it was a he—was dressed in clothing as dark as the car itself.

When I was about twenty feet away, the engine started and the headlights came on. I jumped out of the street and ran across the sidewalk. I crouched behind a tree, gun in hand, as the car began to move. The front passenger window came down, and someone said something in a low, harsh voice that I couldn't understand.

Then something silver flashed through the open window and thunked into the tree. I glanced at it and saw it was a throwing knife. I dropped to the ground in case he had another one and improved his aim a bit.

The car gained speed, going away from me. I lifted my head and thought about trying to shoot one of the tires, but the angle was poor and the car was moving fast by then. I tried at least to get the license number, but someone had disabled the tag light, so the plate was too dark to read.

As the car screeched around the far corner, I rose and tucked away the pistol. I glanced around and didn't see anyone reacting to the situation, either outside or standing at windows. I used the bottom of my shirt to pull the knife from the tree and slide it, hilt first, into my pocket.

I went to my apartment and opened the door as quietly as I could. Then I stood to one side, listening. I heard nothing, but I waited for five minutes before going inside and searching the place, my gun back in my hand.

No one was there, and nothing looked disturbed. I put my gun on a table and used my shirt again to put the knife beside it. Then I locked both locks on the front door and put on the door chain. I knew the chain itself wouldn't keep anyone out who really wanted to get in, but the sight of it hanging across the doorframe made me feel better.

A little better. I suddenly realized I was more shaken than I'd thought. I drew several deep breaths and fixed myself a drink. I gulped it down and made another.

I sat and drank the second one more slowly. When it was half gone I pulled out my phone and found the card Connolly had given me.

He answered after one ring. "Connolly."

"Hi, it's Wendy Lu."

"Oh, hello." There was a touch of warmth in his voice that I hadn't heard before. "How are you?"

"Fine except that someone just threw a knife at me."

"Did it hit you? Are you hurt?"

"No, a close miss. Then he drove off."

"Did you get the license number?"

I told him the whole story, including the part about the car having followed me earlier. He listened, not interrupting, until I'd finished.

Then he said, "You should have told me about that car."

"Given what happened tonight, I guess so."

"Do you want me to come and get you, take you to a motel?"

I knew he meant for safety reasons, not sex. "No, I'll stay here. I've got my gun, and I don't think the guy will try anything else tonight, not now that I'm alerted."

"I wish you'd sleep somewhere else."

For a moment I wondered whether he knew I could take that remark two ways, but then I figured he wasn't trying to be subtle. Connolly didn't strike me as the kind of guy who did subtle.

"I'll be fine. Really."

"Okay, but I'm going to send a patrol car to your neighborhood and keep it there in case he or they—whoever it is—comes back."

I knew I couldn't talk him out of it, and the idea of a patrol car cruising the nearby streets did make me feel safer, so I didn't protest. "Thanks. I appreciate your looking out for me."

"Forget it. I'm just doing my job."

"Sure. If I remember anything about the guy or the car, I'll call you tomorrow."

"Call me regardless. Let's arrange a time for me to pick up that knife. I assume you've been careful about prints."

"Of course. I know the drill."

"Right."

I thought he'd end the call then, but he didn't seem to want to say goodbye. I really didn't either, but I also didn't want to drag the conversation out and seem unprofessional. "Well, thanks again. And good night."

"Good night, Wendy." The phone clicked in my ear and then was silent. I held the phone for a moment, liking how he'd said my name. Softly, like maybe I meant something to him, like I wasn't just another citizen phoning the police. But then I caught myself and realized I was being silly. The man barely knew me, and he clearly thought I was on a fool's errand in trying to clear Fontaine.

Well, maybe I was. But I still liked the way he'd said my name.

I finished my drink and then went around the apartment, checking the locks on all the windows. I slid the knife into the table's drawer, again without touching it with my bare fingers, and picked up my gun. Leaving lights on in the living room and the kitchen, I went into the bedroom.

At one time there'd been traces of Bobby here—a change of socks and underwear, a razor and aftershave, a picture of the two of us walking on the beach that I'd asked a tourist to take. But I'd put those things away after his death. Even the picture—because I cried every time I saw it.

Now the room had an austere feeling and always seemed a little colder than it actually was. Maybe I'd change that someday—I didn't know. I had that same uncertainty about a lot of other things about my life. I didn't like the feeling, but I had learned to live with it.

I put my gun on the nightstand, brushed my teeth, stripped to my panties, and put my clothes away. Then I pulled on an over-sized tee-shirt with the ODU logo.

Norfolk's Old Dominion University was where I'd finally earned a B.A. in criminal justice, neither the school nor the major my parents would have preferred. ODU was a good school, but it wasn't Cornell, where Chong had gone, or even William & Mary, where Meihua, to my parents' carefully concealed surprise, had gotten in and somehow managed to graduate.

I'd started college while I was still in the Navy, first taking some classes on my ship and then going to ODU at night when I rotated to shore duty. I'd finished during my first two years as a cop and thought that perhaps the degree would help me make sergeant or even lieutenant. Of course that was before ... what had happened.

I got into bed and considered following my usual routine of reading until I fell asleep. But I knew I was too keyed up to focus on a book and would just read the same page over and over again.

So I switched off the bedside lamp and closed my eyes. The light spilling in from the living room and kitchen was an unaccustomed distraction, but it wasn't bright enough to bother me. I lay there for a while and then got up, restless.

I went to the bedroom window and parted the curtains enough to see the street. Nothing was moving out there, but I waited. After several minutes a police cruiser went by, moving slowly. Connolly had done what he'd said—not that I'd doubted he would.

I got back into bed and closed my eyes. Seeing that police car had relaxed me a bit, and after what seemed like a long time, I finally fell asleep.

◻ ◻ ◻

I was running down a long, dark hallway, and someone far back was chasing me. I stopped for a moment to turn and look, but it was too dark to see much. My pursuer was a man, judging from his size and stride, and appeared to have something in his hand—a gun or maybe a knife. He was coming up quickly, so I began running again.

I'm a reasonably fast runner—I did cross-country in high school—but this guy was a little faster, and he was gaining on me. My breath was growing ragged in my throat, but I couldn't hear him breathing. Then I realized I couldn't hear my own footsteps, much less his.

I glanced over my shoulder, and he was almost on me. I tried to run faster, but I tripped on something and went sprawling on the hard tile floor. It hurt, but I was so scared I didn't feel it as much as I would have otherwise.

He jumped over me and clamped my throat with one hand. Then he brought his other hand up, and, yes, there was a knife in it. A knife that looked exactly like the one thrown at me earlier.

I tried to scream, but his hold on my throat was so tight that I couldn't make a sound. I struggled, but he was tremendously strong and I couldn't breathe, so I couldn't break free. And I saw the knife coming closer and closer to my face.

Closer and closer .... Then somehow I managed to get enough breath in my lungs to scream.

My scream woke me.

I was tangled in the bedclothes and had sweated through my tee-shirt. I was panting as though I actually had been running. The dream had been so real ... so terrifyingly real.

I checked the time on my mobile—yes, I know you're not supposed to sleep with your phone by the bed, but everyone does—and saw that it was a little before six. I smoothed out the covers and tried to go back to sleep, but after a couple of minutes I knew I was awake for the day.

I got up, changed into a sports bra and a dry tee-shirt, and started coffee. While it was perking I pulled on running shorts and shoes and went outside to pick up the newspaper left by the steps. Then I leafed through the paper while I drank a cup of coffee.

I had most of a second cup while I made the bed. Then I put the cup in the kitchen sink and went out for a run.

On weekends I like to run early before the world wakes up, when the streets are empty of cars and the grass is wet with dew. The sun had risen but was still low in the east. I did my usual perfunctory stretches—my track coach was always annoyed that I didn't stretch more before running—and set off down the street.

I was careful to look around, to check whether my friend from last night was back, but I saw no sign of him. I did see a police cruiser parked nearby, and I gave the cop inside a little wave as I jogged by. In reply he made a slight gesture with an index finger, and I saw him pick up the radio mic.

Probably reporting to Connolly, I thought. I disliked the idea that the police were devoting time and attention to me, but I did like the idea that Connolly wanted to keep me safe. I could take care of myself, but having some backup never hurt.

I ran for two miles, following my usual path along the Elizabeth River. There was almost no traffic, and not many people were out, just a few folks walking their dogs. I saw two or three other joggers, and we nodded at one another, acknowledging our common membership in the runners' society.

I tried to keep my mind blank and focus on my stride and my breathing. It worked to some extent—sometimes I went a whole minute without thinking about the Fontaine case. When I got to my usual turnaround, I stopped to catch my breath and do the stretching I should have done at the outset.

I gave myself permission to think about the case then, and I went down the list of what I'd done and then the list of what I should do next. The second list was a lot shorter than the first, but one thing on it was phoning the server who'd had Fontaine's table on Saturday night.

I jogged back to my apartment and saw that the police car was gone. The sun was higher then, and the world had finished making the transition from night to day. I walked the last hundred yards to cool down before I went inside.

By the time I'd showered and dressed, eaten half a bagel, and loaded and started the dish washer, it was after nine a.m. I figured that wasn't too early on a Saturday to call someone, so I went through my notes, found the number, and dialed.

"Hello." The voice sounded slightly hoarse. Maybe she was a smoker. Or maybe that was just how she sounded on a weekend morning.

"Louise Rossi?"

"Yes."

"This is Wendy Lu. I'm a private investigator working for Whitaker Fontaine's lawyers."

"Oh, that rich man who shot his wife."

"Well, he's charged with shooting her. That doesn't mean he's guilty."

"Nooo ... I guess not."

She sounded as though she thought he was guilty as hell. I ignored her tone and pressed ahead. "Mr. Fontaine and his business partner hosted a dinner at the Lynnhaven Dock House last Saturday night. They were entertaining some Japanese investors. I understand that you had their table. Is that right?"

"Yes, there were five of them—the two Americans and three Japanese. All men."

"What did they talk about?"

"Well, I ...."

"It's okay, you can tell me. Your coworker Judy gave me your name and number." I glanced at my notes. "Judy Wagenaar. She may have mentioned that I interviewed her."

"Yes. Yes, she did."

"And now I'm interviewing you. It may help Mr. Fontaine. You don't want an innocent man to be convicted, do you?"

"Oh, no, of course not. Do you really think he didn't kill his wife?"

I forced myself to be patient with her. "That's what I'm trying to find out. Now what did the men discuss over dinner?"

"Oh, business things. Where to put up buildings and how to pay for them. How to make money from them."

"Anything specific? Any particular buildings or projects?"

"No, not that I remember. Of course I was pretty busy. I mean, I had four other tables, so it wasn't like I was standing there listening to them."

"I understand. Is there anything else you can tell me about them, anything that seemed out of the ordinary?"

She paused, and I kept silent, letting her think. "Well," she said after several seconds, "there was one thing."

"What?"

"Oh, just something odd. But I'm sure it didn't mean anything."

"What was it?" That came out more intensely than I meant it to. In a calmer voice I said, "What did you notice?"

"One of them was missing part of his little finger."

I'd seen Fontaine and McKenna and hadn't noticed anything unusual about their hands. "One of the Japanese men?"

"Yes, I saw it when I served the entrées. It looked like about half of that finger had been cut off."

"Which hand? Can you remember?"

"Oh, sure. It was the left."

I froze. Thinking hard, trying to recall where I'd read or heard about that … what it meant.

She didn't seem to notice my silence. "I remember that because we always serve the traditional way—food from the left. Not all restaurants do, but here the owners are particular about little things like that. And about our uniforms. Why, one time I forgot my—"

Then it hit me. "Louise, I'm sorry to interrupt, but I need to go. Was there anything else?"

It took her a moment to regroup, but then she said, "No. No, I don't think so. Just that about the little finger. Is it important?"

"I don't know. Maybe. I'll have to see. Thanks for your help—I appreciate it."

"No problem. Good luck with the case."

"Thanks. 'Bye."

I hung up, went to my laptop, and began clicking keys. In a minute or so I found what I wanted—yubitsume, ritual finger shortening. Also known as yubi o tobasu, or finger flying, as in "he made his finger fly."

And when "he" did it, he did it as a member of the yakuza, the common name for Japanese crime syndicates. He did it because he'd messed up, made a major mistake about something, and had to atone for it. Had to cut off a joint of his left little finger and present it to his boss, his oyabun. In kendo, Japanese sword fighting, the little finger tightly grips the hilt, so a person missing part of that finger cannot fight as well and becomes more dependent on the oyabun.

A first offense cost the first joint, and more offenses cost more joints. Some yakuza members lost that finger entirely. One of the articles I found said that the penalty for any further infraction was death.

What were Japanese gangsters doing in Virginia Beach? And why had Fontaine and McKenna taken them to dinner? I didn't know.

But I wanted to find out.

CHAPTER TWENTY

I phoned Marcus and briefed him. He agreed the information was interesting but didn't react to it as strongly as I had.

"First, they may not be gangsters at all. Maybe that guy just had an accident that cost him part of a finger."

"That would be an amazing coincidence, don't you think?"

"Maybe, but stranger things have happened. And second, even if they are gangsters, that doesn't prove they killed Susan Fontaine. What would be their motive? Can you think of one?"

"It could be something to do with Fontaine-McKenna—the business, I mean."

"Hard to see what. If there was bad blood between the partners, you'd think the bad guys would kill one of them, not Fontaine's wife."

"Maybe Fontaine hired them to kill her."

"Sure. And then Fontaine let himself be found next to her body with his gun near his hand. You're reaching, Wendy."

I sighed. "I know it. I just want to find something that says our client didn't do it."

"Of course you do. I know you take your job seriously. I appreciate that. But dedication takes you just so far—and that shouldn't be past the facts."

"You're right." I thought a moment. "What if McKenna hired them? And framed Fontaine to avoid being suspected?"

"Again, what's the motive? What did he have against Susan?"

And again I was stumped. "I don't know. But maybe there's something there. I want to talk to him again."

"Couldn't hurt. I'd like to know if those guys really are—what did you call them?"

"Yakuza."

"Yeah, I'd like to know."

"So would I."

"Well, see if you can get McKenna to talk to you. He's the one who brought them into the picture, so he should know something about them. I'll let Scott and Jackie know what you've found so far."

"Thanks."

I said goodbye and started looking for McKenna's mobile number. When I found it, I punched in the digits, and he answered right away.

"Hello." Unlike most people, he made it a statement, not a question.

"Mr. McKenna, this is Wendy Lu. I need to talk to you—in person."

"About the Fontaine case? I've told you all I know."

"Some new information has come to light, and I want to discuss it with you."

"What new information?"

"I'll tell you when I see you."

He paused, and I thought he might suggest we meet at his office on Monday, but he said, "Okay. I'm at a job site in Virginia Beach. Can you come here?"

"Sure. What's the address?"

He told me, and I jotted it down on my notepad. "I'll be there in about forty minutes."

"Fine." He hung up without saying goodbye, probably annoyed that I was going to interrupt him at work on a Saturday. But both as a cop and as a private investigator I'd gotten used to talking to people who didn't necessarily want to talk to me.

I put my pistol in the small briefcase along with my phone and notes and a pen. Then I took the knife from the drawer, put it in a plastic bag, and added that to the briefcase. I picked up my keys and left.

Driving out to Virginia Beach I watched to see whether anyone was following me. I didn't spot anyone, but that didn't mean no one was on my tail. A trained driver can hang pretty far back and be hard to detect. I liked the idea that maybe no one was following me, but I didn't like the idea that perhaps someone well trained was doing it. Someone who might be well trained in other things.

The job site was several blocks off the interstate with a few turns along the way, but I found it without too much trouble. They were putting up a six- or seven-story office building in a park of similar buildings already constructed. They'd finished the skeleton of the building and were beginning to put in the walls, starting at the bottom. Next to the building was the recently started foundation of something, but I couldn't tell what it was going to be.

I parked past the ten or twelve cars and trucks that must have belonged to the construction workers. As I walked back, I saw a dark, four-door Ford parked in a spot headed by a sign reading "Reserved for Fontaine-McKenna Associates." It looked like one of Norfolk's new police cruisers, the ones that had replaced the Crown Vic, the classic cop car, but I knew it must be McKenna's or maybe a company car he was driving.

Because it was the weekend, there wasn't a lot of activity, but I saw a few people moving inside the structure. I pulled out my phone and called

McKenna again.

"Wendy Lu?"

"Yes, I'm here."

"Find Jake, the foreman, tell him to get you a hard hat, and take the construction elevator to the top. I'm up here."

Something about the situation bothered me, but I wasn't sure what. It was after eleven, and the workers, who would have started the day early because of the summer heat, were beginning to pack up their tools and drift toward their vehicles. Apparently they worked a half day on Saturdays.

I wandered around until I spotted a man carrying a clipboard and looking up at the building as if to gauge the progress the crew had made that day. I walked over to him. "Are you Jake?"

He turned toward me, and his eyes narrowed, seeing a stranger on his job site. Maybe he thought I was a reporter here to do a story on some safety problem the building posed.

"Yes. Can I help you with something?" His tone was considerably cooler than the words.

"I'm Wendy Lu, here to see Mr. McKenna. He said I should ask you for a hard hat and take the elevator to the top floor."

He thought about that for a moment, then pulled out his phone. "Wait a minute."

He took a few steps away and turned his back to me. He poked at his phone, paused a few seconds, and spoke softly into it. I could just hear his voice, but I couldn't make out what he said.

Then he seemed to be listening. I could see him nodding his head. He spoke again, briefly this time, and put the phone away as he turned and walked back to me.

"Okay. Come with me."

I followed him over to a big plastic bin. He opened it and took out a pristine hard hat prominently labeled "Visitor" on the front. He handed the hat to me, saying, "We keep these for VIPs."

He kept his expression neutral, but I could still detect the hint of sarcasm. "Guess I've been promoted then."

He chuckled at the joke and in a slightly more friendly tone said, "Sure. Congratulations." Then he led me over to the construction elevator, a wire cage with a scarred wooden floor. He opened the door and waved me inside. I thought he might ride up with me, but he latched the door behind me and pointed toward the top button on the control panel.

"Press that one—it'll take you to the top. You press the bottom one to come down. Okay?"

"Got it. Thanks."

"No problem. Tell Tom we're packing up for the day. He can lock the elevator when he comes down."

"Okay." I pressed the button and the elevator jerked into motion. Jake watched me go up a few feet before he turned and walked away.

The elevator rose slowly and noisily. I looked down at the world receding beneath me, and soon I could see farther and farther into the distance, the reds and grays of nearby buildings blending in with the green of treetops now below me. It was a nice day, and I would have enjoyed the ride if I hadn't been wondering who'd tried to kill me the night before.

When the elevator reached the top floor, I saw McKenna standing there, waiting for me. The cage clanked to a stop, and I unlatched the door.

"I hope this won't take long," he said, visibly irritated.

I ignored his rudeness, stepping out of the cage and looking around. There were no walls on this floor, just some framing where interior walls would be. Orange cones were spaced along the outside edges of the floor to remind people not to get too close. Looking out over the edge opposite the cage I could see for miles and miles, office buildings and then houses receding into the distance under the blue dome of an enormous sky sailed by a few fat white clouds.

"Good morning, Mr. McKenna. I appreciate your agreeing to see me on such short notice. And on a Saturday."

That reminded him of his manners. "Uh, you're welcome. Of course I want to help Whit in any way I can. But I think I've already told you everything I know about his situation."

I thought McKenna might lead us away from the elevator and that edge of the building, but he didn't. I don't have acrophobia stronger than the average person's rational fear of falling, but I would have felt more comfortable farther away from that long drop to the ground.

"Actually, I want to talk to you about something else, something that may be related to his ... situation."

His eyes narrowed. "What's that?"

"I understand there's something unusual about one of your Japanese guests."

"Such as?"

"He's missing part of his left little finger."

McKenna was a good actor, but he couldn't cover it completely. "Oh, that—uh, I mean, he is?"

"Yes."

"How do you know?"

"A witness told me."

"Who? Not Whit. He was too drunk to notice anything like that."

McKenna sounded contemptuous of his partner, and I filed that remark away. "No, someone else. It doesn't matter who it was."

"Well, what difference does it make? I've done business with a one-armed man and a blind woman. These Japanese have money to invest—that's why I took them to dinner."

That's why *I* took them? I filed that remark away too. "Did you know they're yakuza?"

"What's that?"

If he was lying, he did it well. Maybe he'd had enough time to recover from his surprise at my initial question. "Gangsters—sort of like the mafia."

"No, I didn't. I still don't. I just know you're claiming they are."

"So what *do* you know about them? Where did they get the money to put into one of your development projects?"

That put him on the defensive. "What the hell does that have to do with Whit Fontaine's killing his wife?"

I gave him a moment to cool down. "Maybe nothing, Mr. McKenna. I'm just asking questions, doing my job."

"Look, I've told you all I know about what happened that night. I'm happy to help Whit if I can, but I'm very busy trying to run the firm by myself, and I don't appreciate your prying into business affairs that have nothing to do with Susan's death."

"So you won't tell me about these men?"

"Damn it, there's nothing to tell! I don't know where they got their money, and I don't care. All I care about is that they seem willing to invest in one of my projects."

"The casino in North Carolina?"

"What? Why, you damn little snoop!" His expression became ugly, and he moved toward me. "Did Whit tell you about that?"

Without thinking, I took a step back, closer to the edge. "Yes, he did." I paused, wondering how far I should go and not just with my questions—I was already closer to the edge of the building than I wanted to be. "He doesn't seem to think much of the idea."

McKenna's lip curled. "He wouldn't. Not enough vision."

"He had enough vision to found the company with you."

"Sure. Build three houses here, a small office building there. That's all Whit would've ever done."

"But you think bigger."

He moved closer again, and I took another step back. I glanced at the edge. Two more steps and I'd be there.

"Yes, I do. You have to in this economy."

"And this casino is part of thinking big?"

"Sure. I think it will make me—us—a lot of money."

He was studying my face and flexing his fingers. He was thinking about something, and I was pretty sure I knew what.

"If the Japanese put up the money to build the thing."

"They will."

His natural cockiness had made him say it, but I sensed that he regretted the remark. Rather than underscoring his mistake, I said, "Hasn't Mr. Fontaine's situation made them hesitate?"

He smiled, coldly. "No, I don't think so. They're quite pragmatic. They know I can go ahead without Whit. They might even like it better if ...."

"If what?"

"Nothing. Now I'm through answering your questions."

He took another step toward me, but I stood my ground. "Okay, Mr. McKenna, I can't make you talk if you don't want to. That's what I told Marcus when I said I was coming here to the job site."

That stopped him.

"And your man Jake knows I took the elevator up here to see you—you, all alone on this floor."

"I can handle Jake."

"If I come down without using the elevator? I don't think so. I doubt he'd help you cover that up."

He paused. "You have a vivid imagination, Ms. Lu, if you think I'd try anything like that."

"I don't know what someone who has thrown in the yakuza might be willing to do." I looked him in the eye. "Maybe you don't either."

He said nothing to that.

"And keep in mind that these guys play for keeps. If they put money into the casino, they're going to want a big return on their investment. If you don't come up with that ... well, just remember they know how to do more than cut off fingers."

"You can't scare me."

"I'm not trying to. I just hope you know what you're letting yourself in for. If you had to go to them for funding, I'm guessing no bank would lend you the money. Which tells me that Fontaine-McKenna Associates is in financial trouble."

His look of surprise told me I'd guessed correctly.

"So you must see this casino as a way out."

"You don't *know* any of this—as you said, you're just guessing. And there's nothing illegal about any of it."

"There isn't? You think the North Carolina authorities will approve your casino if they know where the money is coming from?"

"It will come from our firm. Where we get it is our business."

I thought about that. Maybe his plan would work and maybe not. It wouldn't if the gaming officials in North Carolina found out about the yakuza "investors," but nobody knew about them but McKenna himself and Fontaine, who didn't know which project they might fund and apparently didn't even know they were gangsters.

And now me—Wendy Lu, the nosey woman who keeps asking questions. No wonder McKenna had eyed the distance from my feet to the edge of the building.

"Well, good luck with the project." I didn't mean it, and he knew I didn't. I started for the elevator.

As I unlatched the cage and stepped inside, he came over to stand by the door. "And good luck with your investigation." He didn't sound any more sincere than I had.

"Thanks."

"But I'm done with answering your questions."

I didn't want to debate the point with him, so I didn't disagree. I simply said, "Goodbye," and pressed the bottom button.

He didn't say anything, just stood there watching as the elevator carried me down and out of his line of sight, back toward the world where I still had no idea who—besides my client—might have killed Susan Fontaine.

CHAPTER TWENTY-ONE

In the car I phoned Marcus. I started to tell him what I'd learned from McKenna, but he told me to save it.

"We're meeting with Scott and Jackie this afternoon. One o'clock, their office. They want an update on the case."

"Will Fontaine be there?"

"I don't think so. They'll probably want to talk to him separately. That way they can use a lot of lawyer words and bill more time."

"Not that you're cynical."

He chuckled. "Who? Me? I'm just a realist—and someone who's seen over a lot of years how lawyers work."

"Okay, one o'clock. See you then."

The time was close to noon, and my stomach was reminding me how long it was since my half bagel. I stopped at a fast-food place and ordered a grilled chicken sandwich. Fries came with it, so I told myself I really had no choice but to get them, but my little voice of guilt—which often sounded remarkably like my mother's voice—whispered that I was really taking the fries because I wanted them.

I told the voice to shut up, reminding it that I'd gone for a run that morning. It didn't shut up entirely, but it muttered so low that I could barely hear it, especially when chewing on a hot French fry dipped in ketchup.

Comfortably full, I finished my iced tea on the way to the Law Office of Cushman & Taylor, which was located in a small, two-story professional building in Virginia Beach. When I got there at five till one, I saw Marcus's car parked in front. I parked next to it, walked to the entrance, and pressed the button by the front door. The lock clicked, and I went inside.

There was no one in the small reception area, but after a moment Jackie appeared. She was dressed casually, but I figured her designer jeans cost more than my best suit. Well, I said to myself, that's what you get for rejecting your parents' suggestion that you go to law school.

"Hi, Wendy. We're in the conference room. Want some coffee? Tea?"

"No, thanks, I just had lunch."

"Okay, come on back."

I followed Jackie down the narrow hallway and into the conference room. Scott was sitting at the head of the table—naturally—and Marcus was beside him. The table was littered with file folders and documents, and I saw a couple of copies of my most recent case summary.

Scott rose as we entered, which prompted Marcus, who was polite but not courtly, to do the same. Scott came over to give me the usual kiss on the cheek, and Marcus winked at me as Scott did it.

Then we all sat down and Marcus asked me to summarize what I'd learned from Louise Rossi and Tom McKenna.

As I spoke, Scott interrupted me with a few questions but mostly let me tell the tale. When I finished, he looked at Marcus. "Well, what do you make of it?"

"Sounds like the business is in bad financial trouble and McKenna may be trying to find a way out by using gangster money for financing."

"You don't think he might be ignorant about who he's dealing with?"

Marcus shook his gleaming bald head. "No, assuming they actually are yakuza. If they're anything like the mafia guys I've met—not that many but some—they've made sure McKenna knows exactly who they are. And what they'll do if the deal doesn't work out the way he's presented it."

"What about Whit? Is he in on this?"

"He told Wendy he didn't know much about these guys, that McKenna brought them in." He looked at me. "Right, Wendy?"

"Yes—in fact, he seemed to want nothing to do with them."

"McKenna would probably be better off if he'd had nothing to do with them," Marcus said. "But I guess he'll have to find that out for himself."

Jackie looked puzzled. "Why would these Japanese gangsters—if that's what they are—get involved with a Native American casino? Why wouldn't they just stay in Japan and do what they do? Rob, kill, whatever—make money there?"

Scott started to speak but then stopped. Maybe he was embarrassed that he hadn't thought to ask the same thing.

"Good question," Marcus said. "I can think of two reasons. First, our police aren't aware of them the way the Japanese cops are, so they don't get as much scrutiny here. Second, they need to launder their money, and they're maxed out in Japan. So they're starting to do it in America. To some extent in Europe also, but they blend in better here."

"Sounds like you've made a study of it," Scott said, and I could tell he was not happy that Marcus had upstaged him. Scott liked to be the star of every show he was in—that was probably one of the main reasons he'd become a trial lawyer.

If Marcus sensed Scott's annoyance, it didn't seem to bother him. "No, not really. I just do a lot of professional reading, and I came across an article on organized crime in Japan. Interesting stuff."

"Well, that's fine, but how do these guys tie in with Susan Fontaine's murder?"

"Maybe they don't." Marcus looked at me again. "What do you think, Wendy?"

"I don't know. There's no obvious connection. But maybe it's not a coincidence that McKenna gets involved with criminals, which means that Fontaine does by extension, and then Mrs. Fontaine dies."

"Are you suggesting that one of these ... uh, whatever the word is ... killed her?" Scott sounded half skeptical but also half hopeful.

"Could be."

"Hmm." Scott thought for a moment, then turned to his partner. "What about it, Jackie? Can we do anything with that?"

"Not just with the suggestion. There's too much circumstantial evidence against Whit. We'd need a witness or a confession."

"Well, we certainly don't have a witness—not yet, anyway." Scott thought some more, and I could practically hear the legal gears grinding. "But a confession ... maybe. Marcus, what if the police picked up these guys and questioned them, questioned them hard. Might one confess to the killing?"

"Not likely unless one of them really did it, and perhaps not even then. If they are yakuza, that means they're pretty bad boys and have undoubtedly been questioned by the police before. They wouldn't crack like some kid facing it for the first time."

That made me think of the Norfolk Four again. No, yakuza wouldn't talk as they had.

"And anyway," Marcus said, "what would the police pick them up for? One guy missing part of a finger? They're not wanted for anything in this country or they wouldn't even be here."

Jackie leaned forward. "Wendy, could you talk to them? Find out if there's any connection with Susan Fontaine's death?"

Marcus held up his hand in a traffic cop's "halt" signal. "Wait a minute. I'm not sure that's a good idea. Maybe I should talk to them."

"I'm not afraid," I said, and it came out louder than I'd intended. "I'll talk to them—if I can find them and they'll talk to me. But I doubt they'll tell me anything helpful."

"Of course you're not afraid," Marcus said. "I know that, Wendy. It's just that I've had more experience with things like this."

"Dangerous things? But isn't that part of the job? And how will I get experience if I never do it?"

Marcus sighed. "Okay, *we'll* talk to them. How's that?"

I would have preferred to go alone, but at least I was going. "All right, both of us will do it. Now we just have to find them."

"Whit may know where they're staying," Scott said. "I'm sure McKenna does, but he probably won't tell you."

"Maybe there's a way to make him."

Marcus gave me a quizzical look. "How?"

"He doesn't want his connection with these guys to become public. If he thinks I might expose it otherwise, he might be willing to tell me how to find the Japanese."

"Wait a minute," Jackie said. "If he doesn't, and a ... yakuza connection does become public, won't that hurt our client's business? Wouldn't that create a conflict?"

"Seems to me that Fontaine is a lot more worried about being charged with murder than how his business is doing," Marcus said.

"Yes, but Jackie has a point." Scott looked at me. "Wendy, is there any other way you can get to these ...."

"Yakuza. Perhaps. I'll try Whit first—maybe I'll get lucky." After I talk to Connolly, I added mentally. I knew Scott and Jackie wouldn't like the idea of my talking to the police about our case even if the goal was to help our client.

Scott didn't seem satisfied with that answer, but he didn't debate it with me. After a moment he said, "Okay, here's what we have. My lab guy tells me that they've established Susan Fontaine's time of death: about eleven p.m., based mostly on body temperature. Obviously, that's not good for our client."

"'Not good?'" Marcus shook his head. "Hell, it's probably fatal. That's when Fontaine got home, isn't it?"

"Maybe a little before," I said. "He didn't leave the restaurant until almost eleven."

"Close enough," Marcus said. "The prosecution will kill us. Time of death is usually approximate anyway. We're supposed to argue that someone shot her with Fontaine's gun, left it there, and Fontaine just happened to pass out next to her body?"

"If we have to argue that, we will," Jackie said. "We'll argue whatever we have to argue to put on the best defense for our client."

Scott seemed surprised that Jackie had spoken up so forcefully, but I gave her an approving nod. When she saw it, she smiled at me.

"Right," Scott said, "we will. But we don't know yet what we'll have to argue. So let's keep going, okay?"

No one else said anything, which seemed to be the reaction Scott wanted. "Good. So to continue, we know that Fontaine-McKenna

Associates isn't doing well financially, McKenna brought in these Japanese guys to help with the Hail Mary casino project in North Carolina, Whit wants nothing to do with it, and Whit's been having an affair with Maxine Walters, who takes it more seriously than he does."

He paused, then looked at me. "Did Fontaine or McKenna say which Native American tribe is nominally behind the casino?"

"No." I gave myself a mental kick for not asking one or both of them that question. "I'll see if I can find out."

"We can probably do that easier than you can. Jackie, why don't you make some calls, talk to the North Carolina gaming commission, anyone else in the state government who might have to approve a new casino? See if Fontaine-McKenna Associates or any tribe has filed an application, maybe some disclosure documents?"

"Sure." Jackie nodded. "I'll get right on it."

"Good." He seemed pleased to have thought of something Marcus and I hadn't. "Anything else?"

"Well," I said, "there is one thing." I began telling them about the guy who'd thrown a knife at me the night before.

Scott tried to interrupt me with questions, but Marcus held up his hand again to silence him. Then the three of them listened as I finished the story, including that I'd reported it to the police.

"Why didn't you tell me too?" Marcus didn't raise his voice, but his cold tone told me how angry he was.

"I didn't see any point in ruining your sleep. And Simone's. Especially when I'd told the police and they'd put a watch on my place."

"You should have told me, Wendy. This is serious."

"I know it is, and that's why I'm telling you now. But don't worry about me—I know how to take care of myself."

"That'll be a great comfort to your parents at your funeral. Goddamnit, you tell me right away if anything like that happens again." He looked me in the eye. "That's an order."

"Aye, aye, sir." I smiled to try to defuse things. Marcus didn't smile, but after a moment he nodded, and I knew he wouldn't keep rehashing what I'd done. Or, more accurately, hadn't done, something I now saw had been a mistake. I hadn't realized that Marcus would feel responsible for any harm that came to me. I'd just assumed risk was part of the job, and it was, of course, but that didn't mean I had to be a lone wolf.

Scott looked from Marcus to me and back to Marcus to make sure that we'd finished our exchange. Then he said, "Well, in any event this is evidence that Whit didn't kill his wife. He has no reason to go after someone trying to clear his name."

"It might be helpful in that regard," Jackie said, "but the prosecutor will claim that the attack wasn't necessarily related to this case. Wendy has worked on a number of other things, and it could have been about one of them."

Scott frowned at Jackie's caution, but what she'd said made sense, and he didn't argue with her. Suddenly I realized why they made such a good team—Scott came up with a lot of ideas, some better than others, and Jackie vetted them for him, applauding the good ones but gently critiquing the ones not so good. As she'd just demonstrated by pointing out the weakness in his theory about the meaning of the knife attack.

"We can at least raise the point," Scott said, apparently not willing to concede completely.

"Yes, we can do that." Jackie made a note. "We don't have much else to raise."

"But we're still looking."

Marcus turned toward me. "Sure, Wendy. If there's anything to find, we'll find it. Now, is there anything else we need to talk about?"

"I can't think of anything." Scott looked at Jackie, who shrugged. "No, I guess that's it for now."

Marcus stood and I did likewise. As we left the conference room, Scott said, "Let us know if you find the Japanese men, Wendy."

Jackie rolled her eyes and shook her head at the remark. I wanted to do the same but limited myself to saying, "Will do, Scott."

Marcus walked me to my car. As I began to open the door, he put his hand on it to stop me. "Somebody's pissed at you, Wendy. And that somebody may try again—maybe with a gun instead of a knife."

"I can handle it."

"Look, I know you're brave. But don't be stupid. Don't take any foolish chances."

"I won't."

"I mean it, Wendy."

I reached up to touch his shoulder, his muscles straining against the cloth of his shirt. "I know. And I mean it too—I'll be careful."

"That's a promise, and you better keep it."

I smiled at him. "Thanks, boss. I love you too."

He didn't smile back, but his expression softened a bit. "Okay. Just remember what I said. And if you locate those guys, call me, and I'll meet you wherever they are."

"Got it."

He nodded and waited while I got into the car. Then he closed the door, more gently than I would have predicted, and went to his own car. We drove away in opposite directions.

CHAPTER TWENTY-TWO

I called Connolly and told him about the Japanese. He didn't have a strong reaction to the information—veteran cops seldom get excited about anything—but said he'd look into what they'd been doing around town. I didn't tell him that I planned to talk to them that afternoon—if I could find them.

"Do you want to have dinner?"

His question caught me by surprise. "What?"

"I asked if you want to have dinner with me this evening."

"Uh, okay. I guess that would be fine."

"You don't sound very enthusiastic. Maybe it's a bad idea."

I heard the disappointment in his voice. "No, I'd like to have dinner with you. It's just ... unexpected. That's all."

"Well, I want to get that knife from you. And we both have to eat."

"Sure." I tried to be as matter-of-fact as he was.

We agreed to meet at Mickey's at seven, have a drink, and figure out where to go for dinner.

After the call I found myself smiling, so I told myself sternly not to make too much of having dinner with someone. It's simply a business meeting in the evening, I thought. And as Connolly had said, we both had to eat.

I wasn't sure I'd convinced myself, so I called Vanessa to get a second opinion. I wasn't surprised to find her in the office on a Saturday afternoon.

"I've got a big project due on Monday, so I don't have much choice. What about you? I hope one of us gets to enjoy the weekend."

"Not this time. I'm doing an investigation for a couple of criminal-defense attorneys, and we don't want the leads to get cold."

"That sounds like something from a TV show."

"Yeah, I guess it does. Anyway ...."

"What?"

"A police detective working the opposite end of the case asked me to dinner. Tonight."

"Are you going? Is he cute? Answer the second one first!" She laughed, a pleasant musical sound.

"Yes, I'm going. And, yes ... well, I wouldn't call him cute. Handsome maybe. Kind of rugged-looking."

"What's his name?"

"Connolly ... Sergeant Ryan Connolly."

"Oh, *Sergeant* Connolly, is it? I hope you don't have to call him 'sergeant'."

"Not when we're alone."

"You've been alone with him? This is getting interesting, Wen."

"We talked about the case at the police station. And then had drinks. That's all."

"Well, you must have made quite an impression if he asked you out."

"It's just dinner, Vanessa."

"Sure, it is. That's how these things always start—with dinner. And where are you two having this dinner?"

"I don't know yet. We're going to meet for a drink and then decide."

"My best friend having drinks and dinner with a rugged police detective—what an exciting life you lead! I'll be working late on a Saturday and grabbing some carry-out on the way home. Want to swap?"

"Sure, if your salary comes with it."

"If we did swap, you'd find the money isn't as great as you think."

I paused. "Probably so. I'm beginning to see what money can do to people. Some of it isn't very pretty."

"No, it isn't. I've seen that too. Well, have fun on your date."

"It's not a date, Vanessa, just a business dinner."

"Okay, enjoy your dinner and see if it turns into a date."

"Well, if it does, you'll be the first to know." I told her not to work too late and said goodbye.

Then I phoned Whit Fontaine. He was home, and I said I was coming over to talk to him.

"What about?"

"I'll be there in twenty minutes, and I can tell you then."

In just under that time I pulled into his driveway. I turned off the engine and sat there for a moment, looking at the big house surrounded by manicured lawn. The guys mowing the yard two houses down showed me who was doing the manicuring. There was probably a housekeeper too, someone who came in at least once a week to dust and vacuum. I wondered whether Fontaine had considered himself lucky to live this way, insulated, even pampered by his money. And hers, of course.

Well, even if he was innocent, he couldn't consider himself lucky now.

I rang the doorbell, and he answered it, looking almost as stressed as he had in prison despite wearing his own clothes instead of an orange jumpsuit.

"Hi." He took a sip of something golden from the short, thick glass in his hand. "Working on Saturday, I see."

"Yes. Something's come up that I need to discuss with you."

"What's that?"

I glanced toward the street, where one of his neighbors was walking a dog. "May we talk inside?"

"What? Oh, certainly. Sorry. Please come in."

He stepped back, and as I passed him I smelled vanilla on his breath—the familiar scent of bourbon. Given what he had hanging over him, I wasn't surprised. And I didn't judge him for it—I was in no position to do that.

I thought he might suggest that we sit in the living room—a sunny space beautifully decorated with antique furniture, subdued oil paintings, and an enormous oriental rug—but he led the way toward the den at the back of the house.

From my previous visit I remembered that the den was a darker room, shaded by the big trees in the back yard. As we entered it, I glanced at the big, expensive-looking TV with external speakers that took up much of one wall and the large stone fireplace that took up much of another.

A third wall was mostly glass to give a view of the yard with its flower beds, swimming pool, and broad swath of emerald grass that led down to the boat dock. Deep leather chairs and a matching leather sofa were grouped around a glass-topped coffee table covered with boating and lifestyle magazines aimed at the sort of the people who could afford this house, this room, that view.

I wondered how much longer Whit Fontaine would be one of those people.

Maybe he wondered too. He went to the bar and refreshed his drink from a cut-glass decanter. As he poured bourbon over what remained of the ice he said, "Can I get you something?"

"No, thanks."

"A soft drink?"

"No, I'm fine. I need to ask you about a couple of things."

"Sure." He brought his drink over to the coffee table, put it on a UVA coaster, and sank into a chair. He moved as though he was tired and probably was after spending a week in jail.

I sat where I could see his face easily and took out my notebook and pen. "Tell me all you know about the Japanese investors."

I didn't mean to stress "investors," but the quick, searching look he gave me showed I must have done it anyway.

"What about them?"

"Anything. Everything. It may be important."

"You don't think they killed Susan?"

"Not necessarily. But if you didn't, someone else did, and I don't think they're Boy Scouts."

He picked up his glass, perhaps to give himself a moment to reflect, and took a long swallow of the whiskey. "I don't think they are either, but that's all Tom's doing. It was his idea to pitch them on investing in the casino."

"Which you're not sure you should build."

"No. But I think Tom's going to do it anyway."

"Well, you're his partner—can't you stop him?"

"He says he'll set up a separate corporation to do it. He says he'll do it independently of our firm. Use his own money and what he can raise."

"Do you believe that? About him using his own money?"

"Hell, no. I think he's been cooking the books, siphoning money out of the business."

"Do you have proof?"

The whiskey was loosening him up, and he gave me an angry look. "No, not yet. He's pretty damn clever. Or thinks he is. But I'll get the goods on him—just you wait and see."

Clearly, the partnership was over in fact if not in law. I couldn't see these guys working together in the future or even the present. So was Tom McKenna the murderer? Maybe, but more likely not. He was a jerk, sure, but that didn't make him a killer.

"Okay, you get the goods on him. Meanwhile, I need to talk to these Japanese investors. Where are they?"

"How should I know? Tom's dealing with them, not me."

"Where are they staying?"

"Staying?" He looked at me with bloodshot eyes. "I don't know. They've been by the office a couple of times. Christ, they're scary—such cold looks, like they have ice in their veins."

"I assume Mr. McKenna put them up in a hotel someplace."

"Probably." He frowned, staring down at his glass. "Maybe the Hilton near the airport? That's what we usually book for out-of-towners."

"Do you have a name?"

"What?"

"A name—someone I can ask for at the hotel."

He frowned harder. "A name? Their names all sound alike to me."

"You're sure? You can't remember even one name?"

"Well, I think the head guy goes by something like 'Want To Be'."

That made me frown. "Want To ... do you mean 'Watanabe'?"

"I guess. That sounds like it."

"That would be his surname. Do you know his given name?"

"No. I probably heard it, but I can't remember."

As Fontaine raised his glass and drank, I thought about what he'd said. *Watanabe.* How many people named Watanabe could there be at that hotel at any one time? I pulled out my phone, searched for the Hilton's number, and hit the button to call it.

When the operator answered, I said, "I'm trying to reach one of your guests—a Mr. Watanabe." I spelled it for her.

"Yes, one moment. I'll connect you."

After a couple of clicks, I heard the phone ringing in Watanabe's room. He might not be there, of course, but it was worth a try.

Someone answered. "Yes," a man said in accented English.

"Mr. Watanabe?"

"No. Who is calling, please?"

"Wendy Lu. I'm a private investigator working on a case, and I need to talk to him."

"About what?"

"I told you: a case I'm working on."

"He will want to know what case."

I thought for a moment. I didn't know who this guy was, but he was in Watanabe's room, so he must one of the crew or whatever the head man called his gang. And it seemed as though I wouldn't get to talk to Watanabe unless I gave at least some detail.

"The death of Susan Fontaine."

"Who?"

"The late wife of Whitaker Fontaine."

After a pause, he said, "Wait."

I waited. As the seconds stretched into over a minute, I looked out at the carefully tended yard, thinking my father would approve of how the flower beds balanced and shaped the grass and how all of it led your eye down to the water at the end of the lawn. I wondered who had done or, more likely, directed the landscaping, Susan Fontaine or her husband. Probably Susan—Whit didn't seem like the gardening type. Especially now, sitting there getting drunk instead of doing something to clear his name.

I noted that between sips of his drink Fontaine was looking at me. His eyes were bleary as well as red, so I couldn't tell whether he was looking at me the way men do when figuring their chances of getting you into bed. Maybe he was, or maybe he had something else on his mind.

Such as who might have killed his wife. I hoped he was thinking about that and could come up with an idea. Something—anything—to help me find a way out of the dark maze this case had become.

After several more seconds I hear a rustling sound and then a more heavily accented voice said, "Yes."

"Mr. Watanabe?"

"Go ahead."

Cagey, I thought. He doesn't know whether the phone is tapped or whether I'm recording this conversation. A careful man, not someone to underestimate.

"My name is Wendy Lu. I'm a private investigator, and I need to talk to you about a case I'm on."

"The murder of the Fontaine woman."

It wasn't a question, but I answered it anyway. "Yes, her murder."

There was a long pause. I was beginning to wonder if he was still there, but finally he said, " I do not know anything about that."

"I still need to talk to you."

"Why?"

"You may know something that could help me. For example, what you're doing with Fontaine-McKenna Associates."

"That has nothing to do with her murder."

"Maybe, maybe not. I won't know until I've talked to you."

"You can ask Mr. McKenna about our business relationship. Or Mr. Fontaine."

"I've asked both of them, and they've told me. Now I want to hear it from you."

"I do not want to talk to you."

"Would you rather talk to the police?"

There was another long silence. "Why should the police want to talk to me? I have done nothing wrong. My associates have done nothing wrong."

"Oh, sometimes the police just like to talk to people. Especially yakuza who have come to this country for some reason."

"What makes you think I am yakuza?"

"Several things—including that you don't deny it. Shall I call the police now or come to see you?"

I thought he might pause again, but he didn't. "Come to see me. I will talk to you for a few minutes."

"Fine. Meet me in the bar of your hotel in forty-five minutes. One of my colleagues will be with me."

He laughed softly. "The bar? A public place? And you are bringing someone with you? I do not think you trust me."

"I don't," I said. Then I hung up.

Fontaine looked at me. "You're going to talk to him? Why?"

"Because that's what I do—talk to people. Sometimes they tell me useful things."

"I don't see how anything those guys say could be useful."

"Mr. Fontaine, if you really didn't kill your wife, you better hope I turn over every rock until I find something to clear you."

He frowned. "I didn't kill her. You believe me, don't you?"

"I believe evidence. Right now all of it points to you. But my job is to keep looking, so that's what I'm doing. Maybe you should think about helping instead of sitting here feeling sorry for yourself and pickling yourself with booze."

I got up and left the house.

CHAPTER TWENTY-THREE

I called Marcus and summarized my conversation with the yakuza boss. "Well, then, I guess they're what you thought they are." He sounded pleased about that as if perhaps things were finally beginning to break our way.

"Yep. So let's go talk to them."

"Okay, I'll meet you at the hotel."

I drove to the Hilton and sat in one of those lobby chairs that hardly anyone ever uses. Leftover cop caution made me sit with my back to the wall. Just like a real gunfighter, I thought, even though I didn't have much in common with one.

The Woman with No Name? Too late—I already had one. 陆文. Lu Wen. "Continent Literature." Whatever. No one was going to confuse me with Clint Eastwood.

After a few minutes Marcus walked in, spotted me, and came over. I stood as he approached.

"Hi, boss. We're going to meet them in the bar—it's over there."

"All right. You take the lead, and I'll speak up if there's something I want to ask them."

I'd thought Marcus would take that approach, but I liked hearing his confirmation. "Okay, let's go."

We went into the bar, which was almost empty at that time of day. We were early, as I'd planned to be, and so had arrived before the Japanese. A server came over and took our order—club soda with lime for both of us. She had just dropped off the drinks when three Asian men entered the bar.

One was big, a bear of a man who walked stiffly and held his arms out from his sides. One was smaller and more slightly built but looked strong as though he had stretched his muscles instead of pumping them up. The third, the one in the middle, was older, solid but not stocky and with a full head of iron-gray hair. All three of them were well dressed without being overly so, and all three had hard eyes.

They looked around, checking out everyone in the bar, and then came toward our table. As they got closer, I could see that the big man was missing part of his left little finger. He must have noticed my glance, because he gave me a look cold enough to freeze a cup of hot sake.

The older man sat without asking permission or even asking who we were. Maybe he'd seen enough cops to know we'd worn the badge. Then the two other men sat, flanking Marcus and me.

The older man started to speak but stopped when the server came over to take their order. All three men ordered American beer.

The man waited until she had left to get their drinks and then said, "What do you want, Ms. Lu?"

"It's nice to meet you too, Mr. Watanabe. This is my colleague Marcus Jefferson. And these men are …?"

He nodded at Marcus. "My associates. You do not need their names. I will ask you again: what do you want?"

"Who killed Susan Fontaine?"

He smiled, reminding me of a shark that had spotted a tasty morsel. "I do not know. But what makes you think I would tell you if I did?"

"I don't think you want the police poking into your business, trying to find out what you might know about the murder."

"And what makes you think I might know something about it?"

Marcus said, "It just seems quite coincidental that Japanese gangsters show up and right away the wife of one of their business partners is killed."

He turned from me to Marcus. "If you are trying to insult me by calling me a gangster, you will not succeed. I have lived a long time and have been called worse things—including by some people who are dead now."

That gave me another chill, but I hoped I didn't show it. "We're not trying to insult you—we're just speaking the truth."

"*The* truth? Is there only one?"

His question surprised me. I hadn't expected a yakuza to delve into philosophy. I told myself again not to underestimate this man.

"Maybe not in *Rashomon*, but here there is, at least when it comes to who killed Susan Fontaine."

"Ah, you know *Rashomon*. Very good. What else do you know about Asian culture? Probably not much, like most Americans."

I forced myself to ignore his insult as he had mine. "I am Asian American, the daughter of Chinese immigrants, so I have a foot in both cultures."

"I see. That must be an awkward way to stand."

Philosophy again. I was beginning to see how he'd survived and prospered in a dirty business where most people valued brawn over brain.

"Sometimes. Do you know of any reason why Whit Fontaine would want to kill his wife?"

"No. I met her only once, and I could tell that she wanted nothing to do with me. Or us." He made a circular motion that included the other two gangsters. "Although apparently she didn't forbid her husband to use our money."

"What about Tom McKenna?" Marcus asked. "Might he have killed her?"

"I do not know why he would have wanted to. Besides, he remained with us that night after Mr. Fontaine left the restaurant."

"Yes, but for how long?"

Watanabe turned from Marcus to the smaller of his two colleagues. "An hour?" The man nodded. "Yes, an hour," Watanabe said. "Then he left in his car, and we took a taxi back to the hotel."

Marcus pressed him. "You're sure it was that long—a full hour?"

"Yes, that is what I said." Watanabe's tone was cool, and I could tell he didn't like to be challenged.

I made a note on my pad. Judy Wagenaar, their server, had told me Fontaine left half an hour before the rest of them, and I'd put that in my report. The discrepancy might be important or it might not. Perhaps she just remembered the evening differently.

"What else can you tell us about that evening?" I asked.

"What do you mean?"

"How did Mr. Fontaine act?"

"Drunk. He acted drunk because he was."

I studied his face. "You don't like drunks."

"No, it is undisciplined to drink so much."

"You do not let your men do it."

He glanced at the big one, then the smaller one. The big one did nothing, but the smaller one smiled slightly, as if he knew what Watanabe was thinking.

"No, if they drink too much, they do not last long with me."

"How did you get into this ... business?"

Suspicion showed in his face. "You mean my business with Mr. McKenna and Mr. Fontaine?"

"We'll get to that, but I meant this business of being a ...."

"Yakuza." He finished for me.

Under the table Marcus gave me what was probably a warning nudge, but I wanted to keep going. "Yes."

He was silent for a moment, looking intently at me. Then, after glancing at Marcus, he said, "Most people I would not tell, but I trust you for some reason. At least enough to tell you a little. I started by running errands for them when I was young, just a teenager. I must have done all right because soon they used me for other things, more important things."

"Such as?"

"Such as things I will not describe. I am sure you can guess what I mean."

"Yes, I think I can."

"Some of those things were hard to do, especially for one so young." He paused. "But I did them."

"And it changed you?"

The question seemed to surprise him. "Yes, it did. I did not realize at the time, but, yes, it changed me." He paused again. "I suppose I did those things well too because after a couple of years they put some men under me, just a few, but I was in charge."

"Their boss."

"Yes, I was the boss. And I have been a boss ever since, moving up, always moving up."

"So here you are now, in the United States, investing in a legitimate business."

He nodded, seeming pleased that I understood him. "Yes. And talking to you, a bright young Chinese woman."

"Chinese American."

"If you like. But you are more Chinese than American. Were you born here?"

"No, in China."

"I thought so. You are smarter than most Americans, more …." He turned to the smaller man and said something in Japanese.

"More perceptive," the man said.

"Exactly," Watanabe said. "More perceptive." He studied me for a few moments. "What is your Chinese name?"

"Lu Wen. It means—"

"Yes, I know. I speak some Chinese. It is useful when dealing with my … counterparts in China and Taiwan." He paused. "Do you like this work?"

The question caught me off guard. "Uh, I think so. Of course, I'm still learning it."

"This man—he is your boss?"

"Yes."

"Does he pay you well?"

I looked over at Marcus, whose scowl told me what he thought of this gangster and his smooth conversation.

"Let's just say not as well as I'd like."

Watanabe smiled again. "I am sure. So why do it?"

"I was a police officer once, and old habits are hard to break."

"You were? You, a Chinese woman? Here?"

"Yes. Here all kinds of women do all kinds of things. I do not believe it is that way in Japan."

"No—at least not so much." He studied me again. "Would you like to work for me? I could use a smart woman like you."

I was surprised he'd ask me that with Marcus sitting right there, but he didn't seem to care much what other people thought. I would have laughed off the question except that I could tell he was serious and I didn't want to hurt his feelings.

"Doing what? Not the kind of thing you have these men for?"

"No, not that. As you say, that is why I have them. No, I could use you as a guide, someone who understands this crazy country, the people, the language." He paused to gauge my reaction. "Someone who understands the customs here. That is important in my business."

"In any business."

"Yes, that is true. So, will you work for me?"

I searched for a diplomatic answer. "Hmm, I'll think about it. How's that? Right now I have a job I want to finish."

"One she has to finish," Marcus said. "Because it's important."

"I see. Well, I will keep the offer open. You could do much better working for me than for ... people who do not understand you as I can."

I knew what he meant, and maybe he had a point. But I decided to get back to what we were there for.

"Thank you for the offer—it's flattering. But about that evening at the restaurant—did either Mr. Fontaine or Mr. McKenna seem distracted?"

"Distracted?" He said the word as though he didn't know what it meant. The smaller man started to speak, but I interrupted. "Preoccupied. Thinking of other things."

Watanabe frowned, thinking. "Mr. McKenna did not. Perhaps Mr. Fontaine did—he was so drunk it would be hard to say what he was thinking about. But he did not seem very happy to be there with us."

"Perhaps he does not like us," the smaller man said. Watanabe looked at him but said nothing. "How does he treat you?" the smaller man continued.

"Like the hired help that I am." I flipped though my notes, thinking of what else to ask. "I understand that you're planning to finance a casino in North Carolina."

Watanabe frowned again, but I sensed it was for a different reason. "Who told you that?"

"Let's just say I heard it in the course of my investigation. Is it true?"

Now Watanabe looked at the big man, who leaned forward and put his massive hands on his knees. He made me think of a sumo wrestler just beginning to bulk up. "I will not talk to you about our business. It has nothing to do with that woman's death." He gave me a cold smile. "America is widely known to be a violent country, and you say you are an American. Then you should look among your fellow Americans for the killer."

I didn't back down. "I've been doing that. But it's only natural that I'd want to ask you too."

"You have asked, and I have answered." He stood and his men did likewise. The big one towered over me, practically casting a shadow, so I stood too. Then Marcus got to his feet and took a step forward, making the big man move back slightly.

"Do not ask me anything more." Watanabe looked into my eyes, and I saw my reflection in his. "It would not be healthy for you. Do you understand?"

"Yes." I knew exactly what he meant, and I also knew he wasn't bluffing.

"Good."

Marcus gave Watanabe a hard look but didn't say anything. I tried to think of a parting line that would reassert our authority, but I couldn't. I figured it was better to say nothing than to say something stupid, so I kept quiet. I just nodded and followed Marcus out.

CHAPTER TWENTY-FOUR

"Well, what do you think?" Marcus asked once we were in the parking lot and walking toward his car.

"Hard to say. They're probably guilty of racketeering and money-laundering. Maybe some other things. But I don't see why any of them would kill Susan Fontaine. Do you?"

"No. Unless someone paid to have it done—Fontaine or someone else. Then they might have done it."

"That seems like a big risk if they're trying to get into business here."

"Yeah, it does, but guys like that are used to taking risks. Well, we needed to talk to them, and you did a good job with the interview."

"Thanks. And thanks for having me take the lead."

"It's your case, Wendy. I've said that all along."

"I know." I smiled at him. "Maybe I'll turn down Watanabe's job offer after all."

"You better. Okay, what's next on your list?"

I paused. "I'm not sure. I want to go over my notes, see if there's something I might have missed. I'll give you a call, okay?"

"All right. I'll wait to hear from you."

He got in his car and drove away. I went over to mine, wondering what I should do next.

I didn't have to wonder long. Watanabe and his men must have been watching us from the lobby, because seconds after Marcus left, they emerged from the hotel and started my way.

Their sudden appearance startled me, and I thought about getting in my car and leaving. But then I decided they weren't likely to attack me in broad daylight in a public parking lot, so I stayed where I was. Maybe Watanabe had something more he wanted to say to me.

As they approached, another car, a Lincoln SUV, roared into the lot. I recognized the driver—Whit Fontaine. He looked at me and swerved in my direction.

Watanabe and his men froze as Whit parked sloppily across two spaces and jumped out of the SUV. He slammed the door and strode over to me.

"Okay, I'm here! I'm taking your advice and looking for the bastard who killed Susan."

He was more sober than when I'd seen him at his house, but he still had enough alcohol in him to make him aggressive. For him to confront the

Japanese would be like throwing a lit match into gasoline.

As that thought went through my head, Watanabe and his men resumed walking toward me. When Whit noticed them, his expression grew ugly and his fists clenched.

"There those fuckers are now. I'm going to—"

"Stay calm and not start anything. You're in enough trouble already."

"But you said—"

"I said help, not harm. And those men are really dangerous. They may have killed Susan, and they won't hesitate to kill you if you give them a reason."

I'd kept my voice down as the Japanese approached. They came up to us, Watanabe in the middle again with his men flanking him. Watanabe frowned at Whit.

"What do you want here?"

"I want to find out who killed my wife, damn it!"

"Then you should ask someone else. We did not do it. And is not this woman trying to find the killer? You should leave and let her do her job."

"She's not getting anywhere!"

Thanks for the support, pal, I thought, but I didn't say anything. I let the scene play out.

"I am not so sure. She found us and asked some interesting questions. I think she is making more … ." He turned to the slim man, who said only, "Progress."

"Yes, progress. She is making more progress than you think." He looked at me and smiled slightly. "An impressive woman. I asked her to come to work for me."

Whit's jaw dropped. Then he gave me an angry look. "You didn't tell me that."

"It just now happened. Anyway, I didn't accept."

"No, she did not," Watanabe said. "But if I keep asking, and especially not in front of her boss, I may get a different answer. In my business I have sometimes seen that."

He said it calmly, but as the words sank in, I thought of the Godfather, making offers people couldn't refuse.

"Well, she's working for me, so you leave her alone!"

Watanabe's expression showed he wasn't used to being spoken to that way. He turned to the big man and made a slight gesture.

The man advanced on Whit, who didn't retreat. Instead, he curled his hands into fists and struck a boxer's pose.

That made the big man pause and study Whit for a moment. Then he made a sudden slashing motion toward Whit's head, using the edge of his hand, his fingers straight.

Whit parried the chop with his left hand and hooked his right into the big man's belly, driving the wind out of him. The man staggered back, took a couple of deep breaths, and charged.

Whit danced out of the way and drove a hard punch into the man's ribs, making him lurch to the opposite side. Then Whit managed to get in an uppercut to the jaw before the big man grabbed him and began to squeeze. Whit got his left arm free and pounded the man on the head, but he didn't let go.

Whit flushed and groaned in pain. He unclenched his fist and drove two stiffened fingers into the man's eyes, making him scream and put his hands to his face.

Whit stepped back, breathing hard, his face still flushed. After a few seconds the big man lowered his hands, tears streaming from his eyes, and shook his head like a bull. Then he spun with surprising grace to launch a sweeping kick toward Whit's legs.

Whit tried to jump out of the way, but he was still winded and the kick connected, knocking him to the ground. The big man fell on Whit, grabbing him by the throat with one hand and hammering him in the side with the other.

Whit tried twice to buck him off, but the man was too big and heavy for that. Whit's face grew redder than before, and his movements became visibly weaker as the man kept his huge hand locked on Whit's throat.

When Whit stopped moving, Watanabe spoke sharply in Japanese. The big man relaxed his grip and slowly stood, rubbing his eyes.

I thought Whit might be badly hurt or even dead, but after several seconds he rolled onto his side and vomited onto the pavement. Then he wiped his mouth with the back of his hand, took a few deep breaths, and got shakily to his feet.

He glared at the big man, balling his hands into fists again and taking a step toward him. But the smaller man intervened, darting a hand into a back pocket to pull out a knife identical to the one in my briefcase. He pricked Whit's back with the tip and said, "Stop! That is enough."

Whit turned his head and looked at the man, then at the knife. "Two against one, huh? And bringing out a knife in a fistfight? You call that fair?"

The fight had taken only a couple of minutes. I glanced around the parking lot, but we didn't seem to have attracted any attention—yet. I knew we would if we stayed there much longer.

Watanabe said, "I call it saving your life. If you do not stop, we will have to kill you."

That got Whit's full attention, and he slowly lowered his hands. "Your man started it."

"I know. But now it is finished, so you should leave."

Whit started to speak, but the smaller man prodded him with the knife again, and he said nothing. He looked at me, but I didn't say anything either, so he got in the SUV and, after giving the Japanese an angry, disdainful look, drove away.

As he left, I thought that although getting into a fight with the big man hadn't been very smart, at least Whit had gotten off his ass and tried to help find his wife's killer—or killers. He'd even been ready to go after the big man again after the beating he'd taken. I liked him better that way than as a sad sack sucking on a bourbon bottle. I knew where that path led.

"I think your client is a reckless man," Watanabe said as the smaller man put away the knife and helped the big man to his feet. "Brave, yes, but reckless."

"Most of us are reckless sometimes," I said, "and he is under a lot of stress right now."

"I suppose. But you must control him, at least with respect to us. I will not allow this sort of thing again."

"I can't control him, but I'll give him the message."

"Good. I meant what I said about giving you a job. You would make much more than you must be making now."

"I'm doing all right."

"How about respect? How much of that do you get?"

"Respect is something you have to earn, and I'm trying to do that."

"With me you would have respect from the beginning. In fact, you have it now."

"Thank you. But—"

"You do not want to work for yakuza, for gangsters."

"I don't want to offend you, but … let's just say I'm happy where I am."

"Very well. If you ever change your mind, the offer will still be open."

"Thanks."

Watanabe turned to the smaller man. "Take her to her car."

The man nodded and gestured for me to precede him. I walked toward my car, the man following close behind me as Watanabe and the big man went back into the hotel.

When I got to my car and reached into my briefcase for my keys, the man pulled out his knife again. I sucked in my breath and the man smiled.

"I think you have seen a knife like this before."

"You know I have—you must be the one who threw it at me."

"Maybe." He held the knife down by his side,

Anger flashed through me and made me stronger—or, as I had said to Watanabe, reckless. "Too bad for you that you missed."

"Oh, I do not miss, but sometimes I give a warning. Here is another one, your last one: leave us alone."

"I'm not going to stop my investigation."

"Do what you like with Fontaine, even McKenna. But leave us out of it."

"I'm not trying to drag you into anything. But I have to go where the evidence leads."

"I will not debate this matter with you. You heard what Mr. Watanabe said—he has no more patience for questions about that woman's death." He glanced around to make sure no one was watching us and then, striking like a snake, used the knife to flick a button off my shirt. "If you do not leave us alone, you will simply disappear."

"That sounds like a threat I should report to the police."

He frowned. "It is not a threat—it is a prediction. One that will cause you pain if it comes true. And if you talk to the police about us, well, that would be a serious mistake on your part." The knife flashed again, and even though I flinched, he took another button off my shirt.

I put a hand on my shirt to keep it closed. "You've made your point." I found my keys and unlocked the car. I put my briefcase on the passenger's seat, slid inside, and started the car. Then I reached into the bag, searched by feel, and found what I wanted.

I lowered my window and showed him the pistol. "I think you have seen a gun like this before."

The man said nothing.

"If you come after me, you may be the one to disappear."

He still said nothing. I put the pistol down and drove away. In the rearview mirror I saw him watching me go.

CHAPTER TWENTY-FIVE

I stopped by my place to change clothes, which I would have done anyway to go to dinner with Connolly but now had to because of the yakuza knife work. As I thought about what to wear, I told myself again that our dinner wasn't a date—it was just two people in the same line of work having a meal together.

But if that was the case, why did I put on a short black skirt and a red silk blouse? And why did I add jewelry, apply makeup, and even dab on a little perfume? Because I want to look nice in public, I said to answer those troublesome questions.

But I couldn't convince myself. I might be able to fool others once in a while, but I couldn't fool me.

I picked up a true purse, black to match my medium heels, and put my wallet and gun into it. There was just enough room left for the knife. As I closed the purse I thought of what my mother would say if she knew I carried a throwing knife around with me as well as a gun. That bothered me some but not too much until I realized my father would probably think the same thing.

I drove to the office, unlocked the front door, and went inside. I was surprised to see Simone sitting at her desk, wearing earphones and typing away. Larry and I often worked on the weekend and Marcus did occasionally, but there was rarely any need for her to be in the office then.

When she saw me, she removed her earphones and said, "Hi, Wendy."

"Hi, Simone. What brings you in today?"

"Oh, transcribing a surveillance report Marcus wants to send out on Monday. I would've worked at home, but we're having some painting done and I'd be in their way."

"Is Marcus here too?"

"No, he took a prospective client, an insurance executive, to play golf this afternoon." She glanced at the wall clock. "By now he's probably got the guy in the clubhouse and is trying to close the deal over a couple of beers. He calls that 'work', you know."

"Well, it would be for me. I'm sure Larry will be tracking some straying spouse tonight, so everyone in the agency is on deck today."

"Looks like it. How's the Fontaine case going?"

"Okay, I guess." I tried to sound more positive than I felt.

"Tough one, huh?"

"Yep, a tough one. But I'm still working it. I came by to type up my notes."
She smiled her familiar warm smile that always made me feel better, and I went on back to my office. Without Marcus or Larry there, the place was empty and quiet. That should have helped me to concentrate, but instead it gave me a creepy feeling.

I wasn't surprised—the whole case gave me that feeling. I was swimming in molasses, getting nowhere and exhausting myself. I picked up a metal pen and threw it across the little room. It bounced off the wall, making such a sharp bang that I thought Simone might come back to see what had happened, but she didn't.

Feeling foolish, I picked up the pen and put it back on my desk. Having a temper tantrum wasn't going to solve anything.

I finished typing my notes a little after six. I read back over everything I'd written, trying to see something, a clue, even a hint I'd missed before. It seemed clear that Tom McKenna was stretching and probably breaking the law, using gangster money to fund his casino and perhaps pay off some state and local officials in the process. Whit Fontaine didn't like the idea of the casino, but simply by being McKenna's partner, he was part of what McKenna was doing.

Still, that didn't mean McKenna had killed Susan Fontaine or had his yakuza friends do it. I couldn't see a motive—Susan wasn't involved in the business in any way, and killing her to frame Whit and get him out of the partnership seemed too far-fetched, not to mention risky.

Then there was Maxine Walters. She loved Whit and wanted him free of Susan so that he could marry her, but she didn't have any motive for framing Whit—quite the contrary.

That left me where I'd started and where Connolly had said I'd end up—with Whit Fontaine as the only person who'd had a motive as well as the means and the opportunity to kill his wife.

Maybe he had done it. He swore he hadn't, but that might not mean much. People lied to me all the time in this job. They'd done it so much I'd gotten used to it—actually expected it from many if not most people. And why not? Everyone had something to hide. I did.

And if I were brutally honest about it, I even tried to hide things from myself.

As I was sitting there thinking—and wishing I had a drink to lubricate my thoughts—Simone came to my office to say goodnight.

"You're working late," I said.

"And so are you. Why don't you go home, get some rest?"

"Do I look like I need it?"

I said it as a joke, but Simone didn't laugh. "Well, yes, you do. You look tired, Wendy. Like this case is getting to you."

"Maybe it is."

"Do you want Marcus to step in? I'm sure he wouldn't mind, and he wouldn't think less of you for it."

"No! It's my case, and I'll handle it one way or another." I paused, noticing the surprised expression on her face. "I really appreciate your concern, Simone, but I've got this. I don't need Marcus to do more than he's doing."

She looked at me for a long moment. "All right. I won't say anything to him. But maybe you should if you think that's in the client's best interest."

"I will." I sort of meant it.

She held my gaze a bit longer, then said, "Well, I'm going home. How about you?"

"Having dinner with someone."

"Oh, a date? That's why you look so nice."

"No, it's not a date. He's a … friend. Someone in the business."

"Another investigator? I probably know him."

Simone would have made a pretty good investigator herself. She certainly knew how to question people without being too direct, too pushy.

"His name's Connolly. He's a Norfolk police sergeant."

"I've heard of him. Good-looking guy, a little flashy, right?"

"That's him."

"Wait—didn't Marcus tell me he's the detective in charge of the Fontaine murder investigation?"

"Uh, that's right."

She shook her head. "Girl, what *are* you thinking?"

"I might learn something—about the investigation, I mean."

"More likely he'll learn something from you."

That stung. "I know how to keep my mouth shut."

"Sure you do, but he knows how to make people talk. All cops do. You're sure this is a good idea?"

"Look, we're just having dinner."

"Have you told Marcus?"

"No. I just made the appointment with Ryan today." I'd seen Marcus since then, but I didn't mention that.

"Ryan, is it? You must be getting pretty tight with this guy."

"He's just a …." I stopped. I didn't know how to finish the sentence.

"Just a what? A friend?" She arched an eyebrow. "Sure—that's what all women say right before they sleep with a guy."

"I'm not sleeping with him."

"Maybe not yet. But you got all dressed up for a reason, didn't you? I'll bet you're wearing nice underwear too, am I right?"

She was, but I didn't want to give her the satisfaction of confirmation. "Can't a woman try to dress well without everyone thinking she's doing it for a man?"

Simone nodded. "Sure she can. I do that all the time. But let's face it, Wendy: you're no clothes horse. So when you get all dolled up, well, that's unusual, and it makes me wonder what's going on."

"What's going on is that I'm doing my job."

She paused for a long moment. "Okay, I've said enough. But I hope you know what you're really doing."

I didn't know what to say to that except "I hope so too," so I said nothing.

"You going to check in with Marcus by phone before your dinner?"

"What?" I noted the time. "No, not now. I've got to hurry or I'll be late." I stood and started gathering my things. "I'll call him afterward."

Simone paused. "Well, like I said, I hope you know what you're doing."

I stepped over to her and touched her on the arm. "Thanks, Simone. I know you're just trying to look out for me."

"Someone's got to do it. You won't do it yourself."

I wanted to argue with that, but she did have a point, and I didn't have the time. "Okay, *Mom*."

She tried not to smile but wasn't completely successful. "Okay, yourself. Good luck with your … whatever it is. Your not-a-date."

"Right. And thanks."

We walked out together, and I waited while Simone locked the door and got into her car. We waved at each other as she drove away.

Half an hour later I pulled into the parking lot at Mickey's. I didn't see Connolly, so I figured either I was early or he was inside. As I walked to the door, I sensed rather than heard someone behind me. I turned and saw Connolly close enough to touch me.

I must have recoiled a bit, because he said, "Sorry. Didn't mean to startle you."

"Now I know why they call detectives 'gumshoes'. You sure can sneak up on a person."

"Hey, I said I'm sorry. I was just hurrying to catch you."

"And you did." I was calmer by then and smiled to lighten the scene. "Now let's have that drink you mentioned."

"Good idea." He held the door for me and we went inside.

We found a table, and Gina came over almost immediately. I asked for Jim Beam and Connolly ordered Maker's.

After she left, Connolly said, "You look nice, Wendy. Very nice."

"Thanks." I liked hearing him say that, but I hoped I wasn't blushing.

"So, what have you been up to today?"

I remembered what Simone had said. "Oh, just doing my job, asking questions."

"Did you talk to the Japanese guys?"

I couldn't think of a polite way not to answer his question, so I said, "Yes. They didn't tell me much."

"What did they say?"

"Like I said, not much."

That made him sit back and look at me. "Is there some reason you suddenly don't want to talk to me?"

"I'm happy to talk to you. But our conversations about the Fontaine case always seem one-sided. I tell you what I know, but you don't tell me what you know. You're the lead police investigator on the murder, so you must know something."

"I do. I know that Whit Fontaine killed his wife. The initial evidence pointed that way, and I've found nothing since to make me think he didn't do it."

"But how hard have you been looking?"

If I'd thought before I'd spoken, I might not have asked the question or at least would have asked it more diplomatically. Connolly's face darkened with anger, and he exhaled loudly. I could tell he was trying to control himself before he answered me.

"What the hell are you implying? That I'm not doing my fucking job? Of course, I am. I'm working this case just as hard as you are. But I keep telling you that there's nothing to find. Whit Fontaine murdered his wife, and that's that."

I paused to let him cool down. While I did, Gina arrived with our drinks. He thanked her—at little brusquely, I thought—and I took a sip of mine to lengthen the silence between us.

I put down my glass and looked at him. "Okay. You may be right. But I'm doing my job too, and that's trying to find anyone else who could have done it. Anyone."

Connolly took some whiskey in his mouth and rolled it around before he swallowed. "Yes, I know. But I think you've finished your job. You've talked to anyone and everyone who could possibly have been involved with Susan Fontaine's murder. And you're right where you started—right where I said you'd be: looking at Whit Fontaine as the murderer."

I wanted to tell Connolly that he was wrong, but I couldn't. He was right. It looked as though as I was stuck. Our client was guilty, and there was just nothing we could do about it.

I played the only card I had left. "What about Betty Partridge? Fontaine couldn't have killed her—he was still in jail. Surely you don't think he had her killed?"

His expression was grim. "No, I don't. I think she killed herself."

"She may have. But as Marcus said to me, the timing seems suspicious. First Susan Fontaine dies and then Betty Partridge—both of them connected to Fontaine-McKenna Associates."

"Coincidences do happen, Wendy, and I've seen bigger ones than this."

"Well, what about McKenna?"

"What about him?"

"Suppose he killed Betty?"

"Come on, Wendy—you're grasping at straws. There's no evidence of that."

"Did she leave a note?"

"I probably shouldn't tell you, but I will. No, she didn't leave a note. And that doesn't mean a thing—lots of suicides don't leave notes."

"Most do."

That stopped him with his drink halfway to his lips. He put the glass down and looked at me. "Actually, less than half. I'm a homicide detective, so I know."

"Don't be patronizing." I spoke without thinking but didn't take back the words. "I talked to her, remember? And I think she was the sort of person who would've left a note—some sort of explanation. Maybe even an apology."

"Look, Wendy, I don't mean to be rude, but she killed herself. People do it all the time. A lot more often than they're murdered."

"That's possible, of course, but it's also possible that someone wanted to shut her up. Maybe someone didn't want her talking to people—me, for example—about Fontaine-McKenna Associates."

"Did she tell you anything that someone would kill her to keep secret?"

"Well, no, she didn't. But now we'll never know what else she might have had to say."

He finished his drink. I'd barely touched mine. "Like I said, Wendy: you're grasping at straws. I know you want to get a good result for your client, but you can't just make stuff up."

"Damn it, I'm not making things up! I'm just trying to explore all of the possibilities, something you seem unwilling to do."

"I'm a cop, Wendy. Remember cops? You used to be one. Then you should remember that we don't have the luxury of working just one case at a time. That's something you private eyes get to do."

"Yes, I remember." I did remember. I remembered a lot of things ... starting with Bobby.

I looked at Connolly, wondering whether I would ever be free of that memory. Then I decided that, no, I wouldn't be and also that, no, I didn't want to be. But I did want to be free to live my life.

Starting now, I thought. "I remember something else too—I remember you said we were going to have dinner."

He smiled faintly—apparently the only way he ever smiled. "Right, I did. Where would you like to go?"

We talked about possibilities for a minute or two. Connolly wanted a steak, but I didn't want anything that heavy. And I didn't want to suggest a Chinese restaurant—too predictable. Finally I said, "How about the Lynnhaven Dock House?"

"The place Fontaine and McKenna took the Japanese?"

"Why not? It has good food."

"You're not going to ask the staff any questions, are you? About the case, I mean. I want you off the clock."

I didn't know exactly why I had suggested that place. The food was good, but somehow I knew that wasn't the real reason. Some instinct made me want to go back there. But I could tell that Connolly was reluctant. "All right. As of now I'm off the clock for the rest of the evening. Let's go eat."

He looked at me for a long moment, then said, "Okay. Let's go."

CHAPTER TWENTY-SIX

By the time we got to the restaurant, it was almost 8:30, and the dinner crowd was beginning to thin out. The deck was still full, however, and the hostess said we'd have to wait if we wanted to sit outside.

"No, that's okay," Connolly said. "I imagine the bar will get busy soon, so how about something over there by the window?"

He hadn't consulted me, but I agreed with his thinking.

"Fine." She pulled two menus from a rack behind her and led us to a quiet table in a corner. The view of the nighttime bay through the big picture windows wasn't quite as spectacular there, but it was still lovely.

I didn't think Connolly would pull out my chair for me, but he did, seeming only a little rusty as he did so.

"Thanks. Guys don't do that much anymore."

"They should." He hesitated at the chair next to me, then took the one across the table.

"Most women would agree."

"Well, I wouldn't know. I don't know that many women."

"You don't? I'm surprised."

"Why?"

I chose my words carefully. "Because you're the kind of man who attracts women. You've got that strong-but-silent thing going on, you're comfortable in your own skin, and you don't try too hard. I mean, you act like you don't care if you attract them or not, and that in itself can be attractive."

"Oh, really? Does it have that effect on you?"

"Uh, I …." I hadn't expected such a direct question from him, and it startled me. "Well, let's just say I'm glad you invited me to dinner."

"Fair enough. And I'm glad you accepted."

That seemed to be a good place to leave it, so we left it and ordered drinks from the server who'd just arrived. I noticed that her name tag read "Louise."

"Are you Louise Rossi?" I asked.

She seemed surprised that I knew her last name. "Yes. Why?"

"I'm Wendy Lu. We spoke on the phone."

"Oh, yes, I remember. I hope what I told you was helpful."

"It was. Thanks again."

"You're welcome."

When she'd left, Connolly said, "I thought you said you were off the clock."

"I was just thanking her for talking to me—trying to be polite."

Connolly's expression told me that he didn't believe me, but he didn't say anything. He just picked up his menu and studied it, so I picked up mine and did the same. By the time we'd chosen our dinners—medium-rare steak and grilled flounder—Louise arrived with our drinks.

She took our orders, gave me a slight smile, and went away. Connolly drank some of his bourbon as though he needed it, and I had a sip of mine.

After another swallow of bourbon, Connolly put down his glass and looked at me. "So, tell me more about yourself. What made you want to be a cop? That's an unusual line of work for ...." He seemed embarrassed to finish the thought.

"An Asian American woman? You're right it is. And my parents didn't want me to do it. They didn't want me to join the Navy, but I did that too."

"You're a real rebel, huh?"

The question made me pause. "Maybe. I wanted to see if I could do it—be in the Navy, I mean. After I proved to myself that I could, I decided to come back to Hampton Roads and get a college degree. I took a criminal justice course and liked it, so I decided to be a police officer."

To give myself a moment, I had another sip of bourbon. I put down the glass and gazed into it. "That didn't work out too well, as I've told you. So here I am."

"Yes, here you are. And I'm glad you are."

"Thanks. I am too."

Perhaps sensing that I wanted to change the subject, he asked me about my time in the Navy, and I told him about the ports we'd visited on a Mediterranean cruise. Rota, Naples, Venice, Piraeus, Haifa, Naples again, and Lisbon before we headed back to Norfolk after six months. The places, the people, the food. The sights and sounds and colors.

Especially the magnificent colors. The black velvet of the night sky with its scattering of stars. The aquamarine of the dawn when air and water were indistinguishable in the far haze. And the spectacular twilights as the reddening sun sank into the big, black ocean.

Connolly was quiet while I talked, letting me paint pictures for him. But he looked closely at me, maintaining eye contact and saying, "Uh-huh," once in a while to show he was following along. No man had looked at me like that in a while, and I liked it. I liked it a lot.

Then the food arrived, and we were largely silent as we began eating. I didn't know what Connolly was thinking. I was thinking he was a good listener—most detectives are.

As I was thinking that, he took a bite of steak, chewed thoughtfully, and said, "Wendy, don't take this the wrong way, but I think you ought to find a new line of work."

"Why? You don't think I can do this?"

"No, I think you can do it. But I also think it will tear you up inside. I've seen the job do that to a lot of good cops, the ones who aren't armor-plated. The ones like you." He looked into my eyes again, and I held his gaze. "I've even known a few who killed themselves. I wouldn't want you to get to that point."

"Nor would I. But I'm stronger than you think."

"It isn't a question of being strong—it's a question of not feeling too much, of being able to put the job down once in a while. Of realizing that you can't solve every crime, can't stop every bad guy. Or gal."

I put my knife and fork down on the plate. I'd eaten less than half of the fish, but suddenly I'd lost my appetite. "Maybe you're right. It does get to me sometimes."

"Why don't you tell Marcus you've done all you can on this case? Tell him that Fontaine must've killed his wife, and that's all there is to it."

I thought about what Connolly had suggested. There was a lot of merit to it. All of the hard evidence did point to Fontaine, and I didn't seem to be getting anywhere. Doing my job was one thing but refusing to face facts was another.

I looked up at Connolly. "All right. I'll think about it."

He pulled out his phone and handed it to me. "Here. You can call him right now."

That annoyed me. I didn't like to be pushed. "I said I'll think about it. I haven't made up my mind yet."

Connolly frowned, and I could tell that he was used to having people do what he said, even if it wasn't a direct order. I remembered a Navy cartoon I'd seen once—an admiral saying to a junior officer, "It's just a suggestion, but don't forget who it's coming from."

"Look," I said, putting a hand on his, "this was a pleasant dinner. Let's not spoil it by arguing, okay?"

He hesitated for several seconds before saying, "Okay." He put his phone back in his pocket and stood. "Excuse me a minute. Order coffee if you like. Dessert too."

"Do you want anything else?"

"Just coffee." He walked toward the men's room.

Louise came by to clear the table. She picked up Connolly's empty plate and then mine with the half-eaten fish.

"Didn't you like your dinner, honey?"

"Yes, it was fine. I guess I just wasn't hungry."

"Well, I'm glad it wasn't the food. Can I get you anything else?"

"Sergeant Connolly wants some coffee, and I'll have the same."

"I've seen your friend in here before," Louise said, "but I didn't know he's in the military."

"He's not. He's a police officer."

"Oh." Louise blinked several times, and I could tell that Connolly's being a cop, combined with my earlier questioning, made her nervous. That wasn't surprising—it was similar to the way most people get nervous when they see a patrol car in the rearview mirror.

To put her at ease, I added, "But neither of us is on duty now."

She nodded and seemed to relax a little. "Would you like anything with the coffee? Dessert maybe?"

"No, thanks, not this time."

She nodded again and scuttled away with the dirty dishes.

A minute later Connolly returned to the table, holding his phone by his side.

"Checking with the office?" I asked.

"What? Oh, uh, yeah." He didn't look at me as he slid the phone into his pocket. "They keep me on a pretty short leash."

Somehow that didn't seem likely. "Really? You seem like a man who does what he wants."

He sat, his big frame making the chair creak. "I wish that were true, Wendy. But we all have bosses and … obligations."

"True. I guess that's part of life."

"Sure is—a shitty part."

His comment surprised me. He seemed different somehow—not morose, exactly, but resigned. Well, maybe he'd gotten bad news about something he was working on. I remembered how I felt after I'd worked a fatal hit-and-run and the only witness, an elderly woman, died of a heart attack before she could give a statement. Nothing to do but close the file despite knowing that some unknown driver was getting away with murder.

"Have you decided yet?"

The question snapped me out of my reverie. "Huh? Decided what?"

"Whether you're going to keep beating your head against the wall on this Fontaine case?"

"Well, I didn't know I was beating my head against the wall. I thought I was trying to help my client. I said I'll think about whether it makes sense to keep trying, but that's far as I'll go right now."

He sighed. "You're a stubborn woman, Wendy Lu. That can be a good quality but only up a point. In our line of work sometimes we have to bend to keep from breaking."

I wasn't sure what he was getting at, so I said, "Good tip. I'll remember it. Thanks."

Louise arrived with two cups of coffee, and pouring and stirring took our attention for a minute. When we got back to conversation, Connolly changed the subject by asking me whether I was dating anyone.

"No, no one in particular." I realized that was an evasion, so I amended it. "To be honest, I haven't been on a date in a while. For one thing, I've been too busy. For another, no one has asked me out lately."

"That's hard to believe. You're very pretty."

For a moment I wondered if he was trying to flatter me, but he sounded sincere, so I decided to take it that way. "Thanks, but I'm just average compared to lots of other girls. You must not get out much."

I hoped that would get a smile out of him, but it didn't.

"Well, I don't, but I'm surprised you don't either. What are young men thinking these days?"

"Mostly about sports or sex. I like sports, but I'm not obsessed with them, and I like sex too but in the context of a relationship. Some guys aren't interested in relationships. And some of the guys who are—with me at least—just have yellow fever. You know what that is, don't you?"

"Sure." He drank some of his coffee.

"But you don't seem to have it."

That did make him smile. "I like all kinds of women, Wendy. White, black, brown, Asian, you name it."

"So you have catholic tastes."

"What? No, I'm a Lutheran."

I wasn't sure he meant that to be funny, so I didn't laugh. Ryan Connolly didn't strike me as a man who enjoyed being laughed at.

"Well, actually, I don't go to church anymore," he continued, "but that's the church I was raised in. I guess you never really leave it—or it never leaves you."

"Ah, so you believe in God and the devil, in heaven and hell."

He paused, sipping more coffee as I did the same.

"The devil, yes. And hell, yes. I've seen hell, close up. Every cop has. After a while you wonder whether there is a heaven. God? Well, let's just say I hope so. But a God who doesn't judge us too harshly for our sins." He paused. "Of which I have committed many."

Then he drained his cup, clinked it onto the saucer, and looked at me.

"Ready to go?"

"All right."

He looked around to signal Louise, but she was already headed our way with the check. I offered to split it, but Connolly insisted on paying. He took a fat roll of bills from his pocket, counted off what we owed, and left a generous tip.

I was surprised at the amount of money he was carrying. "Guess you're not a credit-card guy, huh?"

"I have one, but I like to deal in cash," he said as he put the rest of the currency away. "I've always liked the feel of money in my hand."

My father had said something similar once, and I'd chalked that up to his having been raised in China before credit cards were common there. But that didn't explain why Connolly preferred cash. Maybe it was just an idiosyncrasy of his.

He walked me to my car. The moon was up, shining a long golden streak on the black water of the bay. The world was quiet except for the sibilant whisper of the cars pushing along the highway behind us.

At the car I turned and looked up at him. He came very close to me, our bodies almost touching, and put his hands on both sides of my face. His palms were slightly rough, and although he held my head gently, I could sense the strength in his fingers.

He leaned down to kiss me, and it was even better than before. He took his time, making the kiss last, and I let him.

When our lips finally parted, I wanted to kiss him again. I suddenly realized that I'd spent enough time grieving for a dead man and needed to spend some time with a living one.

As I was thinking through the implications of that, Connolly pulled his head back and looked at me in the moonlight. "You're very pretty, Wendy, as I said. Smart too—I've seen that."

"Thank you."

"I wish I'd met you sooner."

I wish so too, I thought. "Well, at least we know each other now."

"Yes, we do."

When he didn't add anything, I said, "And thanks for dinner. I enjoyed it."

"So did I. But I wish you'd take my advice about the case."

"We've been over that. Please let it go."

I thought he might continue the debate, but he didn't. He nodded slightly. "All right. At least I tried."

That seemed an odd comment, but I just said, "I appreciate your concern."

I know you mean well." I hesitated a moment, then decided to plunge ahead. "Would you like to come to my place for a drink?"

He seemed surprised—at least he didn't answer right away. After a pause that made me wish I hadn't asked the question, he said, "Sure. I would like that."

I wasn't certain what he meant by "that"—I wasn't certain of anything at the moment. But I was tired of thinking and wanted to stop doing it for a while.

"Okay," I said. "Follow me."

"Fine."

He waited while I got in my car and started it. Then I waited while he got into his car. I led him, as I had two nights before, back to my place. I was nervous the whole way.

CHAPTER TWENTY-SEVEN

I unlocked my apartment door and went in, Connolly behind me. I switched on two table lamps, making the room neither bright nor dim, put my purse on the desk, and gestured toward the sofa. "Have a seat. I'll fix you a drink. Is bourbon okay?"

"Sure. Thanks."

He stood in the middle of the living room and surveyed it. "This is nice. Feminine but not in a frilly way. Like you."

"Thanks—I think." I smiled slightly to let him know I was kidding.

"And you're neat. I expected that, but not all these books. You must like to read."

"Yes, I do. It keeps me from being bored."

"Does it? Well, good for you. I've never been a big reader."

"You should try it." I went to a bookcase and scanned the titles. "Here." I pulled a slim paperback from a shelf. "*Double Indemnity* by James M. Cain. I think you'll like this one—a man commits murder for money. Well, for love too—or maybe only lust. Anyway, it's a great novel."

He took the paperback and studied its cover. "Murder for money. That doesn't happen as often as people think."

"No, but it does happen."

"Yeah, and maybe that's why Fontaine killed his wife. Of course, he didn't plan on getting caught."

I held up a hand. "Truce, okay? No more talk about the case tonight."

"Sure, truce." He paused. "As long as I get that drink."

"I'm on it."

I went into the kitchen and made two drinks, his at normal strength and mine half that. I wanted whatever happened to happen because I wanted it to, not because I couldn't think straight.

By the time I carried the drinks into the living room, he had taken off his sport coat and draped it neatly over a nearby chair and was sitting on the sofa, reading the novel. He looked up as I handed him a glass.

"This book sounds good," he said. "I think I might like it."

"Yes, I think you might." I sat on the sofa, leaving some space between us. "G nb i." I clinked my glass against his, and we each drank some of the whiskey.

"'Gon bay?' What's that?"

"Chinese for 'cheers'. It means 'dry cup'. Chinese people empty their glasses after every toast."

"But you don't do that."

"No. As with a lot of other things, I'm somewhere in the middle." I had another sip of my drink, wondering how to explain it. "Somewhere between the two cultures. I'm not sure how to put it into words."

"Interesting. But we don't have to talk about it now." He put his glass on the coffee table.

"No, we don't." I put my glass down too. "In fact, we don't have to talk at all."

He smiled at that and leaned toward me. The second kiss of the evening led to a third and a fourth, and then he was kissing my cheek, my ear, my neck. I could smell his cologne, faint but pleasant, a woodsy scent that suited him. I could feel his breath warm on my skin, and it made my own breathing faster. I could feel the slight stubble of his late-evening shadow as his face brushed against mine.

Then we had our arms around each other, and I held his shoulders and neck as his hands began exploring my body. A little part of me wanted to tell him to stop, to say that this was too soon, but all the rest of me was lonely and empty and hungry for something besides thoughts of blood and death. So I stopped thinking, stopped doing anything but feeling this strong man next to me, this man who seemed to want me as much as I wanted him in that moment.

I felt myself reclining backward, slowly but inevitably, so that I was lying on the sofa with Connolly—Ryan—above me, kissing me still and moving his hands over me. Big, sure hands that felt good as they touched me where no one had touched me since Bobby had touched me the same way.

And then I felt my clothing coming off, slowly, one piece at a time. I felt hot, flushed, and the air was cool on my skin as Connolly laid more and more of it bare.

I moved my hands on him then, stroking his arms and his chest, fumbling with the buttons on his shirt. He helped and soon threw his shirt on the floor. Then his bare chest was against mine, skin against skin, and our hearts were beating inches apart.

Shamelessly, I reached down to touch him and found what I expected. I began fumbling with his belt buckle. I was never really good at that sort of thing—just as some guys have trouble unhooking bras—and I was out of practice, which didn't help.

Connolly saved me from further embarrassment by rolling off the sofa, standing, and scooping me up in his strong arms. He looked down at me, smiling, and said, "We'll be more comfortable in the bedroom, don't you think?"

I smiled back and nodded, not wanting to speak any more than I wanted to think. I was a leaf floating downstream in a broad river of clear, cool water, and I just wanted to float until I reached the ocean and lost myself in it.

I hoped Connolly would help me lose myself.

He carried me into the bedroom, which was dark except for the faint light finding its way there from the living room. He eased me down onto the bed, and we kissed some more, still taking our time, both of us old enough to know that we had plenty of that and didn't need to rush.

Connolly tugged at the waistband of my brief panties, and I arched my hips to let him slide them off, leaving me naked. I hoped he liked my matching lingerie, the best I owned, but I knew he probably hadn't even noticed it.

He bent to kiss me again, starting with my mouth and then moving down, pausing at my breasts and then continuing his slow tour of my body.

He paused again, further down, and I opened myself to him, closing my eyes and giving myself up to the probing of his tongue. Soon that broad river began to flow faster, and my breathing began to come quicker.

All my nerve endings seemed centered in that one spot, that one perfect place, and I felt a warm tingling that grew into throbbing, pushing everything, every other feeling, aside and becoming all there was for me in the universe.

I put my hands on his head, not to guide him, because he didn't need guidance, but just to touch him, to feel him between my hands, to let him know how much, how very, very much, I liked what he was doing to me.

When the climax came, it was so strong I shuddered. Connolly kept doing what he was doing, and I rode a wave of pleasure for a full minute until the sensation became almost painful.

Then I pulled him up to me and held him in my arms. "Thanks," I whispered into his ear. "It's been a while, and I've missed it."

"You're welcome. Glad you liked it."

"More than just liked it. Give me a minute, and I'll return the favor."

"No hurry. We've got time."

He was right—we did have time, lots of it, and we took it.

☐ ☐ ☐

Later, lying there pleasurably tired, I sorted out my feelings, or tried to. Had I been disloyal to Bobby, the man whose picture I kept in a dresser drawer? I didn't think so. I think Bobby would have understood.

He'd wanted me to be happy, and although I didn't mind being by myself a lot, I realized I'd gotten lonely since he died. No man had been in my bed since then, and I thought it was time to rejoin the human race and live like a normal person.

Well, as normal as I ever was.

I didn't love Connolly—I didn't know him well enough to love him—but I did like him a lot, and it felt good to have him there beside me.

He'd fallen asleep. Not right away, he was too well-mannered for that, but after we'd talked some. Not about the case, because I'd decided to stop thinking about it for a while. Rather we talked about personal things—his kids, my family, our favorite foods and songs.

Nothing too heavy or consequential. Just getting to know each other's personalities better now that we now knew each other's bodies.

His voice got slower and softer, and finally he yawned and closed his eyes. I kept silent, letting him drift off into sleep. I needed some myself, but my brain buzzed, first with thoughts of how nice it had been, making love to Connolly, who was surprisingly patient and gentle in bed. Just as Bobby had been.

Then I thought about Bobby, and I was shocked to find that I had trouble picturing his face in sharp focus. I could still see it in my mind, the close-cropped brown hair, the bright hazel eyes, the angular planes of his jaw. That face I had loved so much.

But now the image was slightly blurry as though I were seeing it through streaked glass. And he seemed to be standing farther from me—not distant but not as close as I remembered.

Well, I guessed that was natural. Bobby was dead, and I was alive, and although I missed him terribly, I wasn't going to dedicate the rest of my life to the memory of a dead man.

Connolly's lying next to me proved that.

I listened to his slow, regular breathing—soothing, like rain falling lightly on the roof—and closed my eyes. I felt myself sliding slowly into sleep, and I wondered if the bad dream would come again.

The dream about that night in the little room with the man and woman and the knife and the gun.

I hoped not.

☐ ☐ ☐

The trilling of my phone woke me. I thought I'd put it on mute, but obviously I hadn't. I fumbled for it, trying to answer quickly so that the noise wouldn't wake Connolly. But then I saw that he was gone.

I was disappointed, but in a way I was also relieved. Both of us might have felt awkward in the morning. Even my limited experience had taught me that one could be more self-conscious sharing breakfast with a new lover than when sharing everything the night before.

I pressed the button and said, "Hello."

"Wendy Lu?" A woman's voice, hushed as though she were whispering. The voice sounded vaguely familiar, but I couldn't quite place it.

"Yes."

"Are you alone?"

"What is this? Some prank call?"

"No, I need to talk to you. Now."

"Who is this?"

"Maxine Walters."

I recognized the voice then, but I hadn't previously heard that strain of fear in it. She sounded scared.

"Okay, go ahead."

"No, I mean in person. Someone might be listening."

"You think someone has tapped your phone?"

"Yes, maybe. Or maybe yours."

"For God's sake, why?"

"Susan Fontaine. The casino. Maybe other things we don't even know about."

I paused, wondering if she was drunk. She sounded crazy but wasn't slurring her words. Maybe she was on drugs. Cocaine can make you paranoid, and other drugs probably can too.

My silence must have rattled her even more. "Hello? Are you still there?"

"Yes, but you're not making much sense."

"I can't tell you over the phone. You've got to meet me!"

"Look, it's late." I glanced at the phone display. "Almost midnight. Why don't we talk in the morning?"

"No! It has to be tonight. For your sake as well as mine."

That last remark got my attention. "Okay, where should I meet you? How about your office?"

"No, I'll come to Norfolk. I don't want to run into anyone I know here in Virginia Beach."

"All right." I tried to think of where we could meet. For some reason I didn't want her coming to my apartment, my private space.

Before I could think of a suitable location, she said, "How about Lafayette Park? You know, over by the zoo? That way we'd see anyone who might be trying to sneak up on us."

Whether or not there was any factual basis for it, the woman was definitely terrified.

"Who would try to do that? And why?"

"I'll tell you when I see you."

I didn't want to go out again, but I realized I had no choice. If she really had something to tell me about the case, I couldn't risk not finding out what it was. I sighed.

"Okay. When can you be there?"

"Thirty minutes. Maybe a little less."

"What will you be driving?"

"A Jaguar—silver."

I remembered seeing a car like that in front of Extra Perks. It figured that she'd drive something flashy.

"All right. When I see you, I'll blink my lights."

I hung up then and thought about calling Marcus but decided not to. I told myself I didn't want him to think I couldn't handle a major investigation without checking with him on every detail. The real reason—and I knew it even if I didn't let myself dwell on it—was that I thought he might tell me not to go, might say it could be dangerous so he'd go himself. I compromised by sending him a text message he probably wouldn't see until morning.

I switched on the lamp, wondering if Connolly had left a note on the nightstand. He hadn't, but then I hadn't thought he would. He didn't seem like a leave-a-note kind of guy. He'd probably call me in the morning, and if he didn't explain why he hadn't stayed the night, I wouldn't ask. Apparently both of us liked our space and were cautious about letting others get too close.

When I got out of bed, I saw that Connolly had left something: his elegant wristwatch, which was lying on the opposite nightstand. I picked up the watch and held it for a moment, seeing its golden glint even in the dim light and thinking that the watch suited him—a functional thing that was also valuable and attractive but understated. Then I carried it to my dresser so I wouldn't forget to give it to him the next time we met.

As I started to lay the watch next to my jewelry box, I noticed an engraved inscription on the back. I brought the watch close to my face, squinted, and read, "To R, from S. Love always."

What had he said his wife's name was? Sarah? Yes, that was it. But she was his ex now, I remembered, and he'd still seemed resentful when he told me about her leaving him for another cop. So why did he still wear the watch she'd given him?

Well, it was a lovely one, and maybe he just liked it. Maybe he no longer thought about the inscription on the back. Or—and I didn't like this idea but couldn't avoid it—maybe he liked having something that reminded him of her.

I wanted to think about that some more, but I had to get going if I was going to keep my appointment with Maxine. I put on black pants, a dark tee-shirt, and running shoes. I doubted that anyone was really after Maxine, but I wanted to be ready just in case. For the same reason I checked my pistol by ejecting and inspecting the magazine. Then I replaced it, racked the slide to put a cartridge in the chamber, and made sure the safety was on.

Connolly hadn't asked me for the knife and I'd forgotten to give it to him, so it was still in my purse. I considered leaving the knife at my apartment—the knife plus my pistol made my purse bulky—but something told me to bring it along. For what, I didn't know, but the knife stayed in my purse.

I turned off most of the lights in my apartment, locked the door behind me, and went down to my car. The day's heat had subsided, but the night air was still warm and had the mugginess that stamps most summer days in coastal Virginia. I cranked up the car's AC and headed for the park.

CHAPTER TWENTY-EIGHT

I arrived at the entrance in less than ten minutes and turned onto the street that led to the small parking lot. There were only two cars there, and neither was Maxine's. Both seemed to be empty, but I couldn't tell for certain. I drove as far away from them as I could, backed into a space, and switched off the engine and lights. Then I waited, letting my eyes adjust to the darkness broken only by the widely spaced streetlamps.

I didn't have to wait long. A car eased down the street and stopped at the entrance to the lot. The car was a silver Jaguar convertible with its top up. I blinked my headlights once, and the car came into the lot and rolled slowly toward me.

The Jaguar pulled into a space one away from mine and shut down. I waited to see if anyone was following the car, but no one else pulled into the lot or even stopped at the entrance. That didn't guarantee no one had followed the Jag to the zoo, but it was a good sign.

After about a minute the driver got out, and I recognized Maxine. She was dressed in dark clothing as I was, but her blonde hair shone even in the low light.

I lowered my window and spoke softly. "Hi, it's me. Come around to the other side and get in."

She nodded and did what I said, sliding into the front passenger seat. After she closed her door, I thought I detected, under the hint of expensive perfume, a whiff of fear.

"Okay, what's going on?"

"I don't know." She held her hands in her lap, twisting and untwisting her fingers. "I don't know, but I think it has something to do with you ... and Susan Fontaine."

"All right." I kept my voice calm, hoping that might help to calm her. "Why don't you tell me about it?"

"You won't tell anyone else, will you? I mean, this is just between us."

Her request put me in an awkward spot. I couldn't legitimately promise not to pass along to Marcus and to Scott and Jackie anything helpful in the Fontaine case. But because I didn't know what she might tell me, maybe I wouldn't have to reveal all of it.

"I won't lie to you, Maxine—I may have to repeat at least some of what you tell me. That depends on what it is. But I'll do my best to keep you out of the spotlight."

She thought about that while still doing that twisting thing with her fingers. I put my hand on both of hers. "You sound like you could use a friend right now. I'll help you if I can." And not be disloyal to my client, I mentally added.

After several seconds she said, "Okay. I guess I have to trust you." She took a deep breath. "They threatened to kill me. And I know they'll do it too—they killed Miss Maggie."

That startled me. "Who?"

"Miss Maggie, my cat. I found her dead when I got home from shopping today. On the kitchen floor. They stabbed her, and she bled to death."

"My God! That's awful!"

"Yes. I cried and cried." She sniffed and wiped her eyes. "After a while I called a neighbor to … to help me …."

"Wrap up the body?"

"Yes." She seemed relieved that she hadn't had to say it. "I'm going to take her in for cremation on Monday. After Donna, my neighbor, went home, I decided to call you."

"I'm glad you did. Who threatened you? And when?"

"It was late yesterday afternoon. An Asian guy—I mean, a man from Asia, not someone like you. He has an accent."

"Where was this?"

"At my office. Well, in the parking lot there. I was walking to my car, and he came up to me. Really close. And he kept his voice low so no one else could hear him."

"What did he say?"

"He said they knew I'd talked to you."

Although it was getting warm in the car, a chill came over me. I was pretty sure I knew who "they" were. "Talked to me about—"

"Who might have killed Susan Fontaine. Yes. And about Whit and me."

How did the yakuza know I'd talked to Maxine? For that matter how did they know about Whit and Maxine? Whit certainly hadn't told them, I thought, so McKenna must have. And maybe when I was driving to Extra Perks I hadn't shaken off that tail after all.

"What did you say?"

"Not much. I was too scared. He showed me a knife and said he'd use it on me if he had to—if I talked to anyone else about Whit or Susan."

I pictured the man who'd walked me to my car at the Hilton, the man who'd showed me a knife too. I pulled its twin out of my purse and held it up in what light there was. "Did his knife look like this one?"

She stared at the knife, her eyes growing big. "Yes, I think so. Where did you get that?"

"Probably from the same man—he threw it at me."

"Oh, my God! Did he hit you?"

"No. He told me later that he meant to miss, and that's probably true." I paused, mentally shuffling the facts I'd learned as though they were cards in my hand. Why did the yakuza care if Maxine talked to me? She didn't seem to know anything about Susan Fontaine's death. Or did she?

"Maxine, have you told me all you know about the Fontaine murder?"

Even in the low light I could see that the question made her uncomfortable.

"I don't know anything! I mean, I don't know who killed her, if that's what you're getting at. I just don't believe Whit did it."

I thought about that for a moment. What was I missing? There must be something there. "Do you know something about Susan? Something that might be a clue about who killed her?"

"No."

She said it quite definitely, but for some reason I didn't believe her. "Are you sure?"

"Uh, yes. Yes, I am."

There it was—the least bit of hesitancy. She was holding something back.

"You don't sound sure. I think you know something."

"No! I've told you everything."

"No, you haven't. You know something about Susan Fontaine that someone doesn't want me to know. That's why the Japanese guy warned you."

She didn't speak for several seconds. Then she brushed her eyes with her hand. "He killed my cat."

"Yes, and they'll do worse than that if we don't stop them."

"Do you think they killed Susan?"

"No, probably not. The crime scene suggests the killer was someone who knew her."

"Whit didn't do it!"

"I didn't say he did. I said I think she was killed by someone who knew her. And I think you may know something that would suggest who that might be."

Again she was silent. Fighting a strong temptation to press her, I waited. Finally she said, "Susan was seeing someone."

That was no surprise, but at least it was an opening. "Yes?"

"Someone who works for the government, I think."

"What makes you say that?"

"His car—one of those big, dark cars, American made. The kind a lot of government officials drive."

"A Ford?"

"Yes, I think so."

I thought about that for a moment. A big, dark Ford. Yes, that was a common government car. Solidly built, roomy inside, and fast. Fast enough for—

"With a couple of extra antennas?"

"Uh, yes, now that you mention it. Maybe that's what made me think it's a government car."

"You may be right. But what makes you think the driver was seeing Susan Fontaine? Maybe it was just someone stopping by on some sort of official business."

"No, it—"

She broke off, and I sensed she was embarrassed.

"What?"

"I just know, that's all."

"No, you don't 'just know'. You have a reason."

She didn't speak, and I knew that if there'd been more light, I would have seen her blushing.

"Come on, Maxine. This is important. Whit's been charged with murder, and if you have any information that will help me to clear him, you need to tell me. *Now*."

She cleared her throat and hesitated some more, but then she told me.

"Well, I've driven by Whit's house a few times and seen the car there. Not every time, but often."

"You mean you were stalking him."

"I don't like that word—stalking."

"Okay, but that's what you were doing."

"No, I was just ... checking on him, making sure he was all right."

I decided not to argue the point. "So how often have been you been doing this checking?"

"Umm, most days."

"Every day, right? Sometimes two or three times a day?"

She started to speak, then simply nodded.

"Sometimes when he was home and sometimes when he wasn't?"

She nodded again.

"Was the government car there when Whit was home?"

"No, never. Only when he was gone and would be for a while."

"You knew his schedule that well?"

"Yes." She lifted her head and looked at me. "We kept in close touch."

"How about now?"

"No, not so much. He said we should stay away from each other for the time being. Just until he's past ... you know."

"Yes, I know. *If* he gets past it."

"But that's your job, isn't it? To find who really killed her? Then they'll drop the charges against Whit."

"Yes, that's my job. I could do it better if you'd told me everything at the beginning."

"But I—" She broke off and did the twisting thing with her fingers again. "I didn't want you to think I was some desperate woman trying to grab a husband away from his wife."

That's what she was of course. The stalking showed how desperately in love she was. So much in love that she'd embarrass herself by compounding the simple shame of adultery.

But, as with Whit's drinking, I didn't judge her for her actions. I hadn't stalked Bobby, but I'd certainly slept with a married man. That he was planning to leave his wife was no excuse, and I had to admit that fact now even though I'd been able to ignore it then.

I sighed. "No, I understand. Life gets complicated sometimes, doesn't it?"

"Yes, it does." She leaned toward me and touched my arm. "I'm glad you can sympathize."

"Is there anything else you haven't told me? Anything that might be useful?"

"No, I don't think so. Like I said, I don't know who killed Susan or why. I'm just sure Whit didn't do it."

"Okay." I paused, thinking. "Have you told the police about this?"

"No!" Now she gripped my arm. "No, I haven't, and I don't want you to. I'm only telling you because it might help you find whoever did kill her."

I sat there thinking, not saying anything.

"Well, will it?"

"I don't know. Maybe. Look it's late, and I'm tired. Do you have anything else to tell me?"

"No."

"You're sure this time? You're not holding anything else back."

"No! I've told you everything. Even about ... Miss Maggie." She sniffed again.

"I'm sorry about your cat. That may or may not have something to do with Susan Fontaine's murder. But if I find out who killed your cat, I'll let you know."

"Thank you. And I hope you can get Whit out of this awful mess."

"I hope so too. But I seem to be going around in circles." I rubbed the bridge of my nose. "Well, I'll get some sleep and then see what I can do tomorrow."

When she didn't move, I said, "You go home too, Maxine. Be sure all your doors and windows are locked. Do you have a gun?"

"Of course not! I hate guns. Why would I need one?"

Ask Miss Maggie, I thought. "I hope you don't need one. But obviously someone is playing a rough game. That can happen when there's a lot of money at stake. Maybe you should stay at a hotel tonight."

"I think I'll stay with Donna. She's already told me I could. She knows I don't want to be alone tonight of all nights."

"Fine. But make sure all her windows and doors are locked too."

"I will." She paused. "Are you going to be okay? I mean, if they'd do something like this to scare me …."

"I know. They might try something worse with me."

"Aren't you scared?"

"Yes, some. But I've been trained how to handle people like this." I hoped I sounded more confident than I felt.

"Okay." She opened her door, then turned to look back at me in the car's interior light. "Good luck."

"Thanks. I could use some."

She got into her car and went away. I sat there for a couple of minutes, doing some more thinking, before I finally I drove home.

CHAPTER TWENTY-NINE

When I got back to my place, I was too wired to go back to bed right away. First I took off everything but my panties and tee-shirt. Then I plinked a couple of ice cubes into a rocks glass, poured some whiskey over them, and added a little water.

I sat in front of the TV and picked up the remote. I didn't want to watch anything—I just wanted the pictures and sound to numb my brain so that I could sleep.

I clicked through the channels, not lingering on the inane talk shows with "celebrities" I'd never heard of or the even more inane infomercials for things I'd never buy. After a minute or so I came across a Hollywood noir from the 1940s, one of those dimly lit films where the men are all tough but some of them are good, the women are all beautiful but some of them are bad, and everyone smokes incessantly.

I took a film class at ODU that gave me an appreciation for those old movies. I hadn't seen this particular one and recognized only a couple of the actors, but the movie was better than anything else on, so I half-watched it while I let my mind wind down.

The complex plot revolved around a bank robbery—the planning for the job, the heist itself, and then the aftermath, when everything fell apart. The twist at the end was that a seemingly good guy knew one of the bad guys from way back and turned out to have been in on the robbery.

When the movie ended, I shut off the TV and stumbled to bed. I was tired and slept soundly.

A dream woke me—an unlikely dream that was neither pleasant nor unpleasant. I dreamed that I was sitting with my father by his fountain and having a conversation about the Fontaine case. We were speaking in Mandarin, and I realized that some ideas came to me more easily when expressed in that language.

But English, with which I felt more comfortable, was better for some things. Such as, for example, describing the way Susan Fontaine had looked lying on the floor with two holes in her chest and blood on her nightgown. Somehow the phrase "the big sleep" didn't have the same awful finality when expressed in Mandarin.

As I slid from sleep into wakefulness, I sat up, looking straight ahead but not seeing anything in my bedroom. Instead I saw little bits and pieces of things I'd come across since Tuesday. This was Sunday morning—had

I been working on the case only five days? It seemed longer.

I was still running over things in my mind when someone knocked on the front door. I glanced at the clock by my bed. Almost nine. A bit early for a Sunday morning but not rudely early.

I got out of bed, pulled on some running shorts, and went to the door. I looked through the peephole and saw Ryan Connolly. That surprised me. I'd thought it was probably my parents stopping by to check on me, something they did from time to time.

But it was Connolly. Somehow I didn't feel the same about him as I had the night before ... still, I let him in. I couldn't think of a logical reason not to, and I didn't want to make him wonder why I wouldn't.

He was dressed casually and carrying a striped bag from a local gourmet shop.

"Hi. I brought you breakfast."

"Thanks. You didn't need to do that."

"Well, I wanted to make amends for leaving last night. I just ... well, I had some things to do."

That sounded weak, but I let it pass. "No need to apologize. I enjoyed our time together, and you weren't obligated to stay." I wanted to add something about his not leaving a note, but I let that go too.

"Thanks. I enjoyed being with you." He looked at me with an odd expression that I couldn't read. The silence drew out awkwardly, and perhaps to break it, he said, "I have coffee, Danish, and a couple of bagels. Which would you prefer?"

"Coffee to start. Maybe a bagel later."

"Okay." He went into my little kitchen, put the bag on the table, and began taking things out of it.

I headed for the bedroom, where I'd left my phone, but he stopped me with, "Hey, where you going?"

"I'm going to check in with Marcus. I'll tell him you stopped by."

He stepped over to me, put a hand on my elbow. "No need to do that. It's Sunday morning. Let the man relax, enjoy his day off."

I didn't like the way he was touching me. I also didn't like the look in his eyes. His gaze was usually intense, but was there something more now? Suspicion? Or even fear?

I got a couple of small plates from the cupboard and put them on the table, adding paper napkins. "Okay, please sit down."

He took a chair and watched me put a cup of coffee in front of him. I followed it with a Danish pasty on one of the plates.

Then I sat, put sweetener in my coffee, and took a sip. The coffee was stronger than I like but still good. It was also still hot, and I hoped it would warm me up inside. There was a cold feeling in the pit of my stomach.

Connolly had some of his coffee and took a bite of the pastry. After he chewed and swallowed, he said, "Working today? I hope not. You need some time off."

"I'm not sure yet. I want to keep moving on the Fontaine case, but I'm still trying to decide what I should do next."

"Not much you can do on a Sunday."

"Maybe not."

He nodded and had some more coffee. Then, after a little pause, he said, "By the way, I think I left my watch here last night."

"You did. I'll get it for you."

I went to my bedroom. I figured Connolly would interrupt any phone call I tried to make, so I didn't go for my phone, but I did take a few seconds to slip my bare feet into running shoes. Then I picked up the slim, gold watch.

As I brought the watch into the kitchen I said, "This is a really good one. It must have been a gift from your ex."

"Sarah?"

"Yes, I noticed the inscription on the back—'from S'."

"Oh, that. Yeah, she gave it to me." He held out his hand.

Instead of giving him the watch, I studied it, tilting it from side to side and seeing how the light flashed off the shiny metal case. "No offense, but this is an expensive gift for a cop's wife to give her husband." Especially a husband she'd cheat on, I added mentally. "Did she have her own money?"

"Yeah, she worked."

"Doing what?"

That irritated him. "What difference does it make?"

I smiled what I hoped what a soothing smile. "None, really. I'm just curious. A curse of my profession." I handed him the watch.

"I think it must be," he said, sliding the watch onto his wrist.

"So was it a Christmas gift? Birthday? Or maybe your anniversary?"

"What?" His irritation hadn't gone away.

"I'm just wondering. When did Susan give it to you?"

"She—." He stopped abruptly. "You mean Sarah."

"No, I mean Susan. Susan Fontaine. The woman you killed."

I knew I was taking a desperate chance—perhaps even a foolish one—but I was sick of my endless wandering in a hall of mirrors and wanted to learn the truth. Confronting him seemed to be the only way, and if he was innocent, he would protest his innocence, long and loud.

Ryan Connolly didn't do that. He just looked at me for a long moment and sighed.

"I was afraid it might come to this," he said, almost to himself.

Then he surged out of his chair, faster than I would have thought possible. I tried to execute my spur-of-the moment plan of running toward the bedroom, where I could lock him out for the few seconds it would take to call 911. But before I took my second step he gripped my wrist like a vice and jerked me toward him.

I swung with my free hand and hit him on the side of his face as hard as I could. It was like hitting concrete and sent a sharp pain shooting through my hand but didn't seem to hurt him at all. Then I tried to knee him in the groin, but he'd anticipated that and turned to block my leg

I swung at him again, but he knocked my hand aside and cocked his big fist. I saw the blow coming straight for my jaw, but there was nothing I could do about it.

Nothing but dive into the deep, black pool that opened up before me.

☐ ☐ ☐

When I came to, I was in darkness, wrapped tightly in some sort of blanket, and listening to a humming sound. I tried to move and found that I couldn't—my wrists were tied together with what felt like a thin cord, and my ankles were also tied. All I could do was roll slightly from side to side, and that didn't get me anywhere.

My head ached, and I was afraid I was going to throw up. But that could kill me because a handkerchief had been stuffed in my mouth and crammed down too deeply for me to spit it out.

I forced myself to lie quietly and breath slowly through my nose. The nausea receded after a minute or two, and I figured out that the humming sound was made by a car traveling down a highway.

So I was in a car trunk, presumably Connolly's car trunk, and he was taking me somewhere. Suddenly, even though the trunk was hot and stuffy, I felt a chill. I knew the trip would be one way.

For a moment I wondered why he hadn't simply killed me in my apartment. Then I realized that, after having his subordinates watch my apartment Friday night and having visited it twice himself since then, Connolly was probably afraid someone would link my dead body to him.

So he was going to make sure no one would find it. A nice, cheery thought to have as we rolled down the highway.

I started to shake with fear but then told myself sternly not to panic. I had to think of something, and I probably didn't have much time.

I did think of one thing, but it wasn't going to help me escape. Being wrapped in a rough wool blanket, the kind the military and the police use, made me think of another kind of blanket, the kind that comes in a zippered plastic pouch. The kind of pouch I'd seen at the Fontaines' house.

An electric blanket. Well, that explained her apparent time of death.

Why had Connolly done it? It couldn't have been for money. Sure, Susan probably had been giving him money. That might explain how a divorced cop paying child support for two kids could afford to dress as well as he did despite losing money—maybe a lot of it—playing poker. But killing her would cut off any cash flow, so there had to be some other reason.

Was she pressuring him to marry her? That was possible. Maybe in the course of her several affairs she'd finally found a man she loved and wanted to make a second marriage with. I didn't think she'd loved Whit any longer. In fact, there was no evidence that either of them had still loved the other.

So maybe she had wanted to divorce Whit Fontaine and marry Ryan Connolly. But if Connolly didn't want to marry her, why didn't he just end their affair? That might have been a little messy, but not as messy as murdering her.

Then it hit me. She must have had something on him, something she was using as leverage. Some information about something he'd done or maybe hadn't done that would get him into trouble as a police officer. His job was obviously his whole life, so he'd have taken any action he thought necessary to protect his position as a detective.

But would that extend to killing someone—especially the woman with whom he was having an affair? Well, maybe so. As Marcus had said, strange things happen sometimes.

Such as my being gagged, bound hand and foot, and bouncing along in the trunk of a car.

I remembered the knife in my purse and wished that whatever instinct had made me keep it there had prompted me to put it in a pocket of my shorts before I let Connolly in. Then, if he hadn't found it before wrapping me in the blanket—not likely but possible—perhaps I could cut whatever was binding my wrists and ankles and get this stupid gag out of my mouth. Of course, I'd still be locked in the car trunk, but maybe I could figure out a way to pop the lid.

Or maybe not. But I felt helpless lying there like a trussed-up animal being taken to a slaughterhouse.

When that image came unbidden into my mind, I felt my eyes grow hot, then wet. I wanted so badly to cry, to give in to the awful fear clutching at my heart with icy fingers. I knew what happened to people who were tied up and thrown into car trunks.

I'd seen it.

I hoped that whatever happened to me, my parents would never see pictures of it. I wanted them to remember me the way I looked in the photos they had of me at home. My senior portrait, the day I graduated from boot camp, the day I graduated from college. The days—the few days—on which I'd made them proud.

This wasn't going to be one of those days. This was going to be one of the days they'd worried about and warned me about and told me to avoid.

But now I could only wish I'd been able to avoid it.

A few tears rolled down my cheeks, and I couldn't wipe them away. I gave myself a fierce command to stop crying, to stop giving in to emotion. I had to *think*, to figure some way out of this awful nightmare.

After a few seconds it seemed to work. I rubbed my face in the scratchy, sour-smelling blanket to dry my tears. Then I told myself to replace the fear with anger, to get mad at Connolly for what he was doing. And for what he'd done to Susan Fontaine.

Well, I'd solved the case. I knew who killed her. The only problem was that I wasn't going to be around to tell anyone.

I still didn't know who killed Betty Partridge—assuming, of course, that she hadn't killed herself, and I didn't think she had. Even though finding her killer wasn't part of my job, I was still curious. Maybe Connolly had done it. If so, why? I couldn't think of a reason.

So someone else must have killed her, but speculating about it seemed useless, especially now. I knew too little about the woman and her life to come up with any likely suspects.

And I was out of time to do anything about that.

CHAPTER THIRTY

The car slowed and seemed to go down a curving ramp as though it was exiting the highway. Then it seemed to move at lower speed, stopping a few times to make left or right turns. I had no idea where we were, but I didn't think Connolly was trying to keep me from finding out. He knew I wasn't going to be around to tell anyone.

Finally the car stopped. I heard Connolly's door open and close and what I thought sounded like shoes crunching on gravel. Then there was hot, stuffy silence.

Was he simply going to leave me in the trunk to die of heat stroke? That didn't seem likely. If I made as much noise as I could, kicking the trunk lid, someone might hear it and get me out. Connolly wouldn't take that risk.

And he didn't. I heard the trunk lock click and the lid go up. Then strong hands began unwrapping the blanket.

Bright sunlight hit my eyes hard after so long in darkness. I blinked several times and tried to see through the glare.

Connolly was standing over me with a grim look on his face. He didn't say anything, and, being gagged, I couldn't. I tried to communicate with my eyes, tried to beg him not to do this thing, but I don't know how much, if any, of my message got through to him.

Or maybe it got through but he just didn't care.

Then another face came into view—the face of a slim, redheaded man. Tom McKenna. He said, "You sure this is the best way, Ryan?"

McKenna sounded nervous and probably was. Killing is a hard thing for most people. Then it hit me: *Ryan*. So they knew each other, apparently well.

How had they met? Suddenly I remembered that photo in McKenna's office, the one with Whit and McKenna in the middle and Connolly down at the end of a line of cops. Maybe they'd met then. Or maybe some other time—Norfolk and Virginia Beach aren't that big, and in certain circles it can seem as though everyone knows everyone else.

Regardless, that made more things fall into place. Such as whom Connolly had phoned from the restaurant. Not that any of them mattered now.

"It's the only way. We've got to make sure nobody ever finds her. And nobody will once she's under tons of concrete."

McKenna sighed. "Okay."

Connolly pulled out a pocket knife and opened it. The blade was short but still long enough to do the job if he stabbed me multiple times.

I wanted to scream but of course I couldn't. In my mind I started to say goodbye to my family. I wished I had just one more chance to tell them how much I loved them.

Connolly didn't stab me though. Instead he cut the cord binding my ankles. He carefully gathered the cord and shoved it into his pocket. Then he folded the knife, dropped that in his pocket, and reached down to pick me up.

He lifted me from the trunk as though I weighed hardly anything and set me on my feet. I was unsteady from having lain in the trunk for so long, so he held me up. His touch was surprisingly gentle, as though he still carried with him some small part of what we'd shared the night before.

I looked around and saw that we were at the construction site where I'd interviewed McKenna on Wednesday. There was the halfway-finished office building with the just-started foundation of something next to it and a bunch of trucks, cranes, and other equipment scattered here and there.

The place was deserted on a Sunday morning. I didn't see anyone else around, and there were only two cars, Connolly's and what I assumed was McKenna's.

Then Connolly cut the cord binding my wrists. As I rubbed them to restore the circulation, I looked down and saw that he'd used his shoelaces to tie me. Any other time his laceless shoes would have made me smile but not this time. No, not this time.

"What are you doing?" McKenna said. "Why untie her hands?"

Connolly balled up that shoelace and put it away. "Just in case she's found. Why leave clues?"

"I thought you said nobody would find her."

"Look, Tom, there are no guarantees in this life. We're not going to take any unnecessary chances."

Connolly drew a small pistol from his hip pocket and showed it to me before holding it loosely by his side. He moved his other hand toward my face. I wanted to flinch, but I had an idea that he wasn't going to hurt me. Not just yet.

"I'm going to remove the gag, Wendy. But don't scream. There's no one to hear, and it'd be easy to stop you."

I nodded, and he gently pulled the handkerchief from my mouth. I spat out some cotton fibers and looked at him.

"Everything's easy, isn't it, Connolly? Killing Susan Fontaine, helping

McKenna cover up what he's doing with the yakuza, and now killing me."

McKenna started at the mention of the yakuza. "Hey, wait a minute. I—"

Connolly silenced him with a gesture. Then Connolly was silent himself for a moment, and I thought I saw a touch of sadness under the determination in his strong face.

"No, not easy, Wendy. Just necessary."

"Necessary to save yourself, you mean."

"Self-preservation is a law of nature. I didn't make it."

"You're good at justifying yourself, Connolly. I hope it helps you sleep at night."

"Oh, I'll sleep just fine, Wendy." He paused before adding, "So will you."

I wanted to cry then, to sob and beg for mercy, but I knew it wouldn't do any good, and I didn't want to break down in front of these men. I closed my eyes tightly to keep the tears from coming and opened them to see Connolly glancing around the construction site.

He turned to McKenna. "Are they pouring concrete tomorrow?"

"Supposed to be. Right there." McKenna pointed toward a trench that paralleled one side of the building under construction. "The last of the footings for what will be the parking garage."

Keeping one eye on me, Connolly took a couple of steps toward the trench, which had vertical metal rods sticking up from it.

"I know what you're thinking," McKenna said to him, "but the rebar is already in place."

"So we'll dig around it. Find a couple of shovels."

McKenna looked as though he wanted to argue the point, but he didn't say anything. After a moment he went toward a portable shed sitting next to the trailer that served as the office for the project.

As he walked away, my gaze darted in the other direction, trying to spot some way I could run to freedom. Connolly saw what I was doing and shook his head.

"Don't try it, Wendy. It won't work." He raised the pistol. "I don't want to shoot you, but I will if I have to."

"What difference would that make? I'm going to be dead anyway."

He didn't answer. There was no answer.

Neither of us spoke during the two or three minutes it took for McKenna to return from the shed with a shovel in each hand. He held one out to Connolly.

"Here. We can take turns digging and watching her."

"No, give it to her. The two of you dig."

Connolly wanted me to dig my own grave. I thought about refusing, but

I knew what that would get me—a bullet from his gun. At least digging would buy me a little time. For what I didn't know, but there was always a chance, however remote, that someone would come along.

Again McKenna looked as though he wanted to argue, but apparently Connolly had him completely cowed now. McKenna handed me a shovel, and I waited while he stepped down into the trench. Then I followed him, careful not to cut myself on a rebar rod. Why I didn't know—getting a small cut, even from a rusty bar, was now the least of my worries.

McKenna started to dig between the row of rebar and the side of the trench. I did the same thing a few feet from him. The ground was like solid rock, baked dry from the summer sun after several days without rain, and I could barely break the surface.

Not that I was trying very hard. I was in no hurry to finish the job.

McKenna was doing some better but not much. Connolly watched us for a couple of minutes and then said, "Hell, I'll have to do it myself. You two are getting nowhere. Tom, you hold the gun on her, and I'll dig."

McKenna, clearly relieved, climbed out of the trench. He handed his shovel to Connolly and then reached to pull me up. I thought of giving his arm a hard jerk to make him tumble back into the trench, but with Connolly still holding the pistol, that wouldn't do me any good.

I came out of the trench and watched Connolly hand the pistol to McKenna and hop into the trench. He raised the shovel with both hands and rammed it into the earth. Then he put one of his big feet on top of the blade and pushed it down and underneath more dirt than McKenna and I had moved together. He tossed the scoop of dirt to one side and repeated the whole evolution.

At this rate it wouldn't take long to dig a shallow grave. The hole wouldn't have to be deep for me to lie in it under a blanket of earth.

And then tomorrow a thicker, heavier blanket of concrete. Connolly was right—I'd sleep just fine. Forever.

I shuddered. I decided to run and take a bullet in the back rather than be buried alive. McKenna probably wasn't as good a shot as Connolly, but he wouldn't have to be with me so close. Well, dying this way would be quicker and easier than what they had in store for me, so I placed my feet and took a couple of deep breaths.

Just as I was about to take off, a black car pulled slowly into the construction site. It was the Lexus I'd seen before, following me.

"Hey, Ryan, we've got company." McKenna kept his voice down, but his tone was urgent.

Connolly stopped digging and wiped his forehead with the palm of his hand. "Yeah, who?"

"I think it's some of my Japanese friends."

"They picked a bad time to come calling."

Oh, so Connolly had already known about the yakuza. But if he'd known and hadn't done anything about it ... well, I could name at least one of the officials McKenna had been paying off. Another piece of the puzzle but also another that couldn't help me now.

"I know that," McKenna said.

"Then get rid of them."

"I'll try."

"Don't *try*. Make them leave."

"They're not real big on taking orders, Ryan. Not from you and certainly not from me."

Connolly let his shovel fall to the bottom of the trench. "Give me that pistol. I'll make them leave."

McKenna turned his back to the car, which had parked some distance away, and handed the pistol to Connolly, who slid it into a front pocket of his pants. "Let me talk to them first," McKenna said. "They'll be less suspicious that way."

Before Connolly could reply, McKenna strode toward the black car. As he approached, two men got out.

The driver was the yakuza who'd threatened me with knives, and his passenger was the older man, the boss. Both were wearing dark suits with white shirts. They looked as though they might have been going to church on Sunday morning, but I knew that wasn't the case.

The older man started talking to McKenna, but after a few seconds McKenna interrupted him and began patting the air in a calming way. I couldn't hear what they were saying, but the older man's expression told me that he didn't like being interrupted. The younger man wore a similar expression, so maybe he just didn't like McKenna.

Connolly watched them for a moment, then looked at me. "Nothing has changed, Wendy. If you try to run, I'll kill you."

"I'm not so sure. Too many witnesses now."

"Gangster witnesses? What makes you think I won't kill them too?"

Nothing, I thought. Nothing at all.

After a minute or so the two gangsters started coming toward us, McKenna following with a big frown on his face.

When they were about ten feet away, the two men stopped, leaving a good distance between them. McKenna came around them and stood close to Connolly—too close if any gunfire broke out.

The small professional part of my brain that could still function noted what an amateur McKenna was. What had ever made him think he was smart enough to pull off the casino deal? If the death of Susan Fontaine hadn't drawn attention to what his company was doing, something else would have.

Using yakuza money to finance it, for example.

The young gangster stood in a seemingly relaxed way, his arms held loosely at his sides. But I noticed the outline of what had to be a gun in a front pocket of his pants. The knife was probably in a hip pocket.

"I know this young woman," the older gangster said, bowing slightly in my direction. "But who is this man?"

"His name is Ryan Connolly," McKenna said. "He's a friend of mine."

"This is a strange place for friends to meet. Especially on a Sunday morning." The man looked at McKenna, then at Connolly. "I wanted to talk to Mr. McKenna, but he did not answer his phone. And he was not at his office or home. So I came here, thinking there might be a slight chance I would find him at this project he showed to us."

He paused, looking at McKenna again. "And here you are."

"Yes, uh, I—I wanted to show Mr. Connolly how we're coming along with it."

"I see. And you, young lady, are you interested in construction too?"

"Not particularly. Mr. Connolly brought me. You might say he was quite insistent about it."

"Ah, I understand. That is why you did not have time to change your clothes."

"That's right."

The man was silent for a moment, seeming to weigh the options. Then he said, "If you have seen all of this place you care to, Lu Wen, we will give you a ride home."

"That'll be fine. I can update you on my investigation. Now I know who killed Susan Fontaine."

Connolly stepped behind me, trying to make the movement seem as casual as possible. The older man glanced at the younger, who leaned forward slightly, balanced on the balls of his feet.

"I assume you have told the police."

"Oh, the police know." I turned my head slightly to speak over my shoulder. "Don't they, Sergeant Connolly?"

The yakuza boss frowned. "This man is a police officer?" He looked at McKenna, who started patting the air again and opened his mouth without making any words.

"Yes, he is," I said. "That's ironic because he's—"
"Wendy!"
I felt Connolly's breath as he hissed in my ear.
"—the murderer."
Things began to happen. Quickly.

CHAPTER THIRTY-ONE

The young yakuza drew his pistol as Connolly clamped a forearm around my neck from behind. With me as a shield, he drew his own pistol.

McKenna stood there speechless, probably thinking of how his dream of a casino cash machine was turning into a nightmare. The yakuza boss looked at him.

"McKenna-san, how do you explain this?"

McKenna worked his mouth, but no sound came out.

"I'll explain something," Connolly said, his voice hard. "You two get back in your car and get the fuck out of here."

"You do not scare me, policeman," the boss said. "I am used to being threatened by the police. Some who did it are dead now, but I am still alive."

"Yeah, well, this girl won't be alive if you don't get out of here."

"That was a stupid thing to say. I do not want her to die, but I think you plan to kill her as soon as we are gone."

"Well, that's my business."

"It was your business. Now I have made it mine. Let her go."

"No."

"Why? Because she thinks you killed another man's wife? Can she prove it?"

"Yes," I said, "and I can prove he's been blackmailing McKenna about you!" I didn't have any actual evidence, but it wouldn't be hard to find.

Connolly put his hand over my mouth, and I bit him, tasting blood. He loosened his hold on me then, and I spun toward him, finally getting my chance to knee him hard in the groin.

He groaned and bent over but didn't drop the gun. I ran for the cover of a nearby forklift, and he snapped a shot at me, missing by inches.

"Stop!" the yakuza boss said. "You will not kill this woman."

"Fuck you," Connolly said, and he shot at the young gangster, hitting him in the thigh and causing blood to spurt from the wound. The young man shot back but missed. Then his bleeding leg collapsed, and he fell to the ground, hitting his head on concrete. He lay still, his pistol a foot or two from his outstretched hand.

His boss held out both hands and took a step toward him. Connolly fired a warning shot that sent up a geyser of dirt at the gangster's feet.

"Freeze, you Jap bastard!"

The man gave Connolly a hate-filled look but didn't move. Then he glanced toward the young man's pistol, measuring the distance with his eyes. I knew it was too far for him to get there before one of Connolly's bullets found him, and he must have known it too, because he didn't try it.

But Connolly wasn't going to take a chance. "Tom, quick! Get that gun!"

I could see McKenna from where I was crouched behind the forklift. He didn't move but at least now he could speak. "No, I don't want any part of this."

"Too late—you're already part of it."

"Not of this. Not of killing her … or them. I need them—their money for the project."

"Forget the project! It's over, done. You'll be lucky to stay out of prison."

"Why? I haven't done anything."

"Yes, you have," I said. "You killed Betty Partridge."

"What?" the yakuza boss said. "He killed someone?"

"Yes, a woman who worked in his office. He was afraid she would tell me, maybe even the police, about you, what you're doing here."

The man turned to McKenna. "Is this true?"

"No! I didn't—I wouldn't …." As the yakuza boss stared at him with hard, cold eyes, McKenna swallowed nervously. "Anyway, she can't prove it."

"Come on," Connolly said, still bent over. "We're wasting time. Get that gun!"

"No, I … I …." He ran toward his car, and Connolly shot him in the back, twice. McKenna's momentum carried him three more steps before he sprawled headlong on the ground, twitched a couple of times, and then lay motionless.

Not thinking of the danger, I raised my head over the dust-caked hood of the forklift. "What're you going to do, Connolly? Kill the whole world?"

He straightened and looked at me. "No, just the people I have to. And you're one of them."

He fired at me again, this time hitting the hood with the force of a sledgehammer and raising a cloud of dust. The bullet ricocheted, shooting slivers of metal toward me. I had closed my eyes instinctively, but I felt the hot shards cut my face. I ducked back down to where I should have stayed and rubbed my cheek, my hand coming away sticky with blood.

I knew I had only a couple of seconds before Connolly closed in on me. Frantically I looked around for something, anything, to use as a weapon. I saw a piece of copper pipe about a yard long, but it was several feet away, out in the open.

I had no choice. I sprang toward the pipe, grabbed it, and rolled, hearing another of Connolly's bullets whizz by me. As I came up, I threw the pipe at Connolly, who'd made the mistake of running toward me when he should have stayed still to shoot.

The pipe twirled toward him, turning end over end, and without thinking, he put up his right arm to block it. The pipe hit him near the elbow, making him yelp with pain and drop the pistol.

The yakuza boss was now kneeling by the young man and using the man's belt to make a tourniquet for his bloody leg. I dashed over to the young man's gun, picked it up, and whirled to face Connolly, who was reaching for his pistol with his left hand, his right arm apparently numb.

I automatically went into the Weaver shooting stance drilled into me at the police academy—my feet spread, my left side turned slightly toward him, the pistol in my right hand with my left supporting it. "Don't! Freeze or I'll shoot!"

Connolly stopped and looked at me. "Good form, Wendy. But I don't think you'll actually pull the trigger."

"Don't bet your life on it."

"You've never shot a cop before, and I don't think you'll start now."

"There's a first time for everything."

He paused. "Yes. Yes, there is. I found that out the hard way."

I guessed he was thinking of Susan Fontaine, what he'd done to her, and images from the crime-scene photos flickered through my mind. I blinked my eyes to get rid of them, and Connolly must have noticed my distraction. It lasted only a second, but even that was too much.

I was between Connolly and his car, so he ran for the partially finished building, crouching low to make the smallest possible target. I tracked him with the gunsight but didn't squeeze the trigger. That was mostly because I didn't think I'd hit him, but I had to admit he was right: it was hard for me to shoot a cop.

So I'd have to force myself to do it. Connolly wasn't going to surrender, and I wasn't going to let him get away.

As soon as he ran through an open doorway, I sprinted toward the building, holding the gun in front of me and scanning all the openings I could see. As I got closer I heard him pounding up the concrete stairs that would eventually be the internal fire escape. Without a gun, he needed the advantage of height so that he could throw things down at me and be a more difficult target.

Connolly might be a murderer, but he wasn't stupid—he was still dangerous, even without a pistol. My pipe-throwing proved there were plenty of things around the construction site that could be used as weapons.

In my head I heard my father's voice telling me not to follow Connolly, to use the yakuza boss's phone to call the police, and I almost did it. Almost.

I ran to the doorway and flattened myself against the wall next to it. I waited, listening intently, but heard nothing from inside. Then I darted through the entrance and ducked behind the first thing I saw, a large tool cart. Before I was crouched all the way down, something heavy crashed onto the top of the cart with a *bang!* so loud it hurt my ears. Whatever Connolly had thrown skidded off the cart, narrowly missing my head. It hit the floor behind me, and I turned to see a hammer spinning on the concrete.

"Nice try, Connolly, but you missed me. Give up—you know you can't get away."

"I won't miss next time! And I've gotten out of tighter spots than this one."

I answered by pushing the cart toward the stairs. Connolly tried twice more to hit me by throwing down heavy tools. The first one hit the front of the cart and made me flinch but didn't hurt me.

The second one almost crushed my skull. Just as I popped my head above the cart to see how close I was to the stairs, a big pipe wrench came spinning through the air. I ducked, but the wrench clipped me on the top of the head, not quite knocking me unconscious but making me cry out in agony.

Connolly heard me. "Got you, didn't I? It'll only take one more. I told you to stop investigating, but you wouldn't listen."

That pissed me off, and I fired a stupid shot up the stairwell. When the reverberation died I heard Connolly laughing.

"Come on, Wendy—you know better than that! You can't hit what you can't see."

He was right, and I knew it. I was just wasting ammunition. I had two choices: go call the cops or go up after him.

I checked the pistol. It was a Smith & Wesson .38 Special, the revolver popular with the yakuza, who reportedly made a lot of their money smuggling them into gun-restrictive Japan. Not a bad weapon, but it held only five rounds, which meant I had three left.

I thought about retrieving Connolly's pistol, which was probably the Glock .45 semiautomatic most Norfolk cops carried. He might have had thirteen rounds in the magazine, leaving up to nine left, and nine would give me much better odds than three.

But if I tried it, Connolly would probably get away somehow. Or he might be able to take me from behind, which would let him kill me and the two yakuza and then cook up some story to tell the police. Maybe his career would be over, but it's hard to convict a cop of murder, and I didn't think a jury would send Connolly to prison over the deaths of two Japanese gangsters, a crooked businessman, and a tarnished ex-cop.

No, I had to get Connolly now or step back and let the police do it.

I pushed the cart the short distance to the stairs. Then I crouched, motionless, listening intently. I heard nothing but the sound of my breathing, and I tried to mute that, forcing myself to take long, slow breaths.

Still nothing. Connolly was up there, waiting, and he'd have some sort of weapon to use against me. Well, I told myself, time to find out what it was.

I took one last breath, held it, and exhaled. Then I sprang out from behind the cart and charged up the stairs. As I neared the top, an enormous wooden reel came barreling toward the stairs, the reel half-full of thick, heavy electric cable. I knew that if the reel caught me on the stairs, I'd be dead.

I took one more step and then jumped, launching myself as high and far to the side as I could. The reel hit one of my feet, and for a terrible moment I thought it might drag me back into the stairwell and crush me, but my foot came free, and the reel crashed down the stairs.

I landed, hard, on my left side, and gasped from the pain before rolling behind the nearest cover I saw, a stack of cardboard boxes containing floor tiles. I heard Connolly cursing somewhere across the second floor of the building.

I wanted to taunt him but didn't, saving my breath and also saving my strength to deal with whatever he might try next. Rolling that heavy reel at me had been a good idea. I hoped his next one wasn't as good.

After a minute or two the pain in my side subsided from piercing agony to a dull ache, and I thought I could move again. From the sound he'd made, I had a fairly good idea where Connolly might be, so I started crawling slowly in that direction, using all the cover I could.

I knew Connolly would try to attack me, but because I had a gun, I didn't think he'd get too close.

He didn't. He waited until I was in the open, hurrying from a wooden pallet stacked with doors to one loaded with plumbing fixtures. Then he popped up from behind a huge roll of insulation and threw another hammer at me.

The hammer hit my leg, making me twist and fall on the same side I'd hurt earlier. This time I felt a rib or two crack as I hit the concrete. I realized I couldn't play this game much longer—I had to get Connolly before he got me.

As that thought sank in, I heard running feet and raised my head to see Connolly dashing for the stairs. After he'd thrown the hammer, he must have circled back toward the stairwell.

I watched to see which way he'd go. I was too banged up to chase him, so if he went down he'd probably get away. But then he'd have to keep running. The only way to avoid that was to kill me.

And apparently that was what he'd decided to do. He went up the stairs, meaning I'd have to go up after him again. And with at least one broken rib, the odds against me were longer now.

Now I wished I'd listened to my father's voice, but it was too late for that. I couldn't, wouldn't, give up. I got to my feet and limped toward the stairwell.

As I neared it, I stopped to listen. Nothing. Not that I'd expected to hear anything—nothing but the blood pounding in my ears.

I swallowed hard and started up the stairs, up to the third floor, where I knew Connolly was waiting for me.

And he was waiting all right. He was to one side of the stairwell, just far enough back that I couldn't see him until I was almost at the top of the stairs. He held a long piece of pipe like a spear and stabbed my right side with it as I took the last step.

The pipe made a big hole right below my rib cage but was too blunt to go in deeply. I managed to swing my gun hand around and fire at Connolly, missing but making him drop the pipe.

Two cartridges left. Connolly backpedaled quickly but not quickly enough. I took careful aim and fired again, hitting him in the left shoulder and making him drop behind a big trash bin close to the edge of the building.

My side was bleeding so badly that I knew I didn't have much time left before I'd be in a hospital—or dead.

And because I now had a single round remaining, the second possibility seemed more likely.

To slow the bleeding, I clamped my elbow over the hole in my side. Maybe that would buy me a couple more minutes before I passed out.

I limped toward the trash bin, my shoes dragging across the floor.

Connolly would have no trouble tracking me by ear. What would he try next? I didn't know, but it was bound to be unpleasant.

It was. The bin had wheels, so when I was a few yards away, Connolly shoved the bin toward me, keeping low behind it.

I didn't have a shot at him, so I did the only thing I could, knowing how much it would hurt but not having any choice. I crouched and tumbled across the concrete floor, the pain almost unbearable, but the bin missed me by inches, leaving Connolly standing in the open. Lying on the floor, I had a bad angle, but I aimed the gun at him anyway.

"Hold it! Right there! Don't move an inch!"

He stayed still, watching me closely. After a few seconds he said, "You're almost done, Wendy. You need a doctor."

"So do you."

He glanced down at his shoulder, where a red patch was spreading on his shirt. "Yeah, I guess you're right. Why don't we call it even? I'll leave and send someone back for you."

"Sure you will."

"Wait and see."

There was no point in answering that, so I didn't. I couldn't wait. I might pass out in another few minutes. I got onto my knees and then onto my feet, trying to ignore the pain and keeping the pistol pointed at him the whole time.

Connolly watched me, his eyes narrow, and I knew he was thinking frantically, trying to figure out what to do.

I needed to retain the initiative. "Put your hands on your head and turn around. Slowly."

He hesitated a moment, then gradually put his hands up, grunting as he lifted his left arm. As he started to turn, I shuffled toward him, painfully, blinking my eyes to keep them focused.

By the time I got there, he was facing out, with his hands just above his shoulders. I remembered a line from my police training: "Hands kill."

"Clasp your hands on top of your head."

He didn't move. "This isn't going to work, Wendy. You don't have any handcuffs."

He was right about that. I couldn't cuff him. But I could hold his belt with one hand and make him walk in front of me while I kept the gun on him. Maybe I could get him down the stairs that way. Maybe not. But I had to try.

He must have figured out what I was going to do. When I was close he spun to the right and hit my forearm with a closed fist. I dropped the gun before I could squeeze the trigger, and the pistol clattered on the concrete. Then Connolly made a mistake, a bad one. He stopped to grin and enjoy the moment when he should have lunged at me. Maybe he thought I was too badly hurt to fight him hand-to-hand.

If so, he was wrong. I immediately dropped into a crouch, gritting my teeth against the agony of the rapid movement, and kicked him in the chest. My "ki hup!" sounded weak, but the kick had just enough power to make him stumble backward between two orange cones marking that edge of the building.

He must not have known how close he was to the edge, because he didn't stop himself before one foot was treading on air.

Connolly teetered there for a moment, trying to shift his balance forward, but there was nothing for him to grab. His eyes grew wide, and he held out a hand to me.

"Help me, Wendy. For God's sake, help me!"

I started to take his hand and pull him to safety, but the image of Susan Fontaine's dead body flashed in front of me again and I didn't move.

I didn't move as Connolly teetered for another second or two and then fell, arms flailing. He tumbled as if he were a high-diver who'd somehow missed his mark.

He screamed all the way down.

I took small steps to the edge of the building and looked at him lying there on the ground three stories below. The yakuza boss had put the young man in their car and was standing by the driver's door. He looked at Connolly, then at me. He might have bowed slightly, but I couldn't be sure. Then he got into the car and drove away.

I looked at Connolly again. He might still be alive, I thought, but he wasn't going anywhere under his own power.

And I realized that neither was I. That kick had taken my last bit of energy. I slumped to the floor and closed my eyes, wondering what I'd see next. Maybe heaven, if there is such a thing.

Or hell. And hell is real all right.

Just ask Connolly.

CHAPTER THIRTY-TWO

I was floating in a warm pool, lying on my back, my arms at my sides. It must have been night, because everything was dark. Perhaps this was how a child felt right before being born.

So perhaps death was like birth? That made sense in a way—transitioning from one state to the other.

You're getting very philosophical, Wendy, I told myself. You'll have to tell your father when you see him again.

If you see him again.

Then I opened my eyes and did see him, sitting in a chair near the bed I was in. He appeared to be asleep. I looked around the dimly lit room and saw that I was in a hospital. My wounds had been bandaged, and some colorless liquid was dripping into me from a long tube connected to a bottle held upside down on a metal rack.

I turned my head to look at the table next to the bed. A small clock told me it was a little after five. Given the dim light in the room and how quiet everything was, that had to be five in the morning. I'd been out for something like eighteen hours.

There was a vase of flowers on the table, a vivid mix of red, yellow, and green. Lucky colors in China, so the flowers were probably from my mother. I glanced around the room and didn't see her—my father must have sent her home to get some rest while I slept.

I was more tired than I had ever been in my life. I closed my eyes and drifted away.

When I opened them again, the room was brighter from the sunlight coming through the curtained window. My father was awake, reading a thick book, a cup of tea on the bedside table.

"That tea smells good." My voice was a harsh croak. "Maybe they'll let me have some."

My father put down his book and came to stand by the bed. He gently put his hand on my forehead.

"I will ask," he said. "Perhaps they will." He looked at me for a long time, not speaking. Then, taking his hand away, he said, "Your mother was here until quite late. She was so upset that I thought she should go home and try to sleep."

"I'm sorry I upset her. I know how she worries about me."

"You did not upset her. What happened to you did."

"Well, I probably look more hurt than I really am."

"The doctor says you will be fine, but you have to take it easy for a while. Let your ribs and cuts heal."

"I can do that. In fact, I don't think I'm up to doing anything else."

He smiled slightly. "I see you have not lost your sense of humor." He paused, then shook his head. "My brave, beautiful daughter ... whatever will become of you?"

I tried to smile back, but even that hurt. "I don't know. I guess we'll have to find out."

He started to speak, but a knock on the door cut him off.

He turned toward the door. "Come in."

The door opened, and Marcus's massive frame filled it. "Morning, Doctor Lu. How's our girl doing?"

My father went over and shook hands with Marcus. "Not too badly, under the circumstances. The doctor says she will need to stay one more night but probably can go home tomorrow."

"I'll arrange to have a nurse stay with her for a few days."

My father bowed slightly. "Thank you, but that will not be necessary. Her mother will insist on taking care of her at our home."

Marcus looked at me and raised an eyebrow. I knew it was useless to argue that I'd be more comfortable in my own place, so I said, "That will be fine, Dad. Thanks."

My father seemed relieved that he wouldn't have to fight that battle. "Wen wants some tea. I will go see if they will let her have some. Excuse me."

Marcus stood aside to let my father out and then came over by the bed. "How you feeling, Wendy?"

"Lousy. But alive. How about Connolly?"

"He's dead. He survived his fall—barely—but died not long after the police got to the job site."

"What made them go there?"

"They got a call on a burner mobile. The caller said you were hurt bad up on the third floor. Otherwise it might have taken the police so long to find you that you'd have died too."

"I'll bet the caller had a Japanese accent."

"Yep, it had to be the yakuza."

"And I'll bet they've cleared out—left the country."

"On the first overseas plane they could catch. The police checked the Norfolk airport, and apparently they didn't leave from there. But they could have easily driven to Richmond or even Washington, D.C. We don't have their IDs—just "Watanabe," a common Japanese last name. They even paid cash at the hotel, so there's no quick way to trace them. They're gone."

Good, I thought. I was glad the boss got away, and despite the nasty cat business I hoped the young man would be all right. He'd looked tough enough to take it. You had to be tough to be in that line of work.

"So the cops talked to Connolly?"

"Yeah. He didn't live long, but it was long enough to confess. When they got to him, he was mumbling some prayer, so maybe he got religion at the end. Anyway, he killed Susan Fontaine."

"I know."

"How?"

"Lots of little things. He wouldn't even consider the possibility that Whit had been framed. He seemed to have more money than he should. And I found out that he'd been having an affair with her."

"He told the police that too. But how did he work the frame?"

"He knew Whit would be at that dinner late and, based on what Susan had told him about Whit, drinking a lot. He shot Susan with Whit's gun—either she'd showed it to him or he found it—and used an electric blanket to keep her body warm until Whit got home. I saw the empty blanket pouch when we went through the Fontaine's house, but it took me a while to realize what had been in it."

"Good thinking, Wendy."

"Thanks, but I wish it'd come to me sooner. After he killed Susan, Connolly probably doctored Whit's bourbon. It was a good bet Whit would head straight for the bottle when he got home, even as drunk as he was. If that hadn't worked, Connolly could've just tapped him on the head with the gun butt—it wouldn't have taken much with him in that condition. That would have left a bruise, but the cops might've figured he got it from falling on the floor. In any event Whit was unconscious when Connolly put him next to Susan. He'd wiped off the gun, so he closed Whit's hand on it, then left it lying there."

Marcus pursed his lips for a few seconds, then nodded. "And walked out, leaving the front door open to invite investigation. Okay, that all fits, but what was the motive?"

"Susan wanted to divorce Whit and marry Connolly. He wasn't wild about the idea of marrying her, so she was trying to blackmail him into it."

"Not a very good start to a marriage."

"No. She must've been very unhappy with Whit—probably had been for a long time. Connolly had a bad gambling habit, and she'd been giving him money to keep him afloat. Also, she knew that Tom McKenna had been paying him off to look the other way when McKenna brought the yakuza in to finance the casino. Connolly's main beat was homicide, but he was too good a cop not to notice Japanese gangsters in Hampton Roads."

"So McKenna was dirty too."

"Yep. Connolly probably pressured him to ask the cops to check the Fontaines' house that night. And then McKenna killed Betty Partridge when he thought she might tell me or maybe the police what he was up to."

Marcus raised one hand slightly. "The police still think that could have been suicide."

"Well, it wasn't. McKenna confirmed that before Connolly shot him. Killing her so soon after Susan's death was stupid, but I don't think McKenna was very bright."

"Then the police will want to talk to you about what McKenna said. When you're feeling better."

"Sure." The conversation had made me more tired, and I closed my eyes again. After a few seconds I thought of something, and I opened them to look at Marcus. "Does Whit know? About Connolly, I mean?"

"I called him after I talked to the police."

"What did he say?"

"Not much. He seemed relieved, of course, but he didn't sound happy."

"I can understand that. His wife is dead, and his life will never be the same."

"No. No, it won't. Of course, he won't have to worry about money—he'll get his wife's fortune."

I almost said, "Lucky him," but then I realized he wasn't lucky at all. Not even with all that money.

Whit wasn't going to prison for a murder he didn't commit, but in a way he'd always be in prison. After I talked to the police, they'd give him the whole picture, and he'd know that his wife and his business partner had betrayed him, played him for a fool. And soon everyone in the relatively small circle of people who run things around here—the bankers, lawyers, and politicians—would know it too. I'd be surprised if he stayed in Hampton Roads.

Marcus interrupted my thinking. "He wanted me to tell you thanks. He said, 'Tell Wendy I know what she did for me and how much it cost her.'"

"Well, at least he's not ungrateful." I mentally reviewed what I'd learned about Whit Fontaine. "He's not guilty of murder, but I can't say he's not guilty of other things. So maybe there's sort of a rough justice at work."

"Yeah, maybe so. But we're all guilty of something, aren't we?"

I thought about Bobby, how I had loved him and how he had … died. I hated that he was beginning to fade in my memory. And now I had another memory—my night with Connolly. I hated that too.

I felt hot tears leak from my eyes, and Marcus touched me gently on the shoulder. "Sorry, Wendy, I didn't mean to get you upset."

"No, you're right—we're all guilty of something. I guess we just have to learn to live with it."

"That's how it works. But this should help: Scott and Jackie are giving us a bonus, and I'm going to allocate most of it to you."

Maybe that shouldn't have mattered, but it did make me feel better. "Thanks, boss."

"Don't thank me. You earned it—the hard way."

My father came back, bringing me a cup of tea, and Marcus left soon after, promising to visit again the next day. My father helped me drink the tea, holding the cup to my mouth as I took small sips.

I slept then, and when I woke up, my mother was there, sitting by the bed and looking anxiously at me.

"How do you feel, Wen?" she said in Mandarin, and I answered her the same way, assuring her that I felt better than I really did.

I thought she might scold me—again—for having the job I had and living the life I led. But she didn't. I didn't think she'd given up on doing that, but I did think she knew it wasn't the right time to hector me about anything.

She held my hand, something she hardly ever does, and stayed with me, speaking only to ask me once in a while whether I wanted anything. I drink some water, took the various medicines the nurses gave me, and slept some more.

I woke again in the early evening and saw a purple-and-red sky through the half-closed blinds of my west-facing window. I remembered the sailors' old saying about a twilight sky and smiled to myself.

My father was back, looking as though he'd gotten some rest during the day. My mother was gone, but I knew she'd return later.

"How are you feeling?"

"Some better," I said, and this time I was truthful.

"Good. Your brother and sister called me to ask when they could visit, and I told them to wait until tomorrow."

"Thanks. I'll feel more like talking to them then."

"Yes." He hesitated. "And to the police—they want to talk to you too."

"I'm sure. There's not much to tell them that they don't know by now, but they'll have some questions."

"Yes, they will." He paused. "I know how policemen work. I had experience with them in China."

I looked at him. "I know you did. That's one reason you and Mama are here. I wish you'll tell me about it."

"I will. Some other time."

"When we are sitting in your garden, by the fountain."

He smiled. "Yes, that would be a good place. Some of the story is ... unpleasant, and being in the garden will help me to tell it the right way. Calmly and without anger."

"Good." I fell silent then, not thinking about anything, just drifting in a warm sea as my body slowly started to heal itself. I was hurt, but I knew I'd be better—maybe better than I'd been in a long time.

"Oh, I almost forgot," my father said. "Vanessa Hoang came by to see you, but you were asleep. She said she phoned your office and that nice lady, Simone, told her you were here." He pulled a small red envelope from his pocket. "Vanessa said to give you this."

He handed the envelope to me. It was a lucky-money envelope with two dollar bills inside. On the envelope Vanessa had written: "Get well soon, Wen. Maybe this will help."

I looked at my father. "That was sweet of her. But it's the wrong time of year."

"It is never the wrong time for luck," my father said, gently taking the envelope from me and putting it on the bedside table. "You should sleep now. When you wake up, your lucky money will be here next to you."

As I closed my eyes, I realized he was right: it is never the wrong time for luck.

THE END

More hardboiled action thrillers by
Timothy J. Lockhart

Smith
978-1-944520-23-6 $15.95

"Smith — just Smith - is a tough as nails killer, a secret operative and tough fighter, and Timothy J. Lockhart makes this adventure a compelling must read."
—Gary Lovisi, *Paperback Parade & Hardboiled* magazines

Pirates
978-1-944520-67-0 $15.95

"...with bullets zinging and baddies converging from all sides, it's anyone's guess who will make it alive out of Lockhart's gruesome, exhilarating adventure."
—Nicholas Litchfield, *Lancashire Post*

A Certain Man's Daughter
978-1-951473-22-8 $15.95

"...an enjoyable hardboiled read with snappy dialogue and a touch of humour."
—Paul Burke, *Crime Fiction Lover*

In trade paperback from:
Stark House Press
1315 H Street, Eureka, CA 95501
griffinskye3@sbcglobal.net   www.StarkHousePress.com

Available from your local bookstore, or order direct with a check or via our website.

www.ingramcontent.com/pod-product-compliance
Lightning Source LLC
LaVergne TN
LVHW011934070526
838202LV00054B/4637